Small Town Rumors

Center Point
Large Print

Also by Carolyn Brown and available from Center Point Large Print:

The Wedding Pearls
The Lullaby Sky
The Lilac Bouquet
The Strawberry Hearts Diner
The Sometimes Sisters

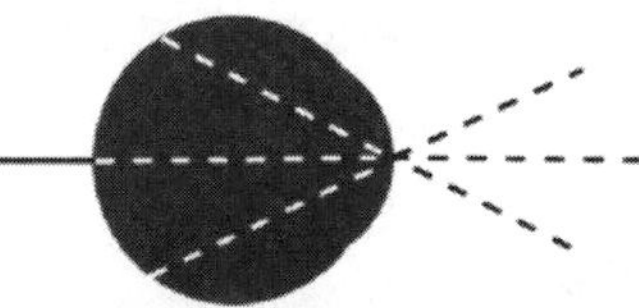

This Large Print Book carries the Seal of Approval of N.A.V.H.

Small Town Rumors

CAROLYN
BROWN

Center Point Large Print
Thorndike, Maine

This Center Point Large Print edition
is published in the year 2019 by arrangement with
Amazon Publishing, www.apub.com.

This is a work of fiction. Names, characters, organizations,
places, events, and incidents are either products of the
author's imagination or are used fictitiously.

The text of this Large Print edition is unabridged.
In other aspects, this book may vary
from the original edition.
Printed in the United States of America
on permanent paper.
Set in 16-point Times New Roman type.

ISBN: 978-1-64358-076-0

Library of Congress Cataloging-in-Publication Data

Names: Brown, Carolyn, 1948- author.
Title: Small town rumors / Carolyn Brown.
Description: Large Print edition. | Thorndike, Maine :
Center Point Large Print, 2019.
Identifiers: LCCN 2018053041 | ISBN 9781643580760
(hardcover : alk. paper)
Subjects: LCSH: Large type books.
Classification: LCC PS3552.R685275 S63 2019 | DDC 813/.54—dc23
LC record available at https://lccn.loc.gov/2018053041

To my editor,
Megan Mulder.
With much appreciation
for continuing to believe in my stories!

Chapter One

Jennie Sue Baker could almost hear the rumors buzzing around the small town of Bloom, Texas, when she stepped off the Greyhound bus in front of the Main Street Café that Monday at noon. On a slow day, gossip hung over the town like smoke in an old western honky-tonk. On a good day, in the opinion of the community, it obliterated the sun.

Today would definitely be a good day for Bloom, but to Jennie Sue, the target of all those rumors, it would be downright miserable.

She wiped sweat from her brow and then picked up the single suitcase that the driver set out on the sidewalk beside her. Glancing around as the bus pulled back out onto the highway, she expected to see her mother's pearly-white Cadillac parked nearby, but it wasn't anywhere in sight.

She set the suitcase down and seriously considered sitting on it. It wasn't her mother's fault—not really, because she hadn't called her until an hour ago, and Charlotte was never on time for anything except her hair appointments. That was because the beauty salon was the breeding ground for the best talk in town.

Well, her mama had better hurry, because Jennie Sue Baker sitting on a suitcase on Main

Street would stir up more than anything the beauty shop could dream up.

The smell of greasy burgers, bacon, and fries wafted across the street from the café. Her stomach reminded her that the package of crackers from a vending machine she'd had for breakfast had long since disappeared. Dragging her suitcase across the street, she was so focused on the café that she didn't notice the vehicle pulling up to the curb only a few feet from her. When the driver honked, she jumped and glared at the car before she realized that it was her mother. She couldn't see Charlotte's face through the tinted windshield, but she could sure enough feel the icy-cold aura coming from the car when she opened the back door and shoved the suitcase inside.

"I've come up with a perfect story," Charlotte started the moment that Jennie Sue was buckled up.

Jennie Sue wasn't surprised at the first words out of her mother's mouth, but she was disappointed. "Hello to you, too, Mama. It's really good to see you. You look as beautiful as ever. Has it really been six months since I've seen you?"

"Don't sass me," Charlotte snapped. "We talk and text every week. And speaking of the last time I saw you, it doesn't look like you've done anything to lose that extra ten pounds you're carryin' around."

"I'd been in the hospital. Besides, I like food," Jennie Sue said.

"Evidently," Charlotte sighed. "Do you like looking like a homeless woman, too? When word gets out that you came in on a bus dressed like that, I won't be able to hold my head up." She eased the car out onto the street. "I bet Cricket was watchin' from the café. Nothing escapes that girl's eye."

"I'm not a movie star, Mama, and I didn't see any paparazzi fighting to get pictures of me. This is Bloom, not Los Angeles. I'm not that important." She shifted in her seat. "So Cricket is still working at the café? She was working there when we were in high school."

"In this town you are, and yes, she is. She don't seem to have much ambition except when it comes to spreading gossip. Her brother, Rick, came back to Bloom a couple of years ago after the army. Folks say he's pretty scarred up from a bomb that went off close to him. Now he's just a farmer." Charlotte slapped the steering wheel. "Dammit! There's Amos closing up the bookstore. He's probably on his way to the library to open it up this afternoon. And he carries tales to Lettie and Nadine Clifford."

"They are still alive? Aren't they over ninety?"

Charlotte nodded. "I think one of them is ninety and the other one is a little younger, like eighty-seven or eighty-eight. But, believe me, they'll both live to be a hundred and spread chitchat every day of their lives, especially if it has anything to do with me or my ancestors. Those old biddies should have died years ago."

It would be easier to alter the way the wind blew on any given day in West Texas than it would be to ever get Charlotte to change her mind, so Jennie Sue shifted the subject. "Okay, Mama, what's this perfect cover story?"

Charlotte turned down the lane to the Baker estate. "You are only here on a visit. Percy is out of the country with his job, and your little sports car is in the shop for repairs. It's simple, but I think it will work. No one needs to know that Percy left you or that you had a baby—or worse yet, that you've been holed up like a hermit since then."

"That's partly right. I *am* just here for a short while. I've gotten my degree and now I'm ready to work. I'm going to ask Daddy for a job," she said.

"The hell you are!" Charlotte's voice got shrill like it did just before she went into one of her famous fits.

"Yes, I am, and if he hasn't got one for me, I'll put out résumés and find one somewhere else. And, Mama, why not just tell the truth when someone asks? That's what I plan to do. I don't care what people think or say," Jennie Sue said.

"You most certainly will not!" Charlotte fumed.

"I'm going to have to ease into this to keep my name out of the mud."

Jennie Sue could feel a headache coming on strong. She pinched the bridge of her nose with her thumb and forefinger. "It's going to come out eventually, Mama."

"Keep your hands away from your nose. If we're careful, no one will know. We covered up all that about the baby last Christmas, and that was bigger than this. Where are the rest of your things?" She glanced at the single suitcase in the back seat.

A pang of guilt stabbed Jennie Sue in the heart. She hadn't stepped up and taken charge of her stillborn child's funeral like she should have done. She'd let her mother railroad her into not having a service, and she hadn't even been to Emily Grace's grave site. This was the first time she'd been back.

"That's all of it in the back seat. The feds only allowed me to take one suitcase full of personal clothing, and they went through every item to be sure I wasn't sneaking anything out that could be sold later. The apartment, my car, and the furniture are frozen until they locate Percy, which I doubt they'll ever do," Jennie Sue said past the lump in her throat.

"I thought when you signed the divorce papers, you kept your apartment and your car. And he was supposed to be giving you an alimony check," Charlotte said.

"Turns out everything was still legally in his name. The last two alimony checks bounced. I had a few dollars put away in a savings account, but that dwindled pretty fast." When her mother parked the car in front of the house, Jennie Sue tried to distract her. "What happened to Lester? That's a new gardener over there."

"I hated to let Lester go, but he'd gotten too old to keep up with the grounds. This new kid is right out of college, with a degree in architectural horticulture. He's a big flirt, too, so you stay away from him. God almighty, the gossip would be devastating if you even looked at him cross-eyed," Charlotte said.

Jennie Sue ignored her. "You haven't gotten rid of Frank and Mabel, have you?"

"Lord, no! I couldn't live without Mabel. She's my right arm. She'll be excited to see you, but stick to the story, even with her. Those damned Clifford sisters are her cousins, and she tells them stuff behind my back." Charlotte got out of the car and tossed the keys at an elderly gray-haired man who came out of the garage. "Dust it off, Frank. There was construction going on down the street from the beauty shop."

"Yes, ma'am." Frank grinned at Jennie Sue.

In a couple of long strides, she crossed the distance between them and wrapped the old guy up in a fierce hug. "I've missed everyone so much."

"Not as much as we have you, girl. And I got the first hug. Mabel is going to be so jealous." He stepped back. "Bet you surprised your mama. How'd you get here? Fly into Dallas? Nicky, would you get that suitcase and take it inside for Miz Jennie Sue?"

"I came by bus and I believe I did surprise her. She was at the beauty shop when I called. And thank you, Nicky. We haven't met." She stuck out her hand to shake with him.

"I've only been workin' here a few weeks," Nicky said.

"Stayin' awhile?" Frank glanced at the single suitcase Nicky was removing from the back seat of the car. "Or is this just an overnight trip?"

"I'm stayin' for a long time," Jennie Sue answered.

"That's good. Place seems empty without you." Frank got into the Caddy and fired up the engine. "Your daddy will be real glad that you're here for his birthday bash. It's comin' up in a few weeks."

"I'll be here." Jennie Sue waved as he drove away.

Mabel bustled out of the kitchen and across the living room floor, grabbed Jennie Sue in a bear hug, and kissed both her cheeks. A short woman who was almost as wide as she was tall, she wore her gray hair in a tight little bun at the nape of her neck. Frank had always been like a grandfather to Jennie Sue, and his wife, Mabel, had been a nanny and surrogate grandmother all rolled into one. "Darlin' girl, if I'd known you was comin', I would have made apricot fried pies for you."

"Whatever you are cookin' right now smells delicious. I'm starving. Haven't had anything but a package of cheese crackers all mornin'. Is that fried chicken?"

"Yes, and this chicken had four extra legs," Mabel teased.

"You used to tell me that all the time when I was a little girl." Jennie Sue hugged her a second time.

Charlotte set her lips in a firm line. "She doesn't need pies or fried foods, for God's sake. She's gained at least ten pounds since we saw her in New York last Christmas. We'll have to work hard on getting those off. So she'll have a salad with no more than a quarter cup of smoked salmon on the top and low-fat dressing."

"She hates salmon." Mabel winked at her. "So how about a side salad and a couple of chicken legs? You do still like drumsticks, right?"

"That sounds amazing. So Daddy is having lunch here today?" Jennie Sue asked.

"I am. Welcome home." Dill stepped into the foyer and opened his arms. "Don't get to see my baby girl often enough. Did you come home for my birthday?"

"Of course she did." Charlotte perked right up. "She's going to help me plan it, and we'll have family pictures made."

That gave her mother the perfect excuse, Jennie Sue thought as she walked into her father's arms. The story of why she was home could also have something to do with her dad's birthday. He smelled like bourbon and expensive aftershave, but what was that scent on his shirt? It sure wasn't her mother's Lalique perfume, but then, he probably didn't buy the expensive stuff for his mistresses, since he changed them more often than Charlotte did Cadillacs—and that was once a year.

When she was a little girl, he'd been on a pedestal so high that he disappeared into the clouds. And then came junior high school, when she found out about his affairs from a couple of students who were whispering in the girls' bathroom at school about what they'd heard from their mothers. The pedestal came crashing down. She still loved him—after all, he was her daddy, and he was so charming. But a part of her heart had never forgiven him and most likely never would.

"Glad you got home in time to eat with me, darlin'. I've got to go to Houston after lunch, but I'll be home day after tomorrow for the Fourth of July party. How'd you get here? Flight into Dallas or Amarillo? You should have called. I'd have been glad to fly up to New York and get you." He draped an arm around her shoulders and led her to the dining room.

When Dill walked into a room, every woman in the place needed suspenders to keep her panties from sneaking down around her ankles. With a light frosting of gray hair at his temples and those crystal-clear blue eyes, tight jeans, high-dollar boots, and a belt buckle as big as his ego, he was a force to be reckoned with. Throw in all that beautiful oil money and he had his pick of young mistresses whenever he wanted to make a change.

Jennie Sue wondered who the newest one was as she watched him pull out a chair for Charlotte. When she was living in New York, she didn't have to think about the secrets in the Baker household—secrets that had turned her into an introvert in high school—but they all hit her smack in the face when she stepped through that front door.

Dill seated Jennie Sue, too, before taking his place at the head of the table. "So why didn't you let us know you were flying home?"

"I came by bus, Daddy, because it was cheaper and it gave me a lot of time to think. I really did want to be here for Mama's birthday and for yours. And"—she inhaled deeply and let it out slowly—"I need a job. Think you might find me one in the firm?"

Dill eyed her carefully. "You have an apartment, a car, and very good alimony from that son of a bitch who left you. Why do you need a job?"

"That's what I thought, too, when I signed the divorce papers. But about a month ago, the IRS audited his company and found a lot of fraud and possibly some money laundering. So a couple of weeks ago he stole a bag of diamonds from the company and disappeared with one of his girlfriends. The government stepped in last week and took everything from me. I really, really need a job."

"Honey." He patted her on the arm. "You are too pretty to work. You can stay right here and do whatever you ladies do all day. Your mama will take care of your time, and I'll start a bank account for you tomorrow. Go down to Sweetwater to the Cadillac dealership and pick out whatever car you want."

"I'm twenty-eight years old. I want to be independent," she protested.

"Nonsense. When me and your mama are dead, this whole empire will belong to you. Your mama can find things for you to do, like fund-raisers, organizin' parties, that kind of thing. Leave the moneymakin' stuff to your old daddy here . . . and to a good CEO when I'm gone." Dill set about eating his lunch.

Jennie Sue had learned years ago to pick her battles—this wasn't the time or place. Right now she had to get through the meal, and that meant enduring her mother's dirty looks every time she took a bite of fried chicken.

• • •

Cricket Lawson almost choked on a bite of cherry pie when she glanced across the road and saw Jennie Sue Baker getting off a Greyhound bus. She swallowed quickly and downed half a glass of sweet tea. Then she grabbed her camera and rushed to the window. She'd for sure think that she'd been dreaming by tomorrow if she didn't have proof that Jennie Sue looked like hammered owl crap.

Flashing pictures as fast as her little camera would work, she took at least forty shots of Jennie Sue in faded jeans, sneakers, and a faded orange T-shirt with the Longhorn insignia on the front. Jennie Sue started across the street toward the café, and Cricket's pulse kicked up at least twenty points. She'd hated the girl in high school, but she'd put the past behind her for half an hour if she could shoot a few more close-ups of her without makeup. No one would believe this.

"Dammit!" Cricket hissed when Charlotte pulled up in her white Caddy and Jennie Sue put a suitcase in the back seat. Leave it to that rich bitch to spoil Cricket's day.

"What are you doin' over there?" Lettie Clifford asked from a nearby booth where she was having a banana split.

"Damn that Charlotte Baker," Cricket sighed.

Lettie motioned toward the place across the table from her. "I like the way you're thinkin'.

Come over here, little girl, and tell me what you mean by that."

Cricket set her camera on the table and slid into the booth. "I've got time now that the morning rush is over. Jennie Sue Baker just got off the Greyhound bus that goes on to Sweetwater. She's got one suitcase with her, and she looks like hell. I swear, she didn't even have on makeup."

"No!" Lettie slapped a hand on each side of her chubby face. Standing at just over five feet, she had her dyed black hair worn in that kinky style that was popular in the seventies. One of the richest women in West Texas, she lived in the same little white frame house she'd been born in more than eighty years before, and she didn't take shit off no one—especially Charlotte Baker and her Sweetwater Belles, or as Lettie called them, the Sweetwater Bitches.

"Take a look at these." Cricket touched a few buttons on the camera and showed the pictures to Lettie.

Lettie flipped through them, shaking her head in disbelief the whole time. "That's sure enough Jennie Sue Baker, but why would she be sneaking into town on a bus? And why only one suitcase? It takes something bigger than that for Charlotte to carry her makeup kit in when she's just going to the Walmart store."

Cricket gasped. "The great Charlotte Baker goes to Walmart?"

"Darlin', everyone needs toilet paper," Lettie giggled.

"I figured she'd send Mabel to buy it," Cricket whispered.

Lettie leaned forward. "I saw her in there with my own eyes. She was buyin' toilet paper, and there was a bag of prescription drugs in the cart, but I couldn't read what they were. Probably diet pills. She's so afraid of gainin' a pound that it's downright crazy."

Cricket glanced around the empty café to be sure no one could hear her. "Lot of good it does her. Dill's keepin' company with Darlene O'Malley, and she's younger than me and Jennie Sue."

"You mean that little redhead who works at the bank?" Lettie asked.

"That's the one. She graduated two years behind me, which makes her twenty-six, and that's younger than his daughter. My cousin who works as a teller says that she's his new personal manager on a couple of his accounts and has to be ready to go with him when he takes trips." Cricket flipped through the pictures again.

Lettie dipped into her ice cream. "Well, he better keep a good supply of them little blue pills in his briefcase is all I got to say."

"I know celebrities go out in public lookin' like crap, but I've never seen Jennie Sue without fancy clothes, makeup, and her hair done perfect," Cricket said.

Amos Jones pushed into the store and wiped the sweat from his face with a red bandanna. “Hello, ladies.” He waved.

“Wonder if he knows something?” Lettie whispered.

“He might,” Cricket said out of the side of her mouth and then waved. “Hi, Amos.”

“Y’all hear that Jennie Sue Baker is back in town and she came in on the bus just before noon?” He raised his voice. “I just saw her riding in the car with her mama a few minutes ago. Wonder what’s goin’ on?”

“Come on over here and sit with us,” Lettie said. “How’s things at your bookstore?”

“Doin’ right good.” He slid into the booth beside Cricket. “I heard that this new group of kids comin’ up into the world is goin’ back to real books rather than readin’ them on them damned devices that they hold in their hands. Millennium, they call them. Don’t know how they got that name hung on them, but it helps my business. Vinyl could be next. I got to be at the library here in a minute, but wanted to grab some lunch to take with me.”

Cricket bit back a sigh and slipped her camera back into her purse. Like lots of older men, he used too much shaving lotion and talked too loud. Her brother, Rick, said it was because when folks got older, their senses of smell and hearing both deteriorated.

"What have you heard about Jennie Sue comin' back to town? She hasn't been here in at least two years," Lettie said.

Cricket perked right up. Amos had a tell when he had good gossip—he puffed out his chest so that his bibbed overalls didn't have a single wrinkle in them. And he grinned even bigger than usual, showing off perfectly white dentures in a face that looked like a cross between Andy Rooney and Mickey Rooney.

"Just that she showed up on the bus. I can't imagine why she'd ride a bus all the way from New York City when Dill has an airplane that he could fly up there and bring her home in style. She's still married to that fancy-shmancy diamond dealer, isn't she?" Amos asked.

"Last I heard, but I'll phone Mabel tonight and see what she knows." Lettie's head bobbed up and down in agreement. "Maybe she's goin' to work for Dill in the company."

"Who knows?" Amos's grin got even bigger. "Right now, Dill is off in his private plane with that business lady from the bank, so he's probably not thinkin' about hirin' Jennie Sue for a job in the oil company." His phone pinged, and he worked it up from the bib pocket of his overalls. "Got a text from Nicky, that new gardener Charlotte hired. He says the news is that Jennie Sue is here to help plan Dill's birthday party. You goin' to it, Lettie?"

"Hell, no! Only way I could get in is if I crashed my pickup truck through the front doors, and I ain't willin' to damage my truck. I've had it forty years now, and I'm right partial to the way my butt sits in the driver's seat. You goin' to ride that tricycle of yours to the party?"

Amos chuckled. "I ain't holdin' my breath for an invitation. What about you, Cricket? Reckon Jennie Sue will invite you to the big wingding?"

Cricket snorted. "That ain't never goin' to happen. I wonder why there's never a big party for Charlotte?"

"Never say never or it'll come back and bite you right on the butt." He shook a finger at her. "Charlotte hates her birthday because it proves she's another year older."

"Gravity eventually gets us all," Lettie said.

"Ain't that the truth," Amos agreed. "Pulls us right into the grave. Change of subject here—y'all two got the Friday-night book-club selection read yet?"

"Oh, yeah." Cricket nodded.

"Me and Nadine finished it last week. We're ready for the discussion," Lettie said.

"That's great. Hey, I heard Wilma done decided to retire from housekeepin'. Y'all find anyone to replace her?"

"Not yet, but we're lookin'. Got someone in mind?" Lettie put another bite of ice cream in her mouth.

"No, but I'll keep my ears open. Charlotte hired two new girls out at the Baker place this week. If they don't work out, maybe you could get them," Amos answered.

"I don't want her leftovers." Lettie's tone could have chilled Amos's tea. "So, you believe this crock of bull about Jennie Sue bein' here for her daddy's birthday?"

"Not for a minute," Amos answered.

Lettie rubbed her hands together. "That's the way I figure it. She wouldn't have had to ride a bus for more'n thirty hours, and she would've needed a U-Haul truck to get her baggage to the house. Who knows? It might be good enough to put Charlotte in her place once and for all. There's for sure something goin' on, and I intend to find out what it is."

"Me, too." Amos nodded.

Cricket slid out of the seat and adjusted her apron. "My late granny used to say that Charlotte comes from a long line of women who think their asses are gold plated."

"My sweet little wife"—Amos glanced up at the ceiling—"before the angels came to get her, used to say that if you could buy Charlotte for what she's worth and sell her for what she *thinks* she's worth, you'd make a fortune. Gert Wilson at the grocery store might know something more about all this Jennie Sue stuff, since one of those girls Charlotte hired is her niece."

"Bless Gert's soul." Lettie made a noise with her tongue like an old hen calling to her chickens. "If she hadn't been born as ugly as a mud fence, she might have gotten a better job than checkin' at a grocery store all these years. She's got a heart of gold, but . . ."

"But brains can only take a person so far." Amos slid out of the booth. "See you ladies later. Looks like Elaine has my tea and call-in order all ready. It's time to be openin' the library for the afternoon."

"Why didn't you show him them pictures?" Lettie asked.

"Because I'm being selfish until we find out what she's doin' here," Cricket declared.

"Don't get your hopes up about that happenin' anytime soon. Them Bakers will close up ranks with all the Sweetwater Bitches and we'll never find out a blessed thing," Lettie said.

"I can always hope that the almighty Jennie Sue Baker will be brought down a few notches. Got to get back to work," Cricket said as she slid out of the booth.

Rick wiped sweat from his brow as he settled into the driver's seat of the bookmobile and drove it toward Bloom. It had air-conditioning when it was running, but with the budget cuts, he'd been told to use the air only when he was driving from one place to another. The patrons had learned to get their books checked in and get more in a hurry.

He'd just gotten it parked in the library lot when his sister, Cricket, pulled up in the truck. Twenty years ago, when he was ten years old and it was new, it had been red, but now it had more rust spots than paint. Still, it was the only vehicle they owned, and the engine still purred like it did when it was brand-new.

She tossed the truck keys his way, and he caught them midair. He limped over to the library door and shoved the bookmobile keys into the return slot for books. On Mondays the town's small library was closed by the time he got home from his run up to Roby. But on Tuesdays and Thursdays, he was back from Longworth in plenty of time to take the keys inside before Amos closed up.

"So did you hear the latest news?" Cricket asked as she got into the passenger seat.

"I hope it's that the library got a big donation, and we can take the bookmobile back to Sylvester again. Those little old folks can't get down here to the library, and I'd love to be able to visit with them again." He started up the engine and headed east of town.

"That would be a miracle, not news," Cricket said. "Jennie Sue Baker came back to town. She got off the bus right in front of the café, and I've even got pictures to prove it."

"So?" Rick raised an eyebrow.

"Jennie Sue, the queen of Bloom High School, cheerleader and all the trimmings? In my class—don't you remember her?"

"Sure I do, but how's it news that she's back in town? Her folks live here." Rick remembered Jennie Sue Baker very well. She'd been one of the rich crowd, but she never came off as uppity or too good to talk to those who weren't on her social level, in his opinion.

"She was on a bus," Cricket said.

"*I* came home on a bus. It's a means of transportation," Rick said.

"Not for the almighty Bakers of Bloom, Texas," Cricket sighed. "The last time she came to town, for one of our class reunions, she arrived in a bright-red sports car with her diamond-dealin' husband. Her daddy has an airplane, and her mama drives a brand-new Caddy all the time. I mean, like she trades it every fall for a newer model."

"And this all is your business why?" Rick asked.

"Because I don't like her. And because someday I'm going to be somebody that looks down on her like she did me in high school."

Rick laughed again. "Let the rich do their own thing and mind your own business, Cricket. Be happy where you are."

She sighed and put her hand out the open window, letting the hot air rush through her fingers. “Don’t you ever want to be something else other than a farmer?”

Rick wiggled in the seat to get his bad leg into a more comfortable position. The IED that almost killed him had left scars that still itched and pulled at his skin. “Sure, I want to be able to take that bookmobile to more people. I want to cultivate readers. I want every house in Bloom to have a little lending library out by the road in front of their house where folks can take a book and leave one,” Rick answered. “Other than that, I want to grow good crops and be able to sell them at the farmers’ market in Sweetwater every Friday and Saturday.”

“You’ve always been such a Goody Two-shoes.” When the truck stopped, Cricket slung open the door and stomped toward the house.

Rick stepped out, bent to rub the pain from his knee, and limped across the yard that had gone brown in the Texas summer heat. Water had to be saved for the crops, and besides, a pretty green lawn had to be mowed more often. In stark contrast, his five acres of gardens stood lush and beautiful. Tomatoes as big as saucers were ripe and ready to be harvested, corn ready to be plucked, and green bean vines loaded. Throw in watermelon, cantaloupes, peppers, radishes, and carrots, and he always had a full truckload of food for the market. The rest of the week, he had regular customers in Bloom.

Cricket had turned on the window air-conditioning unit. It hadn't cooled the small house down much, but it wouldn't take long. Living room, kitchen, three bedrooms, and a bathroom—plenty big enough for him and his sister. Home now, but he couldn't wait to get away from it when he'd graduated from high school and joined the Army Rangers. He'd been on a secret mission when he stepped on the IED that sent him flying into the air. When he woke up, he was in a hospital. Several months later they gave him a medical discharge. Strange how a person's life could make a 180-degree turn in the matter of a split second.

"So what's for supper?" he asked.

"I don't care. I'd be happy with a bowl of junk cereal," Cricket answered as she went to the bookcase in the corner of the living room and pulled out an old yearbook.

"I was thinkin' about fried sweet potatoes and maybe a hamburger patty thrown in a cast-iron skillet so that we don't have to fire up the oven," he said. "You need more than junk cereal."

"Whatever," she huffed. "I'll slice tomatoes and cucumbers soon as I thumb through this. I want to see exactly how many times she got her picture in the yearbook. I'm only in it one time for choir other than our senior pictures."

"Those cheerleader pictures would be in there,"

he said. "I remember that from when I played football."

Cricket flipped through the pages, laid it aside, and sighed. "That's all she was. Just a cheerleader. She wasn't a big shot with student council or in anything else. I wonder why. I remember her on Fridays in that cute little short-tailed skirt and a ribbon around her ponytail. I thought she had her nose in everything that went on at the school."

"I remember her as a sweet girl who didn't quite fit in with the crowd she'd been thrown into," he said. "And, sis, I'm really sorry that you are stuck on this farm when you want to do bigger things, but it takes two of us working on top of what you make at the café and what I get from veterans' disability to keep it going."

"I know," she sighed. "We'd better get supper cooked and over with so we can go pick beans and corn until dark. I bet Jennie Sue's getting her nails done."

"Probably, but I wish you weren't obsessed with her. Be your own person."

Cricket kicked off her shoes and headed into the kitchen. "I'm not obsessed with her. She never even has time to give a common person a simple hello, so don't accuse me of that."

"If she's all that terrible, I'm glad you aren't like her, but I always got the feelin' that she was just a little bit shy." He kicked off his boots and joined his sister in the kitchen.

• • •

Rick never wiped the steam from the mirror on the back of the bathroom door after a shower. He didn't want to see the scars on his body or that long, ugly one that ran from his hip down to his ankle. That the doctors had been able to save the leg at all was a miracle, and he was grateful, but he didn't want to look at it.

He'd gone right into the service after high school with the intention of making a career of it. He'd been on dozens of missions in the nine years before he'd gotten hurt and discharged two years before.

It hadn't been easy to come home to Bloom a broken and scarred man. He'd been the star quarterback on the football team his senior year even though he wasn't one of the jocks. The son of a farmer who didn't fit with the in crowd, he'd always thought he'd return with a chestful of medals. Maybe his sister's drive wasn't too different.

He wrapped a towel around his waist and padded barefoot to his bedroom, where he shut the door firmly. No mirrors in that room—only a bed, a nightstand with a lamp, a chest of drawers, an overflowing bookcase, and an old wooden rocking chair that his grandmother had bequeathed to his mother.

He quickly dressed in pajama pants and a loose-fitting T-shirt and chose a book from the collection. He read six pages before he laid the book to the side with a sigh, got up, and found his senior yearbook on the top shelf of his well-organized closet.

He turned to the page with the sophomores. There was Jennie Sue. The underclassmen's pictures were in black and white, but her eyes looked sad. Why had she come to Bloom on a bus? It wasn't a bit of his business, but he couldn't help wondering. The whole town would be talking about it.

You had a little crush on her when you were in high school, that niggling voice in his head said.

"So what?" he said aloud. "No one ever knew about it. She was way above my league. As if she would have gotten into a pickup truck with me."

He stretched out on the bed and laced his fingers behind his head. So she was in town for Dill's birthday party, was she? That meant a few weeks from now, because he remembered from the social pages in the paper last year, it was right near his own birthday.

The likelihood of their paths crossing was slim to none, but he might catch a glimpse of her in town or having coffee in the café—if he was lucky.

Chapter Two

Jennie Sue awoke on Tuesday morning with a start. She sat straight up in bed and blinked several times before she realized that she was in her old bedroom in the house in Bloom, Texas, and not in her New York City apartment. It seemed like a fitting way to begin a new life, but nothing looked or felt right. And yet nothing had changed in the house or in her bedroom.

Last Christmas her mom and dad had spent the holiday with her in New York. She'd had some free time between her online college classes, so they'd gone to a couple of shows, and she and her mother had done a lot of shopping. It had been a surreal visit ending in the birth of Jennie Sue's stillborn daughter, the baby arriving a couple of weeks ahead of schedule.

A lump formed in her throat and tears dammed up behind her eyelids when she thought of that day. With her head in her hands, she bent forward and let the tears have their way at the memory of holding that precious little body in her arms for an hour before they took her. She'd thought that day that she'd never come back to Bloom and never go to the unmarked grave in the Baker plot at the Bloom cemetery, because she wouldn't be able to stand the pain again.

She'd been in such shock after the birth that she'd never quite figured out why her mother was so adamant about keeping her stillborn grandchild a secret.

Out of nowhere a memory of her dad winking at a young woman at a party when she was fifteen came to her mind, and then she remembered seeing the same gesture from Percy when they went to a dinner thrown by a diamond buyer in Paris. She wiped the tears from her eyes and sat up straight, anger replacing pain. If all men were like her father and her ex-husband, she'd stay single the rest of her life.

Sitting there with a million thoughts swirling around her, she wondered if she'd done the right thing by using part of her slim cash stash to come back to Bloom. But it was either that or live in a box on the streets. She had to get out of the apartment, and even if she'd gotten to keep her car, she couldn't afford the parking-garage bill to keep it if she stayed in the big city. Sure, her dad would have stepped in and given her an allowance until she could find a job, but she couldn't afford to live in New York. Truth was, even though she didn't plan to stay in Bloom, something kept pulling her back there. Maybe if she went to her baby's grave site, she'd get closure and she could move on.

She went to the bathroom and stared at her reflection in the mirror. Red eyes from crying, no makeup, and were her cheeks fuller than they'd been a few months ago?

"Maybe Daddy doesn't want to hire me because I have ten extra pounds hanging on my body," she muttered sarcastically. "Mama will have a hissy if he does give me a job. I'm supposed to be just like her and work on being pretty so I can hang on some man's arm at parties. Tried that, Mama. I didn't like it." She talked to herself as she stretched and rolled her head from side to side to get the kinks out of her neck, and then she washed her face with cold water and went to the bedroom to get dressed.

She'd have breakfast and treat herself to doing nothing for the rest of that day, but tomorrow when her dad got home, vacation was over. If he wouldn't hire her, then she'd find a job somewhere else.

"Good mornin'." Charlotte met her in the hallway and put a glass of something green in her hands. "Drink it up and meet me in the fitness room. We've got an hour with the trainer. You simply must get those extra pounds off before Dill's party. People will talk."

Jennie Sue sipped the green goo and frowned. "I can't stand this stuff. You know I hate the taste of kale."

"You'll acquire a taste for it after a few weeks," Charlotte informed her as she hurried off to the trainer.

Jennie Sue carried the glass into the bathroom and poured it down the drain. Green tea was one thing, but that stuff wasn't fit for toad frogs or cockroaches. Her mother was already on a treadmill when she peeked inside the room. She took one look at the machinery and walked out, thankful that neither Charlotte nor the trainer had seen her.

She sniffed the air on the way down the wide staircase, but nothing, not even a whiff of coffee, floated up to her. Definitely not a hint of bacon or hot biscuits in the oven—she could understand the absence of food since her dad wasn't home, but surely her mother hadn't given up her morning cup of coffee.

"Hey, Mabel, am I too late for breakfast?" she asked when she reached the kitchen.

"Honey, I can whip up something for you, but since your daddy's gone, we don't do breakfast. Your mama drinks one of those god-awful things that she makes in the blender, and she's stopped drinkin' even decaf. Says that she read in an article that it made a woman's face wrinkle up faster," Mabel answered. "I ain't one to meddle, but even the garbage disposal would spit that green crap out. Me and Frank got us a coffeepot out in the garage, and we have a cup before we start our day."

"Well, I'm having coffee," Jennie Sue declared.

"Didn't she bring you a glass full of that liquid grass?" Mabel asked.

"I just cleaned out the drain in the bathroom sink with it. Looked to me like it would work as good as that declogging stuff. How does Daddy get his morning three cups?"

Mabel drew in a long breath and let it out slowly. "Frank keeps the coffee going in the garage all day long. Man couldn't live without it, and Dill goes out there and gets it in the mornin', too. I reckon you could do the same."

Jennie Sue picked up an empty mug and headed to the garage, returning a minute later sipping at the steaming-hot coffee. "What's makin' Mama sick is that green shit."

"Most likely, but you're going to suffer her wrath if she smells coffee driftin' up the stairs. Poor old Dill sure does," Mabel said. "But now that we're alone, tell me, what're you really doin' here, child?"

"Tryin' to talk Daddy into givin' me a job. Percy left me and moved in with his girlfriend months ago. I thought he owned the apartment we had, and I got it in the divorce, but it was leased. Once the alimony checks started bouncing, I had to deplete my savings to finish my business degree online," she answered, finishing with the tale of her ex's diamond-filled escape from the feds.

"I'm so sorry, honey, but I got to admit, I thought that man was shifty from the beginnin'. He had a big name and acted all proper, but there was something about him that didn't add up."

Mabel patted her on the back. “I had a feelin’ you were home for something more than your daddy’s party. You want some bacon, eggs, and hash browns to go with that coffee?”

Jennie Sue nodded. “Yes, ma’am, but you don’t have to wait on me. I’ve been takin’ care of myself ever since he left. You go on about whatever you were doing.”

“Okay, then.” Mabel’s head and all three of her chins bobbed up and down. “Just put your dirty dishes in the sink.”

“No need. Percy had to be in control of everything. Believe me, I know how to keep things spotless. First month we were married, he fired four housekeepers and told me that I’d learn to take care of the place the way he wanted it done, or I could go on back to my Podunk Texas town.” Jennie Sue opened the refrigerator.

“Why did you stay with a man like that?” Mabel’s eyes narrowed into slits.

“Why do you think? I was groomed to be a trophy wife from birth. Keeping a spotless apartment at least gave me something to do.” She lowered her voice. “Truth is, I was glad when he ran off with a bag of diamonds and another woman. I’d had about all I could stand of his cheating, and after . . .” She stopped before she said too much.

“You deserve better than that kind of treatment,” Mabel growled. “I’m sorry about the way things turned out, honey. You go on and make yourself a good breakfast. I've got to go make sure those two girls your mama hired to clean are doing things right."

"This place couldn't run without you, Mabel." Jennie Sue laid six strips of bacon out in a cast-iron skillet.

"Oh, honey, there ain't a one of us that couldn't be replaced," Mabel replied as she left the room.

Jennie Sue had lived on fast food on the bus trip for more than two days, so she was really looking forward to a good, hearty breakfast. When she finished cooking, she carried her plate of crispy bacon, four fried eggs, two pieces of toast, and a nice big hash brown that she'd made from a real potato to the table. She'd just sat down to eat when her mother entered the kitchen.

"What the hell?" Charlotte stopped dead.

Jennie Sue got ready for a lecture about calories and fat grams. "Good mornin', Mama. Care to join me for a healthy breakfast? It's the most important meal of the day, you know."

Charlotte picked up the plate, slid everything on it into the garbage disposal, and flipped the switch. "This is tough love, darlin'. You are going to get back into shape so we can shop for decent clothing for you. You can't go out in public in those ratty cheap jeans and worn-out running shoes. And I'm not buying one single thing for you until you are back in the size you wore when you got married."

Jennie Sue clenched her hands under the table. "And what if I don't lose the pounds, and what if I like my ratty jeans?"

"Don't get pissy with me. This is for your own good. We've got to get you in shape so you can find another husband," Charlotte said. "If I didn't love you, I wouldn't fuss at you."

"I don't want another husband, and I sure don't want another rich one. I'm not you, Mama. I want to eat what I want and live my own life," she said through clenched teeth.

Charlotte grabbed a towel and wiped sweat from her face. "Settle down, darlin'. Of course you want a rich husband. You're just mad at me for takin' care of you. We'll slowly let out the word that Percy lost all his money and you divorced him. By the end of all our Christmas parties, I bet you'll have another good man on the hook. I'll call Mabel to make you an egg-white omelet with tomatoes and fresh spinach if you think you have to eat something. But no more orange juice." She wiggled her finger so fast it was a blur. "Too many carbs, and no toast or biscuits besides."

"No, thank you," Jennie Sue said. "I'll remake my own breakfast."

"Not under my roof." Charlotte raised her voice.

"That can be remedied real easy, Mama." Jennie Sue pushed back her chair and stood.

"You wouldn't dare leave." Charlotte's voice jacked up several octaves. "I'd be the laughingstock of the whole state if you go out in public looking like you do. Gossip has already stirred up over the fact that you came into town on a bus."

"I don't give a damn about rumors. If they're gossiping about me, they're letting someone else rest. I'll be glad to whip up an egg-white omelet for you if you want one." She had learned long ago to stay calm when her mother's voice went all shrill and squeaky.

Charlotte glared at Jennie Sue, who had no doubt that things could start flying through the air at any time if her mother didn't get her way.

"I don't want a damned egg-white omelet. I want you to be reasonable and do what I say. I'm your mother. I know what's best for you," Charlotte yelled, loud enough that it could have been heard all the way up in the attic.

"Oh, really? Seems to me that you liked Percy and thought he was the right man for me. Look how that turned out." Jennie Sue wasn't backing down.

"What happened to you?" Charlotte picked up a cup and slung it at the wall. "You used to listen to me."

"Yes, I did, and look what it got me. I hated

being a cheerleader, but it was important to you, so I endured it. I didn't want a big fancy wedding, and I was a wreck the whole time you planned it. I hated New York, but you said I'd get used to it. Listenin' to you hasn't always worked for me." She went to the pantry and got a broom and dustpan.

"Don't you dare clean that up," Charlotte declared. "That's Mabel's job."

Jennie Sue ignored her and swept the shattered glass into the dustpan. "Is it worth it, Mama?"

"Is what worth it?" Charlotte popped her hands on her hips.

"All these years of ignoring all Daddy's affairs."

"Was it worth ignoring Percy's?" Charlotte shot back at her.

"No, it wasn't, but after living in this house, I'd been trained to think that was life in general. The husband cheats. The wife ignores it as long as she gets all her pretty little things like new cars and jewelry. I hate all this." She waved her hand to take in everything. "I'm glad that Percy left, so I didn't have to leave him. I was sick of what it took to be his wife." She picked up her coffee cup.

Charlotte shook her finger under Jennie Sue's nose. "Don't judge me, girl! I've got everything I want in life."

"Good for you if you are satisfied with a

relationship like this. But I don't want another rich husband if this is part of the package deal. I want to eat what I want and wear what I want, and having a fancy house or a new Caddy every year isn't worth putting up with a cheating husband or a demanding bastard like Percy." Jennie Sue started out of the room.

"Well, good luck with that," Charlotte screamed. "Go on up there and pout in your self-righteousness. Someday you'll learn what life is all about."

Jennie Sue turned around. "Take me like I am or else. That's my new motto."

"Then you can live with the consequences of such a stupid thing, and I'll see to it you don't have a dime to live on until you come to your senses," Charlotte threatened. "I know for a fact that you've got less than a thousand dollars in your purse."

"You been snoopin' in my stuff?" Jennie Sue asked.

"I call it protectin' my daughter," Charlotte said.

"I can always get a job as a waitress somewhere."

Charlotte threw her hand over her forehead and slumped down into a kitchen chair. "You are going to ruin me for sure. I don't know why God couldn't have given me an outgoing daughter that I could relate to, instead of my mother-in-law reincarnated."

"I'm so sorry that you didn't get what you wanted." Jennie Sue heard another cup hit the wall as she climbed the steps, but then there was nothing but silence.

"Tough love," Jennie Sue muttered. "Well, Mama, that works both ways."

In fifteen minutes, she was in the garage with her purse slung over her shoulder and her suitcase in her hand. It was three hours until the daily bus came through Bloom on its way to Sweetwater and then went on to Abilene. She'd buy a ticket for Abilene, spend the rest of the day at the employment office, and then go from that point. Hopefully she could find something—anything from doing waitress work to cleaning hotel rooms—until she could put her degree to use in some kind of business.

But first, she was using a few dollars to buy a decent breakfast at the café. After that she'd go to the cemetery to visit her daughter's grave, and then she'd get on the bus and never look back.

"Hey, Frank, reckon I could borrow a car? I'll leave it at the bus station," she said when she reached the garage.

Frank was bent over her mother's Caddy and raised up slowly with a hand on his lower back. He'd always been tall, thin, and lanky, but right then she realized how much he'd aged in the past couple of years. Working for her mother would age anyone. Hell, he and Mabel had practically raised her. Wrinkles were etched into his long, slender face, and his hair had gone completely gray.

He raised an eyebrow. "Where are you goin'? Mabel told me about your troubles, child. You should stay here where people love you."

"I can't live like this, Frank," she said.

"Wait till Dill gets home, honey. He'll straighten out all this between you and your mama. She'll come around and let you have bacon." Frank grinned. "Don't remember you ever goin' through a rebellious streak as a teenager. Why now?"

"It's more than bacon. I'll gladly drive the old work truck."

Nicky came in from outside and tossed his work gloves in the old truck. "I've got to go to the feed store to get a load of fertilizer, so I'll be glad to give you a ride to Bloom, but the bus don't come through for another few hours."

"Thank you." Jennie Sue threw her suitcase into the bed of the truck.

He brushed his dark hair back with his fingertips. His face was angular with just a hint of a chin dimple, and his muscles testified that he worked hard at his job.

"Now, exactly where do you want to go to wait for the bus?" He opened the door for her before getting into the truck himself, then put on a pair of wraparound sunglasses and started the engine.

"The Main Street Café," she said. "You'll pass it on your way through town."

"Been there lots of times. Love their breakfast. Best pancakes in the state."

"Thanks." The idea of warm syrup over buttered pancakes almost erased the bitter taste of the argument.

The old truck rattled to a stop in front of the café. Nicky hopped out, retrieved Jennie Sue's suitcase, and set it on the sidewalk as she got out of the truck. She picked it up and headed for the first open booth in the café, set it on the seat across the table from her, and picked up a menu stuck between the ketchup and the napkin dispenser.

"What can I get you? Well, my goodness, I didn't even recognize you, Jennie Sue," the waitress said.

"Hello, Elaine. I hear that you own this place now. That right?" Jennie Sue asked.

"Yep, it is. Bought it last year when my husband got killed in a car wreck. The settlement wouldn't support me the rest of my life. All I'd ever known was cleaning house, cookin', and raisin' a couple of kids. Figured I could run a café, so here I am. My mama watches my two boys, and Cricket Lawson stayed on as part-time help," she said.

Jennie Sue glanced over the menu. "I'm sorry to hear about your husband, but good for you for takin' control of your own life. And you're blessed to have family to help you."

"I couldn't do it without them," Elaine said.

"While we were drivin' here, Nicky said I should get the big country breakfast, so I'll take that and maybe a big glass of milk."

"No coffee?"

"Nope, just drank several cups," Jennie Sue answered.

"Then it will be right out."

Elaine hadn't changed much since high school. She'd been a few years ahead of Jennie Sue and had always been super sweet, but she'd never quite fit in with the popular girls. She'd worn her dark hair long in those days, but now it was short and she'd gained probably twenty pounds. Jennie Sue wondered if Elaine's mother ever fussed at her about the extra weight.

"Well, well, well! Are you leaving us already? You only got here yesterday." Lettie shoved the suitcase over and sat down across the table from Jennie Sue. Short, as round as Mabel, and sporting a kinky hairdo that had gone out of style years ago, Lettie hadn't changed since Jennie Sue was a little girl.

"Yes, ma'am," Jennie Sue answered. "How have you been, Miz Lettie?"

"Elaine, I'll have a big stack of pancakes and two orders of bacon," Lettie called out across the café.

"Got it," Elaine yelled.

"So where are you going?" Lettie turned back to Jennie Sue.

"To find a job," she answered.

"What kind of skills and experience do you have?"

Elaine crossed the floor and set Jennie Sue's breakfast in front of her. "Millie will bring out your order shortly, Miz Lettie."

"No rush. Just send me a cup of coffee, and I'll be happy until it gets here." Lettie waved her away with a flick of the wrist and turned back to Jennie Sue. "Now, you were about to tell me about your work experience."

Jennie Sue picked up the saltshaker and applied an unhealthy dose to her eggs. "I have no experience, but I do have a business degree. The only thing I'm good at is keeping a clean house and organizing fund-raisers and parties."

"Hmm." Lettie pursed her lips. "So why didn't you have a housekeeper up there in New York?"

"Percy was never pleased with the way they cleaned."

"Was?" Lettie asked.

"Been divorced for over a year."

"Oh, really?" Lettie cocked her head to one side.

"Yes, ma'am."

"Me and my sister, Nadine, lost our house-keeper a couple of weeks ago. The lady that worked for us cleaned for me on Friday and Nadine on Thursday. You interested?"

Charlotte would probably go into cardiac arrest if Jennie Sue became nothing more than a maid for her archenemies. But hey, it was a job, and Jennie Sue damn sure knew how to clean a house so well that it would pass judgment in the courts of heaven.

"I might be interested if you could point me in the direction of an apartment or a rental house of some kind that wouldn't be too expensive," Jennie Sue answered.

"I got an apartment over my garage. It's pretty small, but it'll work for a single person. I'd be willing to rent it to you furnished. You'll clean for me on Friday each week, but the last week in the month, you won't get paid. That'll be your rent," Lettie said.

Jennie Sue could imagine Charlotte throwing whatever she could get her hands on at the wall when one of the Belles called her with that bit of news. Even if she was angry with her mother over trying to mold her into another Wilshire woman, she couldn't do that to her mother—or could she? How else would she be independent?

She picked up a piece of crisp bacon with her fingers and took a bite while she thought about the offer. It was a job that she could do. It was a place for her to live. She didn't have to live in a shelter or sleep on a park bench. However, her mother would never speak to her again, and the rumors would be so hot that they might burn down the whole town of Bloom.

Elaine arrived with Lettie's pancakes and set them in front of her. "Sorry it took so long. Got a phone call, so the first ones I made were too brown. I wouldn't even take those things home to feed to the kids' hound dogs."

"Thanks," Lettie said and then turned her attention back to Jennie Sue. "I hated to see her husband die, but it's the best thing that ever happened to her mama. The woman was fairly well wastin' away after Elaine's daddy died. Now she keeps Elaine's kids, and she's got a brand-new lease on life."

A surge of jealousy shot through Jennie Sue.

Lettie lowered her voice. "Elaine's doin' a good job of runnin' the café and raisin' them boys." Lettie glanced out the window and frowned. "Sweet Jesus! There's Amos. Sometimes I think that man is stalkin' me."

Amos pushed his way into the café and dragged up a chair to Lettie and Jennie Sue's table without being invited.

"Hey, Millie, bring me a plate just like Lettie's," he yelled across the empty café.

"Will do. Coffee?" she asked.

"Yep, black as sin and strong as Hercules." He grinned. "Now, what are you ladies discussing?"

"Jennie Sue needs a job, and me and my sister

need a housekeeper. She's thinkin' about working for me on Friday and Nadine on Thursday. Says she knows how to clean houses since her husband was a neat freak."

"That so? Well, if you work for them two days a week, I could offer you three days at the bookstore. I'm gettin' too old to work two jobs. Our little library is volunteer and stocked by donation, so I keep it open in the afternoons and work in my bookstore in the mornin's. If I had someone to help me out three days a week, I could keep the store open and have a little time off for myself. It'll only be part-time and minimum wage, but you can read all the books you want for free," Amos said.

"Can I move into the garage apartment today?" Jennie Sue asked.

"It's empty and waiting for you," Lettie said. "But you got to know, Nadine and me are picky. We hate dust and we like our sheets dried on the line when it's not rainin'."

"No problem. I'll take both jobs," Jennie Sue said.

Lettie tapped her finger on the table. "Let's see—tomorrow is Wednesday, but that's the Fourth of July. Why don't you just move in today and get all settled tomorrow, and then you can start work the next day at Nadine's place?"

"Y'all know this is only temporary. I'll start putting out résumés for a job using my business degree and be gone by September or October at the latest. Both y'all all right with that?" Jennie Sue asked.

Lettie cut into the tall stack of pancakes and shoved a forkful in her mouth. "That'll give us more time to find someone permanent."

"I'm fine with it." Amos stuck out his hand. "We got a deal?"

Jennie Sue hesitated, thinking about Charlotte again. She had no desire to cause her mother pain and misery, but she also didn't want to live in a shelter or a dirt-cheap motel while she hunted for a job. She slowly reached across her plate and shook hands with Amos.

"I'll be there bright and early on Monday morning," she said.

"Great!" Amos wiggled in his chair like a little boy. "I'll even throw in lunch on the days that you work for me as a benefit."

"Thank you for that." Jennie Sue looked around the small café. Ten tables for four down the middle and ten booths on one side—not a huge place, but if the burgers were as good as the breakfast, then she might put on another ten pounds by September.

"And my sister and I always provide lunch for our cleaning lady. You'll arrive at nine sharp and work until five, with an hour off from twelve until one. And sometimes in the evening, if you are willin', we pay extra if you'll drive us down to Sweetwater to Walmart or to the movies."

Evidently, Lettie wasn't going to let Amos get ahead of her.

"And you'll have to drive them to our book-club meeting the first Friday of every month. That's this week, so put it on your calendar. Seven o'clock at the bookstore. We're reading *Scarlett*, but we wouldn't expect you to read it in such a short length of time."

Jennie Sue raised a palm. "I've read that book already. *Gone with the Wind* is one of my all-time favorites."

"Great!" Amos said. "You're goin' to fit right in with the rest of our club."

"Yes, she is." Lettie beamed. "When I get finished with my breakfast, you can ride home with me, and I'll show you the apartment. I could use some things from Walmart in Sweetwater, so you can drive me down there this afternoon. You'll need to get a few groceries and things for yourself, I'm sure. Place comes with everything you need in the kitchen except a full refrigerator. You need an advance on your salary for that?"

"No, ma'am, I've got that much covered." Jennie Sue slathered butter on her biscuit and tore the top off a plastic container of strawberry jam.

Lettie was getting a huge kick out of this, but Jennie Sue figured that beggars couldn't be choosers, and neither Amos nor Lettie had mentioned her extra ten pounds or the fact that she was having bacon for breakfast.

Lettie's place was a pretty little yellow house with white shutters and an immaculately kept lawn with colorful lantana, impatiens, and marigolds growing in the flower beds. She pulled into a driveway leading into the garage at the back of the house.

"The apartment steps are inside the garage, so you'll need keys for both garage and apartment." Lettie handed them off to Jennie Sue. "You go on up there and get settled in. I've got to talk to Nadine and tell her that I've solved our problem about a cleaning lady. You have a cell phone?"

"Yes, ma'am, I do," Jennie Sue said, glad that she'd have a paycheck by the time the next phone bill arrived. She wondered why Lettie had chosen such a small house when everyone knew that she and Nadine were among the richest people in town. Maybe it was because she was frugal, or maybe it was because she didn't need anything more since she'd always lived alone.

Lettie fished around in her purse until she found her phone and handed it to Jennie Sue. "Put your number in that. I barely know how to accept calls, and I'll need to know how to get ahold of you if me and Nadine want to go somewhere."

Jennie Sue hit a few keys and handed it back to Lettie. "There you go."

"I'm figuring in about an hour we'll be ready to go to Walmart. We been wantin' to go for a couple of days, but I don't like to drive down there in Sweetwater."

Jennie Sue's eyes shifted to the pickup.

"Nadine has one of them SUV vehicles that seats seven. We always take it when we go places. Trouble is, she's over eighty and done lost her driver's license for too many wrecks. Me, I just hate to drive, so I get out of it any way I can," Lettie admitted. "Right up them steps is your new place. I hope you like it."

"I'm sure I will. Thank you, Lettie," Jennie Sue said.

"Solves a problem for all of us. I'll call you when I'm ready to go."

Jennie Sue carried her suitcase up the stairs, dropped it right inside the door, and immediately called her mother. Charlotte should hear the news from her daughter's lips and not the gossip vine of Bloom, Texas.

"Where the hell are you?" Charlotte answered. "We have appointments to get our nails done at ten thirty and then lunch with a couple of my Sweetwater Belles. I'm hoping to talk them into letting you serve on a committee or two."

Jennie Sue inhaled deeply and spit out the whole story. She got nothing but total silence so long that she thought her mother had hung up on her.

"That's not funny," Charlotte hissed.

"It's not a joke. I'm sitting right here in my new apartment," Jennie Sue said.

"You might as well have taken a gun and shot me through the heart. You know those old Clifford bats hate me. I'm disgraced." There was a shrill shriek, and Jennie Sue heard something hard hit a wall.

"Mama, I did not do this to hurt you. I told you and Daddy both I want a job. I need to be independent so I don't have to shut my eyes to a cheating husband."

"That woman and her sisters were a thorn in my grandmother's side and my mother's," Charlotte said. "I'm coming over. You'd better be ready to come home when I get there."

"Is Daddy going to give me a job in the firm?" Jennie Sue asked.

"No, he is not."

"Why?"

"Because I told him not to."

"Why?" Jennie Sue gasped.

"Because that's low class. Wilshire women do not work, Jennie Sue. You've been raised better than that. And I told your daddy if he gives you a job, then he can't have any more mistresses," she said.

"I'm a Baker, not a Wilshire. You said so yourself this morning," Jennie Sue argued.

“Then have it your way, but don’t expect a dime of your Wilshire inheritance if you feel like that.”

That’s when Charlotte did hang up on her—for real.

Jennie Sue threw the phone at the small sofa and took stock of her new place. The whole thing was smaller than her bedroom at her mother’s house. A small television sat on top of the chest of drawers in front of a sofa that snugged up to the end of a four-poster bed. A galley kitchen was located to her right, with two doors on her left—one into a bathroom and the other into a closet.

A set of french doors led out to a tiny balcony barely big enough to accommodate a plastic lawn chair. She threw her suitcase on the bed, which was covered with a bright-yellow chenille bedspread.

“It beats living in a box in an alley or in a shelter—and it comes with sheets and towels, so I’m not going to gripe,” she said out loud.

Tuesday was Rick’s day to drive the bookmobile to several locations in Bloom, starting at the senior citizens’ center at one o’clock so the elderly folks could turn in books and check them out right after their lunch. He stayed thirty minutes. From there he drove to the bank parking lot and stayed an hour. After that he drove back to the library and spent the time there until it was time for Cricket to get off work.

Reaching the library was his favorite part of the whole week. He could sit in an old, comfortable chair in air-conditioned comfort and read, or else visit with Amos in between customers and replenishing the bookmobile's stock.

He hurried out of the heat and inside the cool library to find Amos grinning like he'd just found a first edition. The short little guy had a perpetual grin, but today the extra twinkle in his eyes said he was up to something ornery. Amos handed Rick a tall glass of sweet tea and motioned to a couple of chairs over by the library's two computers.

"Jennie Sue Baker took a job cleaning houses for Nadine and Lettie Clifford." He sat down, but he could hardly be still.

Rick took the other chair and combed his dark hair back with his fingertips. "Are you crazy? Is this Long Island iced tea or regular old sweet tea?"

"Nope." Amos shook his head emphatically. "I was right there when she took the job. And that's not all. I hired her to help me out on Monday, Tuesday, and Wednesday in the bookstore."

Rick's eyebrows drew down into one line. "*The* Jennie Sue Baker, daughter of Dill and Charlotte, granddaughter of the Wilshires?"

"Yep." Amos was almost giddy.

Rick shook his head and sipped his tea. "I still don't believe it."

"It's the one hundred percent guaranteed gospel truth. Lettie couldn't wait to take Jennie Sue home with her, and I bet the phone lines have been hot with the news."

More than a dozen customers who were more interested in the latest news than checking out books kept Amos hopping up and down from his chair. Finally, Cricket rushed into the library and sank down in the chair beside him. "Did you hear? Jennie Sue is going to clean houses for the Clifford sisters. I keep listenin' for the ambulance on its way toward Charlotte's house."

Rick frowned. "It's good, honest work. What's the big deal?"

"The big deal is that it's their princess cleaning houses and living in a tiny little apartment above a garage. And guess what else? She's been divorced for more than a year. Her husband left her, and the IRS is hot on his trail for income-tax evasion. And he left with another woman," Cricket said.

Jennie Sue was divorced—he wouldn't go there. Not with his scars, the limp, and the fact that the only time he was ever somebody was his senior year in high school, when Bloom went to district playoffs. Add in that he was a farmer, and there was no sense in wasting a single minute thinking about her. Besides, she'd get over whatever rebellion she seemed to have fallen into and go back to her lush lifestyle before long. Once a socialite, always a socialite, right?

"We were busy all day. The news spread fast, and people came to the café to talk about it."

"I hate this behind-the-hands talk," Rick muttered.

"Not me." Amos pulled up a wooden chair and joined them. "I love it. Brings excitement into our lives. Charlotte is probably on the verge of a stroke. Dill might even have to leave his business trip with Darlene and come on back home to settle her down. She gets pretty worked up when she doesn't get her way. Been like that since she was a kid. Jennie Sue never did have that Wilshire temper."

Some things would never change in Bloom. They had put in new curbs and sidewalks two years ago, and some of the vacant stores on Main Street were occupied now, but if the citizens couldn't gossip, it wouldn't be long until the place dried up into a ghost town.

"So what've you been readin'? Did you finish *Scarlett*?" Rick rubbed the scar on his upper arm and tried to steer Amos and Cricket away from the gossip.

"Yep, and then read it again," Amos answered. "You know, Jennie Sue kind of reminds me of Scarlett. She's takin' things into her own hands. I like that in a woman. My sweet wife, Iris, was like that. She didn't let nobody, not even me, tell her what she could or couldn't do. Lord, that woman was as stubborn as a cross-eyed mule in a thunderstorm."

Rick nodded. "I'd say that's pretty stubborn, but I know another woman here in Bloom that's about as stubborn as that, too."

"You'd better not be talkin' about me. In my opinion, Jennie Sue is just plain uppity, Amos," Cricket said.

"Evenin', Amos. I'm glad I got here before you closed." A lady laid a book on the counter. "I hate to keep a book out over the due date. Did you hear that Jennie Sue Baker is going to clean houses for the Clifford sisters?"

"You ready to go home?" Rick asked Cricket under the older folks' conversation.

"In a few minutes," she said.

"I appreciate good patrons, Joyce. Tell me what you've heard." With Amos's hearing going, Rick was surprised people couldn't follow the conversation from outside the building.

"It's closin' time for the library, and we've got work to do," Rick said.

"Oh, okay." Cricket shot a dirty look his way and then called out over her shoulder as they left, "See y'all later."

Amos waved and kept listening to Joyce. Rick wondered if Jennie Sue's ears were burning yet.

Chapter Three

"You look like your grandma Vera Baker," Nadine said as she handed the SUV keys over to Jennie Sue. "Sweetest woman I ever met. She wasn't at all like the Wilshire side of your family. Why, I remember when we'd have a family dinner at the church for funerals, she'd always insist on bringing three or four desserts instead of trying to cancel dessert entirely, and she loved to garden. Sometimes she'd bring sacks full of vegetables to the church and leave them on the table in the foyer so folks could help themselves."

Lettie nodded. "Sad day when she left this earth."

Nadine was tall, thin as a rail, and had sparkling blue eyes. Her gray hair was twisted up into a bun on the top of her head. The sisters were definitely not lookalikes—not by any stretch of the word.

"Thank you, Jesus, for giving us a housekeeper and a driver. I was about to go crazy thinkin' about sittin' in the house another day," Nadine said as she got into the back seat and fastened her seat belt.

"My name is not Jesus, and you've gone somewhere every day since Wilma quit workin' for us," Lettie said.

"Then thank you, sister," Nadine said. "When we get done shopping, let's go to the Dairyland for burgers and ice-cream cones for supper. My treat tonight."

"You're just wantin' to flirt with that old man who carries the trays to the tables," Lettie said.

"The day I quit flirtin' is the day you two can put me in a casket, fold my arms over my chest, and send me on to see Flora up in heaven," Nadine declared.

"How do you know Flora went to heaven?" Lettie asked. "She never set foot in the church after Mama died."

"Because she was too mean and cantankerous for the devil to want her," Nadine answered. "Lord, that girl was wild as a hooker on steroids when she was young."

"And how wild is that?" Jennie Sue asked.

"She came close to breakin' up your great-grandma's weddin'. She was the girl the best man talked into doing a striptease for your great-grandpa's bachelor party. That was what started the feud between the Wilshires and the Cliffords."

"Oh, really?" Jennie Sue glanced in the rear-view mirror.

"Your mama didn't tell you all about it?"

"Guess not," Jennie Sue answered.

"It's a long story," Lettie said. "We'll tell it another time. Right now, we've got to be sure we got everything we need on our list for tomorrow's dinner. You're invited, Jennie Sue, if you aren't goin' home for the party there. If you are, we have dessert after the fireworks, so you can join us for that."

"Thank you. I'm going to my folks' house for their annual party tomorrow, but I might be able to slip away and get in on the dessert," she answered. So the fact that her mother didn't like the Cliffords because they were such big gossips didn't cover the whole story. Maybe on Friday, when Jennie Sue cleaned Lettie's house, she'd hear the rest of the tale.

Bloom was a little less than ten miles north of Sweetwater. The drive usually took about ten minutes unless there was traffic, and that night there was none. The sisters talked about their menu for dinner the next night the whole way to the Walmart. "Where do we meet up when we get done?" Jennie Sue asked when she stopped at the door to drop the sisters off.

"We'll wait for you by the shopping carts," Lettie answered. "We don't never get scattered out when we shop. Tried that once and spent hours trying to find each other."

"You could use your cell phones," Jennie Sue said.

"Honey, I ain't about to use mine anywhere they have fluorescent lighting. I heard tell that the combination of the lights and whatever signals are on the phones mixin' up in a place like this can cause cancer," Nadine said as she got out of the van. "And I don't take chances like that."

"That's hogwash," Lettie declared. "That can't cause cancer or half the people in Texas would be droppin' dead like flies all around us." She lowered her voice to a whisper. "But if there's aliens out there—and I'm not sayin' that they exist or that they don't—but just in case there are, I bet they can listen in on them things. Give me a phone with a cord on it or even one of the cordless like we got in our houses now and there ain't no way them little fellers can hear what I'm sayin'. That's why I don't use my cell phone in public unless it's an emergency of some kind."

Jennie Sue wasn't sure if they were serious or joking with her, so she simply said, "Okay. I'll try to find us a good parking spot."

"Wait a minute!" Nadine dug around in a black purse almost as big as Jennie Sue's suitcase. "Use this so you can park closer to the door." She handed her a handicapped tag.

"Yes, ma'am." Jennie Sue hung it on the rearview mirror. "I've got to get stuff, too, so I'll meet you at the front doors, right?"

"We'll be right there, waitin' on you." Lettie got out of the vehicle and followed Nadine.

Jennie Sue circled the lot once and found an empty handicapped place very close to the grocery-store end of Walmart. When she got inside, Lettie and Nadine were waiting, each with a cart.

"It's my turn to lead the pack," Nadine said. "Then Lettie and you can bring up the rear. We go up and down all the grocery aisles, and then if we need something else, we go that direction. Next time Lettie gets to drive the lead cart." She lowered her voice. "She drives a cart like she does that ancient truck of hers, like a bat out of hell, and I forget half a dozen things because she's going too fast."

"Oh, hush." Lettie took her place behind Nadine. "Nadine drives her cart like she's had six shots of moonshine. I was the good child. She and Flora were the wild ones." Lettie bumped her in the butt with her cart.

Nadine sent a go-to-hell look over her shoulder. "You will pay for that when it's my turn to drive behind you." Then she led the caravan to the deli counter, where she ordered half a pound of shaved ham, two pounds of thick-sliced turkey breast, and a pound of American cheese.

"Hey, Lettie," an older woman yelled and pushed her cart in that direction. "I heard you found a cleaning lady. Want to share her with me? I could use some help every other week on Wednesdays."

"Nope." Lettie shook her head. "Can't do it. She's got a job except on Thursdays and Fridays, and me and Nadine have her on those days."

"Well, rats! And who is this with y'all?" she asked. "Why, bless my soul if it ain't Jennie Sue Baker. You might not remember me—Linda Williams. I was your grandmother's hairdresser for years."

"I'm sorry, I don't, but it's still nice to see you," Jennie Sue said.

"That's all right, darlin'. You remind me of Vera Baker when she was your age. She was the sweetest customer that I had," Linda said as she pushed her cart toward the checkout counter.

Jennie Sue barely remembered her grandmother on the Baker side, and now twice in one day, she'd been told that she either acted or looked like her.

Linda had barely gotten past the doughnut display when she whipped out her cell phone. Evidently she wasn't afraid of cancer or aliens as much as not being the first one to deliver the news that she'd seen Jennie Sue with the Clifford sisters at Walmart.

"Your turn to order deli stuff," Nadine told Lettie.

"Don't need anything here. You go on and get what you want, and then we'll start down the bread aisle." Lettie moved her cart to let Jennie Sue move up in line.

She was so busy deciding whether to buy half a pound or a whole one of pastrami that she didn't even turn around when she heard Lettie talking to someone else. She decided on half a pound and then ordered the same amount of white American cheese. She put her order into the cart and turned around. She recognized Cricket right away and nodded—and then looked into the most gorgeous green eyes she'd ever seen on a man. They were rimmed with thick black lashes that curled upward—entirely too pretty for God to have given to a man. Good Lord, was that Rick Lawson?

"Hello, Cricket and Rick. Looks like the whole town of Bloom came to Walmart tonight," Lettie said.

Rick took all three women in with a single nod. "Hello, ladies. We were out of brown paper bags for the farmers' market later this week, so we decided to make a run into town."

"Don't know if you remember them, but this is Rick and his sister, Cricket. He grows the best vegetables in the area, just like his daddy did before he passed away," Nadine explained to Jennie Sue. "And he has a booth at the farmers' market in Sweetwater on Saturday. But some of us in Bloom get our stuff delivered to the door."

"Of course, I remember both of y'all from high school. I graduated with Cricket, and you were a couple of years ahead of us, right?" She looked up into his eyes again, and a hot little shiver ran down her spine.

He'd been quiet and smart, two pretty crazy

qualities for the quarterback of the football team. Not only had he been a good football player, he'd won every single academic bowl he'd participated in. Neither had run in her circles, Cricket being standoffish, but the Bloom school only graduated about twenty-five kids a year, so everyone knew everyone. But she sure didn't remember him having such gorgeous eyes.

"Hello, Jennie Sue." Rick stuck out his hand. "It's been a while."

She put hers in it and was surprised by the sparks that flitted around them. "Didn't you join the army right after high school?"

"Yes, ma'am, I did." His smile shone warm and friendly.

At least, she thought it did—maybe she was reading too much into a simple handshake, but she thought she'd sure like to get to know him better.

She dropped his hand and turned to face Cricket. "I don't think I've seen you since we graduated ten years ago."

"You were at one of our all-school class reunions a few years ago, and I was there, too." Cricket's tone shed snowflakes.

"Percy and I were on a tight schedule, so we only dropped by for an hour," Jennie Sue said.

"You missed a good time," Cricket said.

Rick pushed the cart in the opposite direction. "Well, you ladies have a nice evening."

"See you at the fireworks tomorrow night." Cricket flashed a sweet smile at Lettie, but it turned into a smirk when she looked back at Jennie Sue.

"Don't mind her," Nadine whispered when they'd gotten far enough away that Cricket couldn't hear. "She's got a burr under her saddle when it comes to you."

"What's that got to do with me?" Jennie Sue asked. "I could feel the icicles comin' off her tone."

"Jealousy," Lettie said. "But don't worry, she'll get glad in the same britches she got upset in. Let's go on to the frozen foods now. We don't buy our fresh vegetables here. Rick's are so much better."

"Why would she be jealous of me?" Jennie Sue said. "I'm divorced and cleaning houses for a living."

"Honey, you are the next Wilshire of West Texas whether you like it or not." Nadine patted her on the arm. "Now let's go get some frozen hash browns for the casserole I'm making tomorrow night."

Jennie Sue picked up a few things as she followed the ladies, but her mind wasn't on grocery shopping. It kept skipping from the chemistry she'd felt when Rick touched her hand to the idea that Cricket was envious of her and the fact that she'd rather be the next Baker of West Texas than inherit the Wilshire crown. She'd rather be known for bringing extra tomatoes to the church folks than having a hand in one of the biggest oil companies in the state.

"You were flirting with her. How could you do that when you know how I feel about her?" Cricket hissed.

Rick pushed the cart up to the express checkout. "Settle down. Your face turns beet red when you are angry. Why would you think I was flirting?"

"The way you were smilin'. I haven't seen that expression on your face since before you got hurt," Cricket said through clenched teeth.

"Jennie Sue is a pretty woman, but I wasn't flirting."

"Good, because she's way out of your league. I hate her," Cricket told him.

"Hate consumes love, sister," Rick said. "The two can't live in the same heart."

"My heart is plenty big enough for both." Cricket began to unload items from the cart.

Hoping to cool her down and get her mind off Jennie Sue, he said, "We could stop by the Dairyland and get a burger and fries for supper. I'll treat."

"I *am* hungry," she answered.

"You're like Daddy. Mama said there wasn't anything crankier than a hungry Lawson." He pulled bills from his wallet to pay for what they'd bought.

Cricket sucked in a lungful of air and let it out in a whoosh. "I'm not cranky. I just don't like Jennie Sue and never will."

"Never say never," Rick said.

"I don't believe that old sayin'."

"We don't get food in you, you'll go postal right here in Walmart," Rick told her.

She nudged him with her shoulder. "Okay, okay. You've always been the one who tried to keep the peace, like Mama was. I'll calm down if I can have a hot-fudge sundae after we eat."

"Deal!" He grinned.

They finished checking out and drove to the Dairyland to find the only booth left was a family-size one that would easily seat six. Cricket claimed it and sent Rick to put in their orders. When he returned with a tray of food, she had her phone up to her ear and a smile on her face. Other than food, gossip was the one thing that could tame the beast in her. She'd make an amazing columnist for one of those newspapers at the checkout counters. But to do that, a person needed a toe in the door.

"Don't you even want to know what happened that caused Jennie Sue to leave her mama's house?" Cricket asked.

"Nope. I don't care why she left," Rick answered.

"Not even a little bit curious?" Cricket bit into a french fry and squealed, "Hot!"

Rick pushed her root beer closer to her. "Right out of the grease. Drink some of that and it'll help."

She gulped several times and then spewed root beer out her nose and across the table on his shirt. "They're comin' in here."

"Who?" Rick asked.

"The Cliffords and Jennie Sue." She grabbed a fistful of napkins from the dispenser and handed them to him.

"She's stalkin' you." He lowered his voice and wiggled his dark brows. "She's jealous of you because you have dark hair and green eyes, and she always wanted to grow vegetables and work in a café. You got to do both of her dreams while she had to be a socialite."

"Don't be sarcastic," Cricket hissed.

"Don't be crazy." He turned around and waved at the ladies. "Y'all want to join us? We got lots of room."

"I'm going to shoot you." Cricket kicked him in the shin under the table.

"I hid your rifle," he said.

"Don't mind if we do, and thank you," Nadine said. "Lettie, you know what I want. Jennie Sue can help carry it back here to us." She scooted in beside Cricket and waited until Lettie and Jennie Sue had reached the counter before she whispered, "So I hear that the Bloomin' Flower Shop sent a bunch of flowers out to Charlotte today."

"Six different bouquets, says one of the girls that works there." Cricket lowered her voice. "Mostly roses, but the last one was a big basket of gladiolas. The Sweetwater Belles sent that one. Guess everyone thinks that Jennie Sue's decision to work for y'all is going to cause Charlotte to die."

"Well, I did wonder when I heard the ambulance goin' through town, but it was just one of Elaine's boys that stuck a bean up his nose and couldn't breathe. They had to take him to the emergency room and sedate him to get it out," Nadine said.

Rick shook his head. "Poor little guy. I remember when Cricket did that. She couldn't get air, and Mama was in a panic."

"Don't you dare tell that story in front of Jennie Sue," Cricket hissed. "They're on the way with the orders."

Nadine patted her on the arm. "Your secret is safe with us, but Jennie Sue seems to be a really nice person. Y'all could be friends."

"You ever goin' to be friends with Charlotte?" Cricket asked.

Nadine sent a dirty look her way. "Maybe when they let Lucifer back in heaven for a visit."

"There's your answer," Cricket said.

"Burger basket with everything for Nadine and one with no onions for me," Lettie said as she set a tray down. "Jennie Sue, you go on and slide in there beside Rick, honey. These old knees like the outside better than havin' to work their way out of the booth after I eat."

Rick wasn't ready for the jolt that shot through him when Jennie Sue's entire side plastered up against his. His tongue knotted up, especially when he thought of the talk that would be flying around the next day.

"I love big old greasy burgers," Jennie Sue said. "This is such a treat."

"It's the one thing I missed the most when I was deployed," he said.

"Where were you?" Jennie Sue asked.

"I could tell you, but then . . . Well, you know the rest." Rick grinned.

"He won't even tell me where he was on that last mission," Cricket said. "You'd think he could tell his sister."

Jennie Sue nudged him with her shoulder. "I always wanted a sister."

"Oh, honey, trust me when I say that you didn't really." Lettie shook her head slowly in disagreement. "They're nothing but a pain in the ass most of the time."

"Especially if you get an older sister who stays in so much trouble that she ruins your name right along with hers," Nadine said.

"So how much older was the other sister?" Jennie Sue asked.

"Flora was two years older than me. If she was

alive, she'd be ninety-two, and I'm two years older than Lettie, who is older than dirt," Nadine said.

"What does that make you, smarty-pants?" Lettie shot a dirty look her way. "If she wasn't old and worn-out, I'd give her to you, Jennie Sue. But you deserve a younger sister."

"If you still want one, I'll give you mine," Rick offered.

Cricket shot a dirty look his way. "Better yet, I'll give you a brother. They're twice the pain in the ass."

"For real?" Jennie Sue asked.

"Oh, yeah." Cricket nodded seriously.

"A brother couldn't be as bad as Flora was," Nadine laughed.

"I really love bein' around young folks. Makes me feel young all over again," Lettie said.

Makes me feel like a king, just sitting here with Jennie Sue Baker beside me, even if it does create more rumors, Rick thought, but he didn't say a word.

Chapter Four

The blazes of hell could never compete with Texas in July. Jennie Sue arose even earlier than usual the morning of the Fourth. She took a glass of iced coffee to the balcony, where she propped her long legs up on the banister and watched the sunrise. There wasn't a city, state, or country in the world that could lay claim to a prettier sunrise or sunset than West Texas. That was one of the many things she'd missed when she moved to New York.

Her cell phone rang, and her father's picture popped up on the screen. "Good mornin', Daddy. Are you on your third cup of coffee?"

"Fourth, baby girl. What's all this talk I'm hearing?" Like always, his deep drawl made her homesick to see him. He might disappoint her horribly with his lifestyle, but there was no doubt that he loved her.

"It's the truth, Daddy. I'm cleaning house for the Clifford sisters two days a week and chauffeuring them around when they need it. The other three days I'm working for Amos in the bookshop, and I'm living in Lettie Clifford's garage apartment," she said.

"Your mama is pitching a hissy," he said.

"I don't doubt it."

"You need anything? Money? A car?" he asked.

"I need to be independent, to stand on my own two feet and figure out exactly who I am. As far as money, I've got a couple hundred dollars left in my purse, and I get paid each week. Besides, Daddy, this town is so small, I can walk most of the places I need to go. Lettie and Nadine take me with them to Walmart, too. But thanks," she answered.

"Why do you kids all have to get on this bandwagon about finding yourself? Why can't you just be happy with what you inherit? And it's three miles out here. You goin' to walk that far?" he asked.

"After my marriage with Percy, I need to be independent, Daddy. I need to prove to myself that I can make it on my own. And yes, I can walk three miles. I used to jog farther than that every day."

"Okay, baby girl. You'll call me if you need help. Promise me that, and, honey, your mama will come around. Just give her time."

"There is one thing, Daddy. You could hire me. I have a business degree." She set her glass on the floor and crossed her fingers.

"That's the one thing I can't do. Wilshire money built my company, and your mama owns more than eighty percent of the stock. She says that she didn't raise you to work in the company. You've been groomed to take her place in the

Belles." Dill's tone sounded sincerely apologetic.

"After what I've been through, the Belles aren't real high on my bucket list. Am I invited to the party this afternoon?" she asked.

"Honey, that's one line I will draw in the sand. You come home anytime you want and stay as long as you want," he answered.

"Can I eat bacon?" she asked.

"I'll make sure there's always five pounds in the refrigerator," he said.

"Then maybe I'll show up. Mama might not be able to stay mad at me if I'm right there, right?" She could always dream, couldn't she?

"Don't count on it. She'll be nice in front of her Sweetwater Belles, though. Can I pick you up or send a car for you?" Dill asked.

"No, I'll find my own way."

"Just promise me one more time to call me if you need anything. Even if it's only to talk," Dill said.

"Promise. Love you, Daddy," she said.

"Right back atcha, kid. See you later."

Dill hated goodbyes and had always ended his conversations with her by saying that he would see her later. She'd asked him about it once, and he'd said that he'd had an argument with his mother and left by yelling goodbye and slamming the door. She'd died that night and he'd never gotten to apologize.

She laid the phone in her lap and decided that she would go to the party that afternoon, but she wouldn't stay for the fireworks. Lettie and Nadine needed her to drive them to the football field for the public show. She finished her coffee and went inside to make breakfast.

"So Mama doesn't work, but she practically owns Daddy's company. I wonder why she puts up with his flings," she mused as she got out a skillet and put half a dozen strips of bacon into it.

The Baker place really was three miles from where Jennie Sue lived now, but she had little choice other than to walk. No such thing as a taxi company in Bloom, population less than twelve hundred. She dressed in her best—khaki shorts, a navy-blue knit shirt, and a pair of sandals. She even took time to polish her toenails so she wouldn't be a complete disappointment to her mother.

She was halfway down the stairs when she saw Lettie standing at the bottom. "Well, hello, Miz Lettie."

"Same to you. Reckon you could drive me over to Nadine's place? We're goin' to do our cookin' over there this morning, and then you can have the truck for the day. Ain't no use in it sittin' here when you need a ride out to your folks' place." Lettie mopped the sweat off her face with a hankie that she pulled from the pocket of her jeans.

Jennie Sue gave a little silent prayer of thanks that she didn't have to walk all that distance. "Yes, ma'am, I'll be glad to drive you to Nadine's. Thank you for the use of the truck."

"Anytime. Wilma and her husband only had one vehicle, and her husband had to take it to get to work down in Sweetwater, so I let her drive it anytime she needed to. I miss her, but it was time for both of them to retire. They were both from Tennessee before they came here to Bloom about ten years ago, so they moved back."

"Do you need me to help carry anything out to take to Nadine's?" Jennie Sue asked, not really caring to hear Wilma's life story, but then, this was Bloom. Everyone knew everything about their friends and neighbors.

"Oh, no, honey, I done got it all in the truck. You can help me take it inside when we get there. Just be careful of that pretty shirt." Lettie talked as she got into the passenger side and hit a button on the garage opener.

By the time Jennie Sue was inside, the door was up. "You could rent out this garage in New York City for a lot of money."

"I wouldn't live in that place for all the money in the world. I like it just fine here in Bloom where I know everyone." Lettie touched the device, and the doors rolled down as soon as they were outside. "It's goin' to be a hot one. Maybe it'll cool down a little bit by dark when we go see the fireworks. You goin' to be back to drive us?"

"I sure will. Shall I bring the truck to Nadine's and we'll go from there?"

Lettie nodded. "That'll be fine, and if you get bored over at your mama's, come on to Nadine's and you can help us get ready for our little party."

"Who all's comin'?" Jennie Sue asked.

"Much as Amos makes me mad with his constant chatter, his dear wife was my friend, so I invited him and the folks that go to our book club. Nadine always invites her Sunday-school class, so we'll have quite a little bunch. Then afterward we have desserts at my house. Already got them made and ready to serve. If you'll help me with them, I'll keep track of your hours and pay the same as when you clean for me."

"My benefit package includes the apartment. Your benefit includes anything I do other than the cleaning responsibilities." Jennie Sue pulled into Nadine's driveway.

From the outside, the house was shaped a lot like Lettie's, only it had a carport instead of a garage with an apartment above it. And instead of being painted yellow, it had white clapboard siding. But the big picture window with lacy curtains drawn back to reveal a table with a lamp in the center was the same and reminded Jennie Sue of the stylized pictures that she'd drawn as a child.

"We'll take the stuff in through the kitchen door." Lettie got out of the truck and headed to the back to open the tailgate. "I put things close to the end, so neither one of us has to climb up inside. You get that box, and I'll take these two sacks and then you can come back for the potatoes. So we can expect you back here by eight o'clock?"

"Or before," Jennie Sue answered as she picked up the box in one hand and the potatoes in another. "Something sure smells good."

"I'm smokin' a brisket, two chickens, and a pork loin." Nadine came from the back of the house. "I just put more pecan chips in the smoker."

"Are you expecting an army?" Jennie Sue asked.

"Maybe, but if there's leftovers, we can eat on them all week." Nadine opened the kitchen door for them. "I love this holiday. Christmas is about presents. Thanksgiving is about families getting together. 'Course since it's just me and Lettie, that's a sad one. But the Fourth is a fun time when friends can all gather up and have a good visit."

Ninety years old and still making a meal for a crowd—Jennie Sue wanted to grow up and be just like her. She tried to imagine her mother or any one of the Sweetwater Belles at ninety, wearing a pair of baggy bibbed overalls and a faded T-shirt. Nope, the visual wouldn't appear, no matter how hard she squeezed her eyes shut.

"Just put all that on the table. Me and Lettie will get busy and make up the sides that go in the refrigerator first. We ain't spring chickens anymore, so we sit as much as we work, but we always enjoy the day," Nadine said.

Lettie poked her thin arm. "Speak for yourself. The only reason we do one big holiday a year is because you are so bossy."

"Well, Flora was the oldest. She said that gave her the right to boss me. When you came along, it was my turn, so stop your bellyachin'. If you'd wanted someone to boss, you shoulda got married and had kids." Nadine pulled macaroni noodles from the box.

"I didn't want a husband tellin' me what to do," Lettie snapped. "Women don't really need a man except for sex, and you don't have to stand in front of a preacher and promise to love and obey to get that when you need it. Jennie Sue can back me up on that, can't you?"

Jennie Sue's face burned. "I think I'll leave you two to discuss that all by yourselves. I'll see you this evening, and, Nadine, I'd love it if you'd save me a slice or two of that brisket."

"Consider it done." Nadine stopped and gave her a quick hug. "I'm glad you've come to work for us, girl."

"Me, too." Jennie Sue nodded.

With her face still on fire, she walked out of the house and got into the truck. Then the laughter started. Those two old ladies were a complete hoot. By the time she'd backed out and was on the road to her folks' place, she was laughing like she hadn't done in years. She braked at a stop sign and laid her head on the steering wheel. Once she finally got control of herself, she saw the little green sign pointing toward the cemetery.

She stared at it until a car behind her honked, and then she made a sharp left and drove down to the cemetery, through the gates, and straight to the Baker plot. Tears streamed down her face and dripped onto her shirt. Her baby had been buried right there in an unmarked grave for more than six months. There'd been no funeral, no saying goodbye—at the time, it seemed like the best thing to do, since she couldn't leave the hospital, and there was no way she wanted her baby buried in New York. So while she was in the hospital with an infection, she'd let her mother take over the arrangements. She'd sent a pretty little white lace dress that she'd planned for Emily Grace to wear home. She didn't even know if her mother had used it.

She opened the pickup door, and hot air rushed inside. She slung a leg out but couldn't make herself move the other one. Maybe if she touched the grass above the place where she knew Emily Grace was buried, she'd have closure. But she couldn't do it that day. She pulled her leg back inside the truck and slammed the door.

"I'll be back, Emily. I promise," she whispered as she turned the truck around and drove toward the Baker estate. She wanted to cry or hit something or maybe just scream. The one thing she didn't want to do was face her mother, so she pulled the truck off on the side of the road a mile from the house and said a silent prayer for strength to get through the day.

After several minutes she started up the engine and drove the rest of the way. She parked in front of the garage and inhaled deeply, let it out slowly, and got out of the old truck. She'd never needed a dose of energy more than she did right then. Going into the house with all the Belles in attendance, plus her mother at the center, would take more strength than even God could give her.

She touched the key to start up the engine again, put it in reverse, and go to Nadine's. But Frank opened the door for her before she could do anything.

"Hey, sweetheart, what's the matter?" he asked.

"It's been an emotional morning. I don't think I can do this," she whispered.

"That's up to you, but if you are going to give it a shot, you'd best make a side trip through the bathroom in the garage. There's black streaks runnin' down your cheeks, and your mama will have a hissy if she sees you like this," Frank told her.

"Thank you, Frank," she sighed. "I might as well go on in and face the music since I'm already cried out."

Rick's truck bed was filled with paper sacks full of fresh produce that morning. With twenty stops to make in Bloom, it would take until lunchtime to get it all delivered. He'd thought about putting in a small produce stand out in front of his and Cricket's house, but then he'd have to man it for several hours a day. A lot of his customers didn't need to be out in the heat anyway.

His first stop was at the Baker place, where he took two huge bags of food up to the kitchen door and rang the doorbell. Mabel opened it immediately and motioned him inside. "Thanks so much for putting us first on the list. It helps so much today. Oh, Rick, these tomatoes are beautiful."

"Thank you. Lots of water, healthy fertilizer, and bug spray. Be sure to wash them good," he said.

Mabel pulled several bills from an envelope marked "Petty Cash" and handed them to him. "This is so much better than what I can get in the grocery store. Dill loves fresh food. Says it reminds him of when his mama had a garden."

"Thank you. Let me know if you need anything

else this week." He was out the door when he saw Lettie's old truck rumbling up the lane. He stopped and leaned on the porch post until the driver parked in front of the long multicar garage. Surely Lettie Clifford wasn't coming to the Baker place to brag about Jennie Sue working for her.

Frank went out to the truck, then Jennie Sue followed him back into the garage. Rick left the porch and met them when they rounded the end of his truck. Jennie Sue. So much sadness filled her pretty blue eyes that he wanted to hug her.

"Are you okay?" he asked.

"I'm fine . . . or I will be," she said.

Her eyes and all that mascara streaking down her cheeks didn't agree with her words, but he wouldn't pry into her business. "Can I help?"

She shook her head and glanced over into the truck bed. "Did Mabel order all this?"

"No, only a couple of bags. I still have to deliver the rest," he answered.

"It all looks good." She forced a smile, but it didn't reach her eyes. "I love fresh better than frozen or canned. Could I get some delivered to my apartment once a week? If you'll give me a couple of minutes, I'll help unload it."

"Wouldn't want you to get those party clothes dirty. But about a delivery—I'd love to add you to my list. Here's my phone number." He fished a business card from the pocket of his shirt. "Just call me the night before you want it and tell me what you need. I can have it there the next day or bring it to you at Amos's store. And I always take stuff to Nadine's and Lettie's on Fridays." His heart kicked in an extra beat as he handed her the card. Jennie Sue would have his phone number. If she ever called, would they talk about anything other than tomatoes and watermelons?

"I'll be in touch tomorrow night, so you can bring mine and Lettie's at the same time," she said. "Right now, I've got to get myself presentable so my mother doesn't stroke out."

"I think you're beautiful even with war paint." He smiled.

She dashed into the garage bathroom and washed off all her makeup. Her reflection stared back from the mirror above the sink. "I like this woman with no makeup, but I expect Mama would have a cardiac arrest if I showed up at her party like this." She talked to herself as she got out an emergency makeup bag from her purse. She redid her mascara, brushed on a minimum of eyeliner and shadow, and then applied lipstick. It wasn't what Charlotte would expect, but at least it was a compromise.

"How mad is she?" she asked Frank when she was back in the garage.

"Not quite as upset as she was when you brought home that guy who was studyin' psychology for the weekend when you was in college. Lord, did that man have thoughts. She's got all her friends around her right now, so she'll keep her temper in check. You here for the party or for good?" He hugged her tightly.

"Just for the party. I talked to Daddy, and he said I could come to it even if I didn't want to move back into the house. I don't know if I can do this, Frank. Facing her after that fight we had would be bad enough, and now the Belles are in there."

"Well, there ain't but two options right here, Jennie girl. You can get in Lettie's truck and drive back to town, or else you go in there and face the bear in her cave," Frank said.

"Guess I'll face the bear. She only gets worse with time." She hurried to the kitchen door before she lost her nerve and pushed inside.

"Darlin' girl." Mabel rushed to wrap her arms around Jennie Sue. "I'm so glad you came today. Your mama's friends are already out on the porch havin' mimosas. They're makin' a day of it to cheer her up. She's been horrible since y'all had the fight."

"Mabel, we need some more orange juice out here," Charlotte yelled.

"I'll be right back." Mabel got a bottle from the refrigerator and hurried out of the kitchen.

Rick pushed through the kitchen door carrying a huge watermelon. "I got to the end of the lane and remembered that I didn't bring in the most important thing for the party."

"Hello again. Just put it right there." Jennie Sue pointed toward the cabinet.

He set it in a position so it wouldn't roll, then turned to face her. "You've still got a smear right under your ear you might want to check."

She quickly wet a paper towel and handed it to him. "Help me, please. If I run into one of Mama's friends, they'll say something about it."

He carefully dabbed at a place and then tipped her chin up with his thumb and turned her head back and forth. "Now you're in good shape."

"Thank you so much." She took the towel and threw it in the trash, but it wasn't so easy to get rid of the feeling his touch created. She chalked it all up to nerves over having to deal with her mother and her friends.

Mabel returned, nodding when she saw the watermelon. "Have you got a couple of extras? I'm beginning to think one won't do the job."

"Sure do. I'll go out to the truck and bring them in," Rick said as he limped out the back door.

"Good boy, that Rick is," Mabel said. "Town should have given him a parade or named a street after him or something when he came home all shot to hell and back. But he wasn't—Well, they didn't."

"Wasn't what?" Jennie Sue touched her chin to see if it was as warm as it felt.

"Honey, this is Bloom. The have-nots don't get much attention or reward for doin' something amazin'. The haves get the glory whether they did something really important or not," Mabel answered. "But that Rick is one of the best. And now you'd best get on out there and play nice with your mama and her friends."

"Where's Daddy?" Jennie Sue asked.

"He's at the office. Said he'd be back in time for food this evening. You want to call him?"

Jennie Sue sighed. There went her support if her mother was still mad. "No, I'll just go get it over with."

Mabel lowered her voice. "She did drink a whole pitcher, so she might be softened up a little bit. Tread easy, though."

"Yes, ma'am." Jennie Sue gave her a thumbs-up sign.

She went to the window and counted all eleven of the other Belles sitting on the porch with Charlotte. According to the charter that had been made when Charlotte's grandmother and several of her friends started the Sweetwater Belles, twelve was the magic number. If a member had a daughter, when she died, that child inherited the prestigious spot. If not, then the remaining eleven had to agree on who was worthy to be admitted into the exclusive club.

From a very young age, Charlotte had instructed Jennie Sue to call all eleven of those women "aunt," but standing back in the shadows, trying to gather the courage to go out there, she wondered if today she'd be disinherited. With her gaze on her mother, she didn't even see Aunt Sugar coming her way until the woman touched her on the arm with a frown.

Sugar Cramer was Charlotte's age, but she looked twenty years older. She wore her blonde hair in a pageboy cut, and she towered above Jennie Sue. Looking more like a rough old girl you'd see hangin' around a lamppost on a bad street, she hardly gave off the impression that she could be a southern belle.

"Jennie Sue Baker, how could you upset your mama like this? I'm glad to see you back home, though. You go out there and make a public apology to her. She only wants what's best," Sugar scolded.

"She thought Percy was wonderful, so maybe she doesn't know what's best for me," Jennie Sue argued.

"But he's so cute and so rich and he treated you like a queen," Aunt Sugar shot back.

"The only thing he ever did for me was teach me to keep a clean house, which got me a job to hold me over until I can find something," Jennie Sue said.

"A southern woman, especially a Belle, holds her head up in adversity and never leaves her husband," Sugar said stoically. "And she damn sure doesn't clean houses. It will take a lot of redeeming for you to ever get into the Belles. If your mama wasn't the good-standing member that she is, we'd all have some major doubts."

Jennie Sue popped a hand on her hip. "I didn't leave him. He left me with nothing. No man is worth what I went through, so believe me when I say I don't want a husband anytime in the near future. The feds are after him for tax evasion and have confiscated my house, my car, my jewelry, and everything I owned. He's also wanted for extortion. Don't give me a dressin'-down over cleanin' houses, Aunt Sugar. And FYI, which is for your information, I don't give a damn about my place in the Belles."

Sugar backed up a couple of feet. "You settle down, Jennifer. That's no tone to take with your elders. You mama said you'd gotten a bad spirit since the divorce. If you'll straighten up, we can forgive one little rebellious week. We've all had our bad days, and we could use you on a dozen committees, with your business degree," Sugar said.

"And I can't serve on those committees unless I'm livin' at home?" Jennie Sue asked.

"That's life, darlin'." Aunt Sugar patted her on the cheek. "You got to decide what's important in the long haul." She disappeared toward the bathroom on the first floor.

Jennie Sue stiffened her spine and walked outside, went straight to the bar, and asked for a mimosa with double the champagne.

"Jennie Sue," Aunt Mary Lou squealed, "I told Charlotte that you were just havin' a little anxiety attack. You should see my doctor for that. He'll prescribe a little capsule that will make you feel at peace with the world."

Carrying her mimosa with her, Jennie Sue crossed the patio and sat down in a lounge beside her mother. "I'm just here for the party, not for good. I start the first of my two jobs in the morning."

"Did Dill send a car for you?" Charlotte asked.

"No, Lettie loaned me her truck for the day, but I need to be back by evening so I can drive her and Nadine to the fireworks." Jennie Sue took a sip of the mimosa.

"Sweet Lord! Housecleaning and chauffeuring around those two old bats," Charlotte gasped. "And driving that truck onto my property? Have you lost your damn mind?"

Jennie Sue took a big gulp. "Mama, I want to forge my own path. I don't want to try to fill the mold that you have all these years. Let's agree to disagree and get along."

Charlotte's expression almost had the plates and cups flying on their own. But she managed to compose herself and say, "You look like crap in that outfit. I swear, you've gained another ten pounds since yesterday, and your hair needs to be styled. Did you do your own toenails? You smeared the polish onto the skin on your pinkies."

"But she's goin' to look better when we take her to the spa tomorrow, right?" Sugar sat down beside Jennie Sue.

Mary Lou came up on the other side and laid a hand on her shoulder. "You need to stop this nonsense. Let's do lunch tomorrow, and afterward we'll all get our nails done and maybe hit that new little boutique in Sweetwater for some decent new outfits."

Jennie Sue set the remainder of her drink on the table and stood up. She bent down and kissed her mother on the forehead. "Thank you both for the invitations, but I have to work tomorrow. You look beautiful as always, Mama. Call me when and if you ever change your mind about what I'm doing. Y'all have a wonderful day."

With her head held high, she walked back into the house and, avoiding even Mabel, went out the front door and circled around to the garage. Frank met her at the truck with his white handkerchief held out. She took it from him and wiped at a brand-new rush of tears flowing down her cheeks.

"Mabel heard what they all said and called me. I'm so sorry, darlin'," he said. "I should call Dill."

"No, don't do that. It would just work Mama up more. He'll be home today and I'll talk to him then. Nadine and Lettie have invited me to their party, and they could use some help getting things ready the rest of the day." Jennie Sue handed back the hankie. "Thanks, Frank. You and Mabel have always been here for me."

"Couldn't have no kids of our own, so we kind of adopted you." He smiled through sad eyes. "We're right proud of the way you've grown up."

"Thank you." She gave him a quick hug. "I'm glad you've been in my life."

"Not *been,* honey—*are* in your life. If you need anything, you can call me or Mabel anytime, night or day. We'll always be here for you," Frank said.

Jennie Sue patted him on the shoulder, got into Lettie's truck, and drove away from the house. How could so much happen in only two days? It seemed like six weeks since she'd gotten off that bus.

Chapter Five

Rick dressed in his best jeans and a mossy-green shirt that matched his eyes. He combed his dark hair straight back and laid a hand over the scar under his jawline on the left side. It had taken sixteen stitches to close that gash, but that was nothing compared to all the scars under his clothes. He looked like a Frankenstein character, with a total of more than a hundred stitches on his body. That didn't count the scar that ran the whole length of his bad leg. Thank goodness for clothes.

A picture of Jennie Sue flashed through his mind. The streaks down her cheeks reminded him of the black on his face that he'd been wearing when he went on his last mission. A warrior in those days, he'd been somebody, not just that farmer's kid from Bloom, Texas.

I wonder what brought tears to Jennie Sue's eyes this mornin'. What kind of mission would make her cry? He picked up his phone and keys.

"Are you about ready?" Cricket yelled.

He made his way to the living room and whistled through his teeth. "Well, it does look like all that primpin' paid off. I just got one question. Who are you trying to impress?"

"Oh, hush." She smoothed the sides of a cute

little sundress. Her hair had been curled, and her makeup was perfect. "I might ask you the same question. You even ironed those jeans." She tilted her chin up a notch. "And that's the aftershave you save for church. You thinkin' that Jennie Sue might give up her place at the Baker party and join us low-class folks? Think again. She's too hoity-toity to stay in a little place like Bloom, and when she leaves, all of us peons will be left in the dust." She picked up her purse and led the way out of the house. "You drivin' or am I?"

"You need to calm down about Jennie Sue. I'm a pretty good judge of character, and I'd bet money that you are wrong about her. I don't think she's doin' any of those things you just said or that she'd treat her friends so hatefully," he said as they went out into the hot night air.

"You'll see. When the time comes, her true colors will come out like a good ol' American flag blowin' in the wind." Cricket got into the passenger seat and fastened her seat belt.

"And if you are wrong, will you admit it?" Rick fired up the truck and started toward town.

"I won't be wrong," Cricket answered.

Rick noticed Jennie Sue's truck parked behind Nadine's van. That meant that Jennie Sue had left the Baker place and would be with them. Cricket wouldn't like it, but he sure did. "Let's not argue. Let's just go have a good time this evening with all our friends."

"I can get into that for sure. You did bring the wine and beer, right?"

"In the cooler in the back of the truck. You go on inside and I'll bring it," he answered.

"Hey, hey." Amos held the door for him. "Nadine said you were bringing the good stuff to go with her brisket and baked beans."

"And I've also got macaroni and cheese, and Jennie Sue's made her fabulous potato salad," Lettie called from the kitchen.

Rick caught Cricket rolling her eyes on the other side of the room and almost laughed out loud. Sometimes karma really did whip around and bite a person right on the butt.

Cricket frowned at her brother and then turned away to find Jennie Sue right beside her. There was nothing to do but speak to the woman, even if she would rather have slapped her. She knew that was the wrong attitude. Just last Sunday the new preacher at the church had delivered his sermon on having a sweet, positive spirit and never letting bitterness into the heart. But dammit! He hadn't had to live under Jennie Sue's shadow all these years. If Cricket had cleaned houses or worked at the bookstore, it wouldn't even be noticed, but let Jennie Sue do the same thing and the phone lines buzzed for days.

"Hello again, Cricket," Jennie Sue said softly. "You look so pretty tonight."

Cricket didn't want to be taken in by Jennie Sue's compliments, but she couldn't help it. "Well, thank you. I thought you'd be at your mama's for that big party."

"I went, but I didn't stay. I've had a really good time helping Lettie and Nadine this afternoon. They're such a hoot." Jennie Sue picked up a plate of chocolate-covered strawberries and cubes of cheese. "We have these little appetizers until Nadine says the brisket is ready. Want one?"

Well, la-di-da! Jennie Sue was now a house cleaner, a chauffeur, and a waitress. Didn't life turn round? "I'd love a chocolate strawberry. These came from our farm. Did you dip them?"

"Yes, but I promise I didn't lick my fingers," Jennie Sue whispered.

Why did Jennie Sue have to be so nice? It sure made it hard not to like her, but Cricket was determined.

"I used to help Mabel and Frank in their small garden when I was a kid. I loved getting my hands dirty and gathering in the vegetables. We never had strawberries, though, and when Mama decided to add a big porch onto the house, the garden had to go. I missed it," Jennie Sue said.

Cricket had just finished eating the strawberry when Nadine said for everyone to gather around and hold hands for the blessing. Cricket made sure that, among the twenty people, she wasn't standing beside Jennie Sue. Yet when she saw that Rick had wiggled in between Jennie Sue and Amos, she wanted to wring his neck. Didn't he have a lick of sense? That's it. He was going to have to find out for himself—the crash would be terrible.

Amos delivered the shortest grace in the history of mankind, followed by Nadine's loud amen. She continued, "Line up, heap your plates, and find a place to eat. If you like to be cool, then stay in the house. But if you don't mind a little heat, there's two long tables set up under the pecan tree out back. As for me, I'm going to sit in my rockin' chair in the livin' room and put my food on the end table right beside it."

"Where are you going?" Jennie Sue asked Cricket.

Wherever you aren't, she thought. But she looked around at all the elderly folks, and it wouldn't be right for her to deprive any of them of a nice cool place to eat. "Probably out under the shade tree. Seems more like the Fourth of July if we eat outside."

"I've been inside all day, so I'd love to join you," Jennie Sue said.

"I'll go out with you ladies," Rick said quickly.

Of course you will. Cricket frowned. *Either you have a crush on Jennie Sue or you're workin' real hard to prove me wrong.* "Then it looks like at least three of us don't mind sweating."

"I'll go with y'all!" Amos raised his hand. "Me

and Iris always liked to eat out under the shade tree."

"It's been years since I've been on a picnic." Jennie Sue added a slice of smoked pork loin to her plate.

"I miss them," Amos sighed as he carried his plate toward the door with the rest behind him. "Iris and I met at a church picnic. I like to think she's lookin' down on this one."

"Maybe she is." Rick grinned. "That's the way I like to think about my mama and dad—lookin' down and happy that we're keepin' the farm going. They would have enjoyed today."

Jennie Sue picked up a beer with her free hand as she brought up the rear. Outside, she chose a place on one side of the table, and Rick set his plate right next to her. Cricket pulled out a chair across from them, with Amos settled in beside her.

"Jennie Sue, it's good to see you makin' friends other than folks with one foot in the grave and the other on a banana peel." Amos laughed at his own joke.

"Age is just numbers on paper," Jennie Sue said.

"You got that right." Amos set about eating.

Rick turned to Jennie Sue. "So how was your mama's party?"

"Don't know," she answered. "I was only there about fifteen minutes. But I've had a really good time here today. Lettie and Nadine should go onstage with a comedy act. They've had me in stitches most of the day."

Cricket kicked Rick under the table and shook her head at him when she got his attention. He raised an eyebrow, and she shot daggers at him.

"So Cricket says that you liked to garden when you were a kid." He moved his legs to the side.

"I loved getting my hands dirty." She glanced at Rick. "When I get my own place someday, if it's too small to have a garden, then I'll plow up the whole backyard and plant vegetables. I love to cook with fresh stuff."

Cricket caught the sly I-told-you-so look that her brother cast her way. Something wasn't right here. Jennie Sue Baker was the next Wilshire in the long line of Bloom socialites. She should be worrying about chipping her nails, not digging in the dirt. What kind of game was this woman playing?

Even with Cricket's mean looks, this is a better party than any I've ever been to at the house. I love all my new friends, Jennie Sue thought. *It would be amazing if I could add Rick and Cricket to the list.*

Why would you ever want that woman to be your friend? an aggravating voice in her head asked.

Because she's got a big chip on her shoulder,

and I'd like to see it gone. She glanced at Cricket, who had her head down, and kind of doubted that would ever be possible. Then she shifted her eyes over to Rick, who was staring right at her. Their gaze met halfway, and she could have sworn there was chemistry between them again. He was a fine-looking man, but even if he didn't feel what she did, maybe they could be friends. They sure shared a love for gardening.

Hey, I wonder if he'd let me come out there and pick my own vegetables?

"This potato salad is amazing."

"It's because I had good fresh potatoes to work with." Jennie Sue blinked and looked down at her food. "Besides, a little bacon makes anything better."

What she didn't say was that it had been Percy's favorite, and she'd made it at least once a month. That brought back the final night they'd spent together. He'd gotten angry when she confronted him about his latest affair—with one of her friends, no less—and told him that she was six weeks pregnant. He'd thrown a whole bowlful of potato salad at the wall, shattering the glass and sending the mixture all over the carpet. Then he'd demanded that it be cleaned up before she went to bed, with not a single bit of stain left on the floor.

He'd slept in the spare bedroom, and when she awoke the next morning, he was gone without even leaving a note. A week later she was served with divorce papers. She'd signed them without benefit of a lawyer, since the alimony he'd set was reasonable, and she got to keep the apartment. It wasn't until later that she realized how little she'd actually received for the years she'd been married to him.

"You okay?" Rick nudged her with his shoulder.

"I'm fine." She blinked away the past and came back to the present.

"You looked like you'd seen a ghost," he whispered.

"I did, but it's gone now." She looked up at him, noticed the scar on his jawline, and had to hold her hands in her lap to keep from touching it.

His hand went to it, and he said, "It's the least of many."

"I'm sorry. I didn't mean to stare."

"No problem, but I believe we were talking about bacon in the potato salad. I figure anything that has bacon or ham in it has to be good." His pretty green eyes lit up when he smiled.

"Amen to that," she agreed. "Have you ever made whiskey bacon?"

"No, but I'd love to." Cricket's tone was almost sweet. Maybe they could find some common ground over recipes.

There could be hope for a friend there after all. "You mix equal parts of brown sugar and whiskey and paint it on thick-sliced bacon. Bake it for fifteen minutes at two hundred and fifty degrees, take it out, and flip it over and do the other side. Repeat that until it's crispy, and then let it cool. Oh, I forgot, you need a rack to put it on while it's cookin'."

Cricket nodded. "That would be something a little different at our book-club meeting—it sounds really good."

"I'm finished eating, so I'm going back inside to help Lettie and Nadine with cleanup. We'll be going to the football field in less than an hour," Jennie Sue said.

"I'll help." Rick pushed back his chair.

"Me, too," Cricket said.

Who would have ever thought that she could win a friend with a bacon recipe and a bowl of potato salad? Jennie Sue's heart lightened as she picked up her plate and headed inside.

The fireworks show might not have been as big or as fancy as the one out on the Baker property, but Jennie Sue loved every minute of it. She sat between Rick and Lettie. Cricket sat right behind her, flanked by Amos and Nadine.

When the first display lit up the sky, she pursed her lips and inhaled deeply. "Ohhh, that is so pretty."

Rick leaned over and whispered, "Not nearly as pretty as you."

She whipped around to see if he'd really said

that or if she was imagining things, and bumped noses with him. They each clamped a hand over their faces at the same time.

"What?" Cricket leaned down and asked. "Don't you like the smell of the smoke?"

"No, we turned at the same time and almost broke each other's noses," Rick said.

She didn't see Rick as a guy who'd use pickup lines like the boys in college the two years that she was there. So where had that come from?

When the show ended, she threw an arm around Lettie's shoulders. "This has been an amazing day. Thank you so much."

"It has been fun, Lettie. Thank you, ladies, for the good meal and the fun." Cricket stood up and got a firm grip on Nadine's arm to help her down the bleacher steps. "We'll all get to meet again at the book-club meeting on Friday, so this is a good week."

"I heard you're bringing a new thing that has bacon and whiskey involved," Nadine said. "I can't wait to try it out."

"It's Jennie Sue's recipe," Rick said.

Cricket gave him another of her looks, and he just laughed it away.

"So what are you bringing, Jennie Sue?" Lettie asked. "The new member should show her worth by showing up with something in her hands."

"And it can't be a vegetable tray, because I'm bringing one of those," Nadine said.

"Make it something sweet, like cookies," Amos said.

"Cookies or cake or both," Jennie Sue said.

"Then make it a cake. I love cake," Amos suggested.

"How about my praline caramel cake?"

"Sounds wonderful," Amos said.

"Need some fresh pecans to make that cake? We've got lots in the freezer. Pralines always have pecans, right?" Rick asked as they made their way down the steps and headed toward their individual vehicles.

"Would love a quart." Jennie Sue nodded. "Just put them in with my vegetable order and add them to my bill."

"Sure thing," Rick said. "Good night, y'all. It's been a great day."

There was definitely something to be said for small towns, the folks who lived there, and their traditions.

Chapter Six

With a bucket of hot soapy water in one hand and a tote of cleaning supplies in the other, Jennie Sue started at the back of Nadine's house. She'd barely gotten one room done when Nadine yelled that she was going down to the church to help with a funeral brunch. She'd be home at noon. Jennie Sue took time to get a bottle of water and her MP3 player from her purse. She chose a playlist of country music and went to work on the second bedroom.

Percy would have fussed for hours if he'd seen the dust on the ceiling fans and the half dozen dead flies between the window and the screen. Just as she thought about one of his last tantrums, Miranda Lambert started singing "Mama's Broken Heart."

Every word sounded just like Jennie Sue's situation. The lyrics talked about powdering her nose, lining her lips, and keeping them closed, but the line that really hit home was when Miranda sang that she should start acting like a lady. She played the song five times as she worked and then listened to "Gunpowder & Lead," and anger boiled up inside her. If Percy had hit her, her daddy would have done just what the song said about loading a shotgun. But her mother would have been a different matter. A little infidelity—that was just a man, right? Going on the run from the IRS—that was only protecting his sorry hide, right? Verbal abuse if one of the cans of green beans had been shifted over to the side where the corn was kept—well, Jennie Sue promised to love, honor, and obey in her vows, right? And he did keep her in pretty jewelry, a nice apartment, and a car, right?

She forced herself to focus on the work and forget about the past, but it wasn't easy. Her playlist stopped when she finished up in the two bedrooms and hung the sheets on the line. She took the earbuds out and put the MP3 player back in her purse. Before long she was humming an old Travis Tritt tune, "Here's a Quarter (Call Someone Who Cares)," and giggling. She really hoped that someday Percy found himself backed up in a corner with a woman who was messy, who hated to clean, and who didn't give a damn what he wanted or thought. She hoped that he had a quarter to call someone. It just better not be her, because she didn't care anymore. Today she had a job and new friends.

"Hey, are you gettin' hungry?" Nadine yelled as she pushed into the house. "It's hotter'n Lucifer's little spiked tail out there. Let's have a beer and take a break; then we'll drag out leftovers for lunch. Wait till I tell you what all I learned at the brunch today."

"Gossip at a funeral brunch?" Jennie Sue asked.

"Honey, you can find it anywhere." Nadine twisted the lids off two longneck bottles of beer, handed Jennie Sue one, then collapsed on the sofa, propping her feet up on the coffee table. "Sit down. You're workin' too fast. You got to pace yourself to make the job last all day."

Jennie Sue sat on the other end of the sofa and sipped the icy-cold beer. "Who died?"

"Laura Mae Watson's sister. She ain't lived here in years, but Laura Mae wanted her to be buried next to their parents. Since there wasn't many at the funeral, and it was a nine o'clock service, we decided to do a brunch. Who in their right mind has a funeral that early in the morning? Ten o'clock is early enough for folks to have to get dressed and put on makeup, don't you think?"

Nadine didn't wait for an answer. "There wasn't but three floral sprays in the church, and those were from the immediate family. Won't even be hardly enough to cover the grave. Whole thing, including the graveside service, was over in an hour; then we served the family for an hour, did cleanup, and visited a spell."

She drank a third of the beer, burped like a three-hundred-pound trucker, and grinned. "Pardon me, but that tasted so good that I'm not even sorry. I also heard that your mama and her Sweetwater Belles are going to some fancy spa out in Arizona for a week. And the last is that you and Rick Lawson had an affair in high school. You came home to pick up where y'all left off, and that could be the reason your husband left you."

Jennie Sue had just taken a gulp of beer, so when she snorted, it came out her nose and ran down her face. Thank goodness a box of tissues was sitting on the coffee table, or she'd have been cleaning beer stains from Nadine's cream-colored sofa for hours.

"That's not true," Jennie Sue gasped. "No wonder Mama is escaping to the spa for a week. Why would people say that? We might be friendly, but we didn't have an affair, and that's not why Percy left me."

Scratch that great feeling of belonging she'd had the night before. With that kind of talk flying around, she couldn't wait to get out of town. But before she did, she had to go to the grave where Emily Grace was buried. She had to have closure before she left Bloom, or she'd never be able to get a fresh start.

Next week, she would definitely get some résumés written up and make a trip down to the Abilene employment office to see if anyone was looking for a woman with a business degree. Maybe she could even borrow Lettie's truck and drive over to Dallas to one of those job fairs that was always listed over there.

Nadine took another sip of beer and went on.

"They say that you goin' to work for us has aged Charlotte ten years. I just want you to know that we didn't mean to cause trouble like this. It isn't a secret that the Wilshires and the Cliffords haven't spoken a kind word to each other in decades, but we sure wouldn't want to do you no harm. We like you, Jennie Sue."

"Well, I like you, too, and this is my decision. Mama will come around. It might take twenty years." The poor old darlings weren't at all how her mother had drawn them all these years. She already dreaded leaving the funny, kindhearted sisters.

Nadine finished off the beer. "Honey, I'm ninety. I won't be here in twenty more years. Oh, and the last little tidbit says that Dill has broken it off with Darlene. She's heartbroken, but he's probably got another woman in his eye. No one knows who it is right now, but there's lots of betting goin' on. I put five bucks on the new chamber-of-commerce secretary that just moved here from Midland. Dill kind of goes for red-haired women." Nadine clamped a hand over her mouth. "That's your daddy. I shouldn't have told you that. Blame it on the beer and the heat. My brain ain't firin' on all the cylinders today."

Jennie Sue patted her on the arm. "It's okay. I've known about his ladies for years. What I've never been able to understand is why, with Mama's temper, she puts up with it."

Nadine laid a hand on Jennie Sue's arm. "Your mama was in love with a really poor kid in high school, darlin'. His name was James Martin, and his folks lived between here and Rotan in a trailer house. Your grandma put a stop to that as soon as she found out, and she picked out Dill Baker for your mama. Theirs was the biggest wedding in the whole county—right when your mama got out of high school."

"What happened to James?" Jennie Sue asked.

"He went right into the army when they graduated and stayed away from Bloom for six years. She married Dill and was faithful during that time and doted on you when you were born, but right after James came back to this area, well, that's when Dill started having affairs."

"Where is James now?" she asked. Had she blamed her father for everything all these years when part of the problem might lie with her mother?

"Cancer got him about five years ago, but until then, he worked at the airport in Lubbock. Charlotte disappeared for six weeks after he died. We all figured that she went to a private place to settle her nerves," Nadine answered. "And I shouldn't tell you all this, but maybe it will help you understand both of your parents."

"I remember when Mama went to a place in Colorado for more than a month. She said she needed some time to rest. She did that pretty often with her Belles, but that time she went alone. Now I know why." Jennie Sue was on her feet in a flash and began to pace back and forth across the floor. "On one hand, I've hated my dad for his affairs. On the other, I loved him just as fiercely. I've never been able to sort it out in my mind, how I could both love and hate him with the same heart."

"We're only human, child, and you didn't know the whole story," Nadine said.

She made two more trips from one side of the room to the other. "How could my mother do this? She loved someone else, but she couldn't let go of that precious Wilshire bloodline and let me love whoever I wanted. She pushed Percy and me together—lookin' back, maybe I married him hoping she would finally be happy with me."

"I'm so sorry that I even brought it up," Nadine said. "Let's forget about it and get out the brisket and make us some barbecue sandwiches. We got enough of your good potato salad to go with them, and then we'll take a little rest for an hour and watch a *Family Feud* rerun on television before you finish up the cleaning."

When Nadine fell asleep in her recliner five minutes into the television show, Jennie Sue eased off the sofa and started dusting the dining room. She couldn't get what Nadine had told her off her mind. How could she have lived in that house all through her high school years and not questioned why her father was cheating? At least now she had a sense of why Charlotte didn't give a damn. Talk about a twisted marriage.

"How could they even be civil in public and live in the same house?" she muttered as she finished the dining room.

What difference would it have made if you'd known? Would it have brought peace or more turmoil?

"I'll never know now, will I?" She headed outside to gather the sheets in from the line. Lettie was right about them smelling fresh. No amount of dryer sheets could give them that scent. She'd remade both beds nice and tight without a single wrinkle and was on her way to the kitchen when Nadine awoke.

"Hey, Jennie Sue, where are you?" Nadine called out. "Are you still here?"

"On my way to the kitchen. Want a glass of sweet tea? I was about to get one for me."

Nadine yawned loud enough that Jennie Sue could hear it. "It's three o'clock. How about some ice cream instead of tea?"

"I ate far too much dinner for anything right now, but I'll get you some. One scoop or two?" Jennie Sue called out.

"Two, and you can sit with me while I eat it. What all is left to do?"

"Vacuum." Jennie Sue headed to the kitchen. "Then take out the trash and mop the kitchen and utility room, and we'll have you all fixed up for another week."

"Okay, then. But, honey, the refrigerator is like an open bar anytime you come to my house. If you'll tell me what you like, I'll have it in there and ready for you." She eased up out of her recliner and worked the kinks out of her neck.

"Thank you, Nadine. I'm sure I won't starve." Jennie Sue turned on the vacuum and made sure every inch of carpet was gone over at least three times. She didn't want to talk or hear any more gossip. She just wanted to get the job done and go home to her apartment and try to sort out everything.

Rick parked the bookmobile at the library that afternoon, made sure everything was shelved and that the doors were locked, and then whistled all the way into the small brick building.

"This abominable heat must have kept the folks up in Longworth from getting out today. Didn't have a single customer." He handed the keys to Amos.

"I hope we don't have to cut that little town from the route because folks ain't interested." Amos hung the keys on a hook behind the checkout counter. "We had a great time last night, didn't we? Did I see a little spark between you and Jennie Sue?"

Rick had already gotten the third degree from

his sister, so he tried to tease his way out of it. "Amos, you need your glasses changed if that's what you were seein'. Had many customers today in here?"

"Nope, and I saw what I saw. Reminded me of the way I looked at Iris back before she said she'd go out with me. Jennie Sue is bringin' cake tomorrow to the book club. What are you goin' to say to her when you deliver the pecans? You could tell her that she looks right nice and maybe pick a bouquet of wildflowers," Amos suggested. "Town is already sayin' stuff about y'all. If you're goin' to have the name, you might as well have the game."

"And what're they sayin' about us?" Rick asked.

"That y'all dated on the sly in high school and that you are the reason her husband left her. She's run home to you." Amos grinned.

"Bullshit!" Rick sputtered.

Amos raised a hand. "Truth. That's just the way I heard it. So?"

"It's just talk," Rick said. "It isn't even reasonable, but then gossip seldom is."

"Amen," Amos said. "But you better be careful, son. If they catch you holding hands with her, they'll start polishing up the silver punch bowl at the church for a wedding reception."

Rick threw a hand over his heart in mock horror. "Now that would be horrible, wouldn't it?"

"For the ladies at the church, it would." Amos nodded. "They'd be real upset if they was to go to all that work for nothing."

Rick patted him on the shoulder. "Seriously, thanks for the advice. I like Jennie Sue and we might be friends, but you and I both know that's as far as it could ever go."

"Stranger things have happened. It's closin' time. Give me a minute to turn off the lights and I'll walk out with you," Amos said. "I also heard that Jennie Sue was seen out at the cemetery visitin' her Baker grandparents' graves. She didn't go to the Wilshires', though. I wonder what's going on with that."

"Guess she didn't have the time." Rick really did like Jennie Sue, and he'd felt more alive with her than he had in years. Maybe it was because he didn't see pity in her eyes when she saw him walk with a limp or noticed the scar on his chin, or maybe it was a mutual love for gardening. Whatever it was—well, he enjoyed being with her.

He walked a couple of blocks up the road to the café. The truck was parked behind the building, so he went in the back door to see if Cricket was finished or if he needed to wait on her. His eyes took a minute to adjust from the blaring sunlight to the dimmer café, but when they did, he noticed that Jennie Sue was sitting alone in a booth toward the back.

The place was almost empty, but Cricket still had her hands full, so he took a seat in the next booth down from where Jennie Sue was sitting.

"Hello," she said.

"Evenin'. What brings you to town?" Though he faced her, a bench and two tables separated them. Surely that was enough that it wouldn't create more problems.

"I'm still full from dinner with Nadine, so I decided that a strawberry shake would make a wonderful supper," she said.

"And here it is." Cricket set it in front of her. "I'll be another ten minutes, Rick. If you want to come sit at the bar, I'll make you a shake, too."

"I'm fine right here," he said.

It didn't take a rocket scientist to know that was not the answer she wanted, but dammit, he was a grown man and didn't need her constant meddling.

"So how's your first day on the job?" he asked.

"Fine. I like working for the sisters." Jennie Sue unwrapped a straw and stuck it down in her milkshake. "But I've told them that it's temporary. I didn't work to get my degree so I could clean houses. I want a job in a firm with benefits. So how was your day?"

"Did some weedin' and harvestin' this morning for tomorrow's deliveries and for the farmers' market in Sweetwater. Then drove the bookmobile up to Longworth this afternoon." He wondered what folks did with false rumors. Did they go into a recycling bin? Change the names and the places and use them all again?

"What are you thinkin' about?" Jennie Sue asked.

"Rumors." He shared his recycling idea.

Her blue eyes twinkled with amusement, and his heart actually skipped a beat. "Think we could start a business reselling them? I could run the office and man the phones, bringing them to my attention. You could sort through them and decide what was real and what was false and then we could sell the untrue ones to other towns."

Cricket brought an order of french fries and a tall glass of sweet tea with a wedge of lemon and set it down in front of Rick. "I've got to stick around a little longer. Elaine had to make a run home to see about her mother. You might as well have something to eat."

"Thank you," Rick said.

"What were y'all laughing about?" she asked.

"Gossip and rumors. We may go into business together recycling them. Want to partner up with us?" Jennie Sue asked.

"You are both crazy, and I wouldn't go into any kind of business with you, not ever." Cricket flounced off.

"Never say never," Rick called after her.

"How long have you been home?" she asked.

"Two years. I was on the West Coast in a

hospital and rehab center for nine months before they discharged me on a medical with full disability. My dad died right after I got home, so I just picked up the shovel and hoe and kept things going."

"I admire anyone who goes into the service and who makes a livin' working with his own two hands in the dirt," she said.

"Well, thank you. I wish you weren't leaving Bloom. I think we could be really good friends," he said.

"I'm sure we could." She hoped that their friendship would endure long-distance when she left Bloom.

Chapter Seven

A short Texas rain on Friday afternoon brought the temperature down into the low nineties but jacked the humidity up, so it seemed hotter than it had been that morning. Jennie Sue made the cake, and after a quick shower, she dressed in fresh jeans and a clean T-shirt and wished she'd brought along a sundress or two when she'd packed. Cricket had looked so cute in the one she'd worn to the Fourth party that Jennie Sue was a little jealous.

She'd seen a rack of brightly colored ones when she'd gone to Walmart with the sisters. Maybe she'd splurge and buy a couple when they went again. Lettie was waiting beside the truck when she arrived, and Nadine was doing the same by her van when she carried the cake down the stairs that evening.

Nadine started talking before she even got the door closed. "I heard about you having dinner with Rick Lawson yesterday evening. He's a good guy—kind of broken since he got back from wherever to hell they sent him, but he'll come out of it." She fastened her seat belt. "Now, wagons, ho! Let's go argue with Amos about Scarlett O'Hara."

"It wasn't dinner or a date." Jennie Sue backed

the van out and started toward the bookstore. "He sat in one booth and I sat in another and we had a conversation. That's all there was to it. We had to talk so loud that everyone who was in the place could hear us."

"Did he pay for your strawberry milkshake?" Lettie asked. "I heard that he did."

"He did not. He didn't pay for his fries and tea, either. Cricket must run a bill in there or else she gets free food for her and Rick, because I didn't see either of them pay, and they left before I did." Jennie Sue pulled in behind a cute little red Smart car. "Who owns that?"

"It's Amos's new toy. He says he gets almost fifty miles a gallon with it. I wouldn't have one of them things, no matter how cheap it is to run," Lettie said. "Get hit with a big car and it's lights out."

Nadine unfastened her seat belt. "I been meanin' to tell you that I ain't never had a housekeeper that cleans like you do. I couldn't find a speck of dust on anything, not even the rungs of the rockin' chair in the spare bedroom. I hope you can't find a job."

"Nadine!" Lettie scolded. "That's not nice. But we love havin' you close by."

"I really like workin' for you and havin' you for friends, too, but I told you in the beginnin' that I was going to look for another job," Jennie Sue said.

"Listen to her, Nadine," Lettie said. "Only been in God's country for a week, and she's already gettin' her Texas accent back."

"Wonderful, ain't it? Let's get on inside and get the discussion done with so we can get down to the serious business. I've got a couple of juicy tidbits, and I ain't talkin' about whiskey bacon and that delicious-smellin' cake in the back of this van." Nadine undid her seat belt. "Y'all hurry up and get in out of this god-awful heat before we all melt."

Jennie Sue held the door open and then followed the two ladies into the used-book store. She set her cake with the other food and sat down at the discussion table beside Cricket. Rick, Lettie, and Nadine were all across the table from them, with Amos taking his place at the head.

"Okay, this meeting is officially in order," Amos said. "For your information, Jennie Sue, we usually have about five or six more, but they called in today with one excuse or another. We really should make a rule that says if a person misses more than two discussions a year, they're on probation, but we can decide on that later. Everyone welcomes you, Jennie Sue."

"Thank you. I'm excited to be here. I love books and I love to read." She shot a sideways glance at Cricket, and the look on her face said that Amos hadn't taken a poll before he spoke.

"And here's the first question on my discussion

list. Do you think that *Scarlett* is a good sequel to *Gone with the Wind*? Did it bring closure to you when you read it?"

"Yes, I love a happy ending," Jennie Sue said.

"I liked it, but I liked Scarlett better in the original book," Cricket said. "She was her own person in both books, but in the first one she had more grit and sass."

"Which brings me to the next question," Amos said. "Do you think that having that child tamed her wild spirit? I realize that none of us here has a child, but we all know Scarlett O'Hara pretty good. What do you think?"

Jennie Sue couldn't speak past the lump in her throat, so she let Lettie and Rick take that question. She focused on keeping the tears at bay as their unheard responses washed over her. She couldn't answer, not when she didn't have the power to even get out of the truck and go visit Emily's grave.

Jennie Sue had tried her best to make her mother happy, and that always meant things had to be perfect. She didn't know why her mother had wanted to keep the baby a secret. After all, she was married when she got pregnant, and there was no shame in having a stillborn baby, but Charlotte always had her reasons. Jennie Sue vowed that the next time she went home or saw her mother, she would make her explain why Emily Grace had to be such a big secret.

"Okay, next one," Amos said. "How many of you have read *Gone with the Wind* more than once, and would you reread *Scarlett*?"

Jennie Sue's hand shot up in the air. Anything to get her mind off her inability to touch the ground where Emily was buried. "I've read them both multiple times already." She didn't tell them that both books and *Rhett Butler's People* had helped her keep her sanity when she lost her baby.

"Got anything to add, Jennie Sue, before we go on to the next question?" Amos asked.

"I'm so sorry. I was woolgatherin'. What was the question?"

"Did Scarlett change because she'd lost Bonnie Blue and she wanted to be a good mother to her daughter Cat?"

"I would think that maybe Scarlett must have felt an extra strong bond with her new daughter after losing Bonnie Blue." Hopefully, she'd answered it well enough without going into detail.

Rick nodded.

"Agreed," Amos said. "It's been a great discussion. Anyone got anything to add?"

"Yes, when are we eatin' the snacks?" Nadine said. "I saw that whiskey bacon over there, so let's get to it."

Cricket pushed back her chair and led the way to the refreshment table. "Good discussion, everyone. Did y'all hear that Belinda, one of the

Belles, almost didn't go on that spa trip because she's been sick? I wonder what's wrong with her."

Rick stepped up behind Jennie Sue and whispered, "If we're going into business together, we need to know the gossip rules. Number one is that you don't discuss the people who are within hearing distance. Belinda is a safe topic because she's not here."

His warm breath on her neck caused tingles to chase down her spine. "What's the number-two rule?"

"I can see that you aren't up on the rumor protocol." He took a couple of steps to the side so he was facing her. "The second rule is to never write anything down or send a text. Phones are fine since no one has a party line anymore, but the best way to spread it is word of mouth. You want plausible deniability."

"Thanks for explaining it to me. I'll need to be up on all the regulations." She kept a serious expression, but it wasn't easy.

"And the last rule is that whatever comes in must be spread real quick. If you sit on it more than a day, you are committing a sin," he drawled. "When it comes back to us, we can sugar it up and resell it."

"Is that a little like reissuing a book? Put a new cover on it and change the title and it becomes new?" she asked.

"What's been reissued?" Cricket asked. "I wish they'd make a law that all reissued books had to have a little sticker on the front cover so us readers wouldn't buy something we've already got."

"We're talkin' about our rumor business," Rick said.

"That again? Y'all are crazy." Cricket turned her back on them.

"Now that you know the rules, you will be held accountable." His eyes sparkled. "This cake looks really good. I love pralines."

Cricket's phone rang, and she fished it from her purse. "Sure I can. Be glad to. See you in the morning." She turned around. "Elaine needs me to work tomorrow. The high school girl who usually picks up a shift on Saturday has that stomach bug that's going around."

"What about the farmers' market?" Rick asked.

"You'll have to run it by yourself, brother. We need the money too bad for me to turn down shifts, and besides, Elaine has been so good to us. I can't turn her down," Cricket said.

"I love farmers' markets. If you want me to, I can help," Jennie Sue said.

The whole place went silent. Finally, Lettie spoke up. "You think that's a good idea with all that's bein' said?"

"I can't afford to hire help," Rick said.

"If we show everyone that we are just friends, then maybe the rumors will stop. And I'll take out my pay in food. How about another bag of pecans and a watermelon?" Jennie Sue said.

"Girl, you are gettin' good at this barterin'," Nadine said. "Clean a house for your rent and now workin' for produce. I like it. We used to do a lot of that when I was a girl."

"Don't get started on the old days, Nadine," Lettie scolded. "We'll be here all night if you transport her and Amos back in time."

"Well, pardon me." Nadine wiggled her skinny neck better than any teenager that Jennie Sue had ever seen.

Rick moved over to the table with Amos, and they started talking about something called Little Free Libraries. She'd seen pictures of them on Pinterest. Folks put little boxes on posts in front of their houses and filled them with used books. The idea was to take a book and leave a book so there was always something to read. She thought it was a wonderful notion, even with a library in town. The Little Free Libraries were open twenty-four-seven, and folks could always find something to read that way.

"Do you have one of those in your front yard?" Jennie Sue asked, sitting down beside Cricket.

"Yes, we do. It's Rick's dream to have them at every house in the whole town. He has this vision of even tourists stoppin' to use them," Cricket said, and then leaned over and whispered, "I'm tellin' you up front, I don't like the idea of you going to the market with Rick, but he needs help, and I've got to do that double shift."

"It's not a date and it's not every week," Jennie Sue protested.

"Thank goodness," Cricket snapped, and then changed her tone. "Lettie, darlin', come over here and sit with us girls. Those guys are all plannin' Rick's stand idea." Cricket turned back to Jennie Sue. "I intend to put out the news that y'all had a big argument at the market and you've broken off your relationship."

"Kind of difficult to break something off that hasn't even begun." Jennie Sue's tone could be every bit as cold as her mother's.

"That's not what the talk in town says—I'm nippin' it in the bud," Cricket said.

"Be careful," Lettie said in all seriousness. "You might cause a bigger problem than if you let the whole thing die in its sleep. We all know that they're just friends, and pretty soon everyone else will know it, too."

Cricket changed the subject without commenting on Lettie's advice. "So what's our book for next month?"

"I'd like to do a mystery this time. Maybe the newest Sue Grafton?" Nadine offered.

"How about instead of the newest, we go back and do the first one, *A Is for Alibi*, and then do one of her newer ones and compare them?" Cricket suggested.

Jennie Sue didn't like to read mysteries, and right then, she wasn't too fond of Cricket. She'd just invent an excuse not to go to the book-club meeting the next month. Maybe by then she'd have a lead on a new job in Dallas or Austin.

Rick tossed and turned for an hour after he crawled into bed. Finally, he got up, made himself a cup of hot chocolate, and carried it back to his room. Cricket was in a snit, but then, she'd never liked Jennie Sue. She might come around someday, but maybe not. It didn't matter anyway. He could be friends, even long-distance friends, with Jennie Sue, whether his sister was or not.

When he awoke before daylight the next morning, he tiptoed around in the house so that he didn't wake his sister. Elaine had offered Cricket a ride, but she wouldn't show until a bit before nine o'clock. While he was being considerate, he also didn't want another lecture. He just wanted to spend the day with Jennie Sue.

He loaded his truck bed, and an hour later, he parked in Lettie's driveway, expecting to go up to the door and knock. But Jennie Sue came out of the shadows and got into the truck before he could even shut off the engine.

"Hello. Don't you just love the smell of early morning?" She held up a brown paper bag. "I brought a thermos of coffee and biscuits stuffed with sausage. They're those kind you buy in the frozen-food department, but I promise I cooked the sausage all by myself."

"Hey, any woman who can cook biscuits without burning them is a star in my book."

She opened up a plastic container and handed him one. "Don't judge until you've tasted it."

"Mmm." He made appreciative noises at the first bite. "Amazing. You are now invited to go with me every Saturday that you want. I'll even throw in an extra cantaloupe for the breakfast."

"Sounds like a plan to me," she said. "But don't pencil me in for every Saturday. The ladies could need me to drive them somewhere, and I sure wouldn't want to take Cricket's job."

They ate in silence all the way to the market, where Rick backed his truck up to his regular stall. Jennie Sue was out of the vehicle and had the tailgate down before he could join her.

"So we put some of each on the table and then keep it replenished as the day goes on, right?" She was already filling one of the small baskets with tomatoes.

"You sure you haven't done this before?" He picked up two huge watermelons and set them at the back of the wooden shelf.

"Nope, but I loved going to the market with Mabel when I was a little kid. I used to play farmers' market at home after we'd been. This is going to be a fun day," she told him.

Why oh why did she have to be so perfect in

every way and so determined to leave Bloom? They were becoming friends, and there was a possibility that could lead to more.

Maybe.

Chapter Eight

Dill sat across the booth from Jennie Sue in the Main Street Café. They'd both ordered the chicken-fried steak special that Sunday afternoon. She didn't mind the silence between them, yet with her father's expression and the way he kept sighing, it wasn't hard to guess that he had something on his mind.

"Spit it out, Daddy." She pushed her empty plate back. "You've got something on your mind. So let's clear the air and then go on to more fun things to talk about. I'm dying to tell you all about the farmers' market and how much fun I had at the book club on Friday night."

His gaze locked with hers across the table. "Your mother is mortified about what you are doing."

"And you?" Jennie Sue asked.

"It's complicated."

She shook her head. "You don't get to use that. It's my generation's go-to, not yours."

He laid his paper napkin on the plate, picked up a half-empty glass of sweet tea, and took a sip. "But in this case, it's the only word that describes the problem. Everything about your mother is complicated."

"And you?"

"The same."

"From the beginning?" she asked. "Were you both this complicated when you first got married?"

Dill nodded. "My grandfather Eugene Dillard Baker founded the Baker Oil Company, and it did very well in the days of the oil boom here in Texas."

"So I get a history lesson?" She raised an eyebrow.

"You get the undercurrent of what it really means when I say it's complicated. Listen and learn. So Gene turns over the company to my father, Robert Dillard, your grandfather Bob, who died when you were a toddler. The bottom fell out of the company, and we were struggling to keep afloat about the time that I finished college. The Wilshires stepped up and were willing to plow a lot of money into the company, but there was a catch—I had to marry your mother. With the marriage, she would retain eighty percent of the company."

"I didn't know they did that kind of thing thirty years ago." She could hardly believe her ears.

"Honey, even these days they still do," he sighed.

"Percy? Did you pay Percy?" That would explain a lot.

He nodded. "Not me. I was against it. I kind of liked that boy you brought home from college, but your mama said that she wasn't havin' a son-in-law that was constantly trying to analyze her with his psychology stuff, and besides, she thought you could do better. So Charlotte met Percy at some fund-raiser and pushed him toward you with the promise of investing in his sagging diamond business. She lost a good chunk of money when he took off."

"She gave him money to marry me?" Jennie Sue's voice sounded like her mother's, even in her own ears.

"Not exactly. She kind of pushed him toward you, and then when he started to back off, she had a talk with him and—dammit, Jennie Sue, I wouldn't have any part of it. But he said he wanted to support you in the style you were used to, and so your mother wrote him a check to buy into the diamond partnership with his cousin."

Dill looked absolutely miserable.

"So basically, when you get right down to brass tacks, they came to an agreement. Did he propose before or after she gave him the check?"

He hesitated.

"It can't get much worse. I guess somewhere down deep in my heart, I knew all along that something wasn't right. Tell me," she demanded in a shrill voice.

"After it cleared the bank," Dill said. "In Charlotte's defense, she wanted to be sure you were taken care of properly. Don't be angry."

"Oh, the naive ship already sailed, Daddy. I'm really, really mad, and I don't know when I'll be over it," she said. Tears welled up, but she'd be damned to hell before she'd let anyone see her cry. Not over this pile of crap. For the first time in her life, Jennie Sue felt like throwing something at a nearby wall.

Dill had trouble looking her in the eye. "You shouldn't know it now, but maybe it will help you understand the way things are."

"Did you love Mama when you married?"

"I did." Sadness peeked around the edges of his smile. "She was so beautiful and full of life. Those first five or six years were amazing. The business was good, and we had you and built our dream house." He stared out the window as if he were looking back into the past.

"And then James came home from the service," Jennie Sue said.

He jerked his head around so fast that she heard the bones crack. "Who told you about him?"

"When a person gets out of the glass bubble called the Baker house, they find out all kinds of things. So what happened when James came home?" Her father had been right when he said it was complicated. This whole thing had more layers than a big Vidalia.

"We hit a rough patch that never got smoothed out." His voice cracked. "Our bubble burst, and we've—evidently you've figured out the rest."

"I refuse to live like y'all have, Daddy. That's not the life I want," she said.

"Don't expect you to, but it will take a miracle to ever get your mother to come around to your way of thinkin', darlin' girl." Sadness filled his words. "Maybe I should just go."

He should for real, but she couldn't tell him that. Another layer of guilt lay on her shoulders. She'd blamed him, and even now, he wasn't totally in the clear because he could have made the choice not to cheat. But at least she was beginning to understand both of her parents' underlying motives.

"Stay," she said. "Daddy, I don't think I ever had real friends before now. Not in school, where I tried so hard to be the daughter Mama wanted. Not in New York, where I was just arm candy for Percy."

"And you think you do now?" he asked.

She nodded. "I really do, and I don't think they care about this Wilshire thing, but I'm not planning to stay here. If you won't give me a job, I'll go somewhere else. At my age, I need to start building seniority, to have benefits and all that. I need a fresh start where no one even knows me. But I've got a feeling the friends I've made this week will always keep in touch."

"You hang on to them, darlin'. That kind of friendship isn't easy to come by," he said wistfully. "And forget the Wilshire curse."

"I heard about the beginnings of the Wilshire and Clifford feud," she said. "So, did Flora have sex with my great-grandfather at the bachelor party?"

"Have no idea. It was a he said/she said situation, but you know how the rumors go in this town. And call your mama in a few days. She's got a hot temper, but she cools down after a while. In addition to everything else, she's going to be fifty this fall, and it's really tough on her to age." He scooted out of the booth and bent to give Jennie Sue a kiss on the forehead. "Do you need anything? Can I take you home or to your apartment?"

"Nope. I'm actually doin' pretty good. After all this, I need to walk and clear my head," she answered.

"I'm here if you need me, and I'm sorry," Dill said.

He was gone before she could answer. Anger topped the list of all the other emotions that she'd experienced that week. Leaving Bloom might not be so difficult after all.

Cricket always went straight to the café after church, changed clothes in the restroom, and got right out onto the floor, and she was in a hurry. The parking places were all filled in front of the café, which meant she'd have to park on the next block. But then she saw a truck pull away, and she quickly grabbed that empty space.

She was running late. People were clustered up around the front of the place waiting for tables or booths. She slid out of the truck and grabbed her purse. In the rush, she didn't even see the crack in the sidewalk until the spike heel of her favorite Sunday pumps popped right off. Then the heel on the other shoe went out from under her, and she fell flat on her butt right there on Main Street in Bloom, Texas. The first thing she did was look around to see if anyone saw her. For the first time, she was thankful that no one was paying a bit of attention to her.

She tried to stand up, but her leg hurt so bad that she collapsed. Her breath was coming in short gasps, and her stomach did a couple of flips with nausea. From the acute pain in her ankle, she figured it was broken. She jerked at her skirt so that her underpants weren't showing, but it was tangled up around her waist. Everything started spinning around her so fast that it was hard to focus—and then she heard Jennie Sue's voice.

"Stay with me. I'll call 911," she said.

Cricket opened her eyes and grabbed Jennie Sue's hand. "Don't. Insurance won't cover it. Just take me to the emergency room."

"I don't have a car." Jennie Sue started digging in her purse.

"Take me in the truck. Keys in my purse." Sticky sweat popped out on Cricket's forehead. "Now! People are looking." She absolutely couldn't bear the embarrassment of people seeing her chubby thighs and white cotton underpants. She'd endure Lucifer if he was shielding her from everyone's eyes rather than Jennie Sue, but he wasn't, so Jennie Sue would have to do.

"I'll call Rick and he can take you, then."

"No! He can't get into town. I have the truck. Are you stupid? If there was any other way, I wouldn't ask you," Cricket moaned.

"Okay, okay, stop your whining." Jennie Sue helped her to her feet and got her into the passenger side of the truck before retrieving her purse from the sidewalk and handing it to her.

Amos knocked on the window as Jennie Sue crawled into the driver's seat and Cricket tossed her the keys.

"You okay? I saw Jennie Sue helping you up," he asked.

She nodded and yelled through the glass, "Just a little twist of the ankle. I'll be fine. Jennie Sue is takin' me home. Thanks for askin'."

Dammit to hell on a rusty poker! Now he'd go tell everyone in town that Jennie Sue was nice enough to take her to the hospital. Everyone would think they were friends.

Cricket shoved her purse across the console. "Center compartment, and please hurry. I'm getting sick to my stomach."

Jennie Sue left at least a week's worth of tire rubber on the pavement when she peeled out, and by the time she reached the city limits sign on the south side of town, she was doing eighty in a forty-five. Cricket opened her mouth to tell her to slow down but only moaned when more pain shot all the way to her hip.

It was normally a fifteen-minute drive to Sweetwater, but Jennie Sue brought the truck to a greasy sliding stop in front of the emergency-room doors in less than ten minutes. She hopped out, rushed inside, and returned with a nurse pushing a wheelchair in what seemed like mere seconds.

"Sit still and let us help you," the nurse said.

"It's only a sprain." The world took another couple of spins when Cricket tried to put a little weight on it.

"That can be worse and take longer to heal than a break sometimes," the nurse said. "Settle into the chair, and we'll go to the business center to get your information."

"My stuff is in my purse. You take care of it," she told Jennie Sue.

"Okay, then," the nurse said. "We've had a slow day, so I can take you right on in."

The nurse rolled Cricket into a triage room and left her sitting in the wheelchair. A guy in blue scrubs looked up from a computer and asked her how much she weighed—she lied by fifteen pounds, just in case Jennie Sue saw any of the records. How tall she was—she stretched it and said that she was an inch taller. Then he glanced at her swollen ankle that had begun to turn purple and took her straight to a cubicle.

"They'll be in and take you down to X-ray in a minute," he said, and disappeared.

Immediately Cricket began to worry about the lies she'd told. If they had to anesthetize her, then would they give her enough to keep her under? She sure didn't want to wake up before they got finished.

Jennie Sue dug around in the purse until she found Cricket's wallet and had almost given up even finding a driver's license when she noticed a small cloth bag. Inside she found an insurance card and all the pertinent information that the lady behind the counter needed.

She took it from Jennie Sue and said, "She will have to personally sign these papers before she is dismissed, but you can put these cards away."

"Now can I go back there with her?"

"Only if you are family," the woman said.

Jennie Sue opened her mouth to say that she was her friend, but then snapped it shut. One of Mabel's old sayings—you might as well hang for a sheep as a lamb—flashed through her mind. So Jennie Sue said, "I'm her sister."

"Then I'll press the button so the doors will open for you," the lady said.

"Thank you." Jennie Sue hoped that lightning

didn't shoot out of the sky and strike her dead on her way out of the office cubicle.

A hunky male attendant was rolling Cricket down the hall in a wheelchair and into the emergency-room area. She didn't have a bit of color in her cheeks.

"What's the prognosis, *sister?*" Jennie Sue asked.

The guy stopped at a door. "I'll go in and tell them we're here."

Cricket looked up with the best of her dirty looks. "I'm not—"

Jennie Sue bent down and cupped her hand over Cricket's ear. "I had to tell them that so they'd let me come back here with you. If you blow it, you're on your own."

Cricket frowned and answered, "Don't know until the doctor sees the X-rays. And—" She lowered her voice to a whisper. "I appreciate you doing this for me, but we are barely friends."

Jennie Sue's shoulders raised in half a shrug. "After the way you've treated me, I'm not even sure I want to be your friend."

"Me neither," Cricket said. "But it seems like we're thrown together all the time. Maybe instead of barely friends, we're civil friends."

"That sounds more like it." Jennie Sue nodded.

The door opened and the guy stepped out. He glanced over at Jennie Sue. "You'll have to wait out here, but this won't take but a minute."

"Yes, sir." She sat down in a folding chair right next to the door.

Mabel used to tell Jennie Sue that everything happened for a reason, that life was like a ball of yarn. She explained that when a person got older, they could pull the loose end and look back at life and see that something that happened on a particular day had changed the course of it. Jennie Sue couldn't think of a single reason that she had to be the one who'd been close enough to Cricket when she fell to help her.

Maybe it was to get your mind off the conversation that you had with your dad. There was no doubt it was Mabel's voice in her head. *You needed a little time to cool your heels. Remember, you do have some of that Wilshire temper even if it doesn't show up very often.*

"I don't have my mother's temper," she muttered.

Be honest.

Before she could argue any more, the man pushed Cricket out of the X-ray lab and headed down the hall. "We'll go back to the emergency room, and the doctor will be here soon to discuss the next step."

"Is it broken?" Jennie Sue asked.

"The lab tech will read it, and then the doctor will talk to you," he said as he got Cricket into her original cubicle and helped her up onto the narrow bed. "Need a blanket?"

"Yes, please," Cricket moaned.

"Can you give her something for the pain?" Jennie Sue asked.

"Not right now. The doctor . . . Oh, here he is now. Ask him."

An older man with a round face, a wide nose, and snow-white hair cut close to his head gently rolled the sheet away from Cricket's leg. "Let's see what we've got here. I checked the picture and there's no broken bones, which means a nasty sprain that's going to keep you off your feet for three to six weeks. For the first week, you'll keep it propped up and only get up to go to the bathroom—on crutches."

Cricket sucked air through her teeth several times when he pressed on the ankle. Jennie Sue grabbed her hand and held it.

Cricket tried to jerk it away, and Jennie Sue leaned down and whispered, "We're civil friends, remember?" Did that subcategory of friends mean that the friendship ended when they left the hospital, or did she have to do more for Cricket? And how was it different from acquaintances?

Jennie Sue was still mulling over the type of friendship she wanted with Cricket when the doctor's deep voice jerked her back to the room.

"Ice. Twenty minutes on and twenty minutes off, three times in the morning, afternoon, and evening," he said. "Second week you can move around the house on crutches, but you can't put the foot on the ground. I'll see you at the end of that week and we'll talk about a walking boot."

"I have to work," Cricket moaned.

"Not for the next three weeks, and then only part-time until I release you," he said sternly, and then looked over at Jennie Sue. "I understand you are her sister. Can I trust you to make her follow my instructions?"

"She's not really—" Cricket snapped.

Jennie Sue squeezed her hand hard. "This time I get to be the boss, so don't argue with me. How much longer will we be here, Doc? And will you please write a prescription for pain medicine? She's an old bear when she's hurting." Jennie Sue talked fast to keep Cricket from saying another word.

"Where do you want me to call the prescriptions in to?" the doctor asked.

"A pharmacy here in Sweetwater that's open on Sundays, since our little drugstore is closed," Jennie Sue answered. "Can we get crutches there?"

"We'll give her some and I'll tell the nurse to call this in to City Drug. Know where that is? And you'll see to it that she makes a follow-up appointment?"

"Yes, sir, I will be sure." Jennie Sue nodded.

"Okay, then, I'll see you in my office in a couple of weeks," he said on his way out the door. "Someone will be in to wheel you out to your vehicle in a few minutes."

"You are not my sister!" Cricket hissed.

"A civil friend doesn't act like a full-fledged bitch," Jennie Sue said. "Let's just get you home and comfortable so you can start that regimen with an ice pack."

A woman came through the curtain with a syringe in one hand and a set of metal crutches in the other. "Doc has ordered a pain shot to help until you get your meds started. Hip or arm?"

"Arm," Cricket answered.

"It wears off quickly, so go ahead and take a pill as soon as you can with food. Here's your crutches. Tuck them tightly under your arms, and don't put your hurt foot on the ground. We'll get you in the wheelchair and roll you out to the car." She looked over at Jennie Sue. "You can go get the vehicle and I'll roll her out to it."

Cricket was barely in the chair when another woman arrived with a sheaf of papers. "You'll need to sign these. We'll bill your insurance and then send a bill with the balance due to the address on your driver's license."

Cricket signed all the places where she was told and glanced over at Jennie Sue. "I sprained the other ankle five years ago. I know what to do. Just take me home and then leave me alone."

"Sisters. You don't get to pick 'em, and there's nothing you can do about what you get when they arrive. So which of you is oldest?" the administrator asked.

"I am," Jennie Sue said. "By ten months."

"Then I guess you've got the God-given right to be the boss," the woman said. "Let's get you out to your car."

Forty-five minutes later they'd been to the drugstore, picked up the medicine, and Jennie Sue was parking the truck in front of a small white frame house. It looked like a picture from Mabel's kitchen calendar with the deep-red crape myrtle bushes blooming all around it. On one end of the porch a swing, wide enough for three or four people, moved gently in the afternoon breeze. On the other end, two bright-red metal lawn chairs, like what Mabel and Frank had on their porch, beckoned for folks to come sit a spell and visit.

"Hey, what's goin' on?" Rick rubbed a hand over his face as he came outside. When Cricket got out of the truck and tucked the crutches under her arm, he hurried to her side. "What happened?"

"I fell. Jennie Sue took me to the hospital. It's a sprain and I'm fine." She started toward the house with Jennie Sue on one side and Rick behind her to catch her if she fell. "What are we going to do? I can't work for at least three weeks and maybe six. And you need help with the crops." Tears began to rush down her cheeks and drip onto her shirt.

"Stop worryin' about all that. We'll survive," Rick answered as she made her way up three steps to the porch.

Jennie Sue wiped away Cricket's tears with the tail of her T-shirt. "I'll make her an omelet and some pancakes if you'll get an ice pack ready. She's got to eat to take a pill."

"You are not my sister. You're only my civil friend, and that don't mean you get to waltz into my house and take over," Cricket fumed.

"Sister?" Rick looked from one to the other again.

"She lied and said she was my sister so she could come back into the emergency room with me. Now she's been bossing me worse than you do." Cricket eased down into a worn recliner when she made it into the house. She popped up the footrest and leaned back. "That pain shot is starting to wear off, and it's throbbin' again."

"Civil friend?" Rick raised a dark eyebrow toward Jennie Sue.

"Friendship comes in degrees. Civil friend is a step below barely friend, but only a step up from not at all and almost hate," she explained.

"I see." He grinned. "Well, thank you for taking her and bringing her home. I can handle it from here. I'll make her some food after I give you a ride home."

"No, it's starting to hurt and I need to eat," Cricket said. "Fix me a peanut butter sandwich or hand me a tomato and I'll eat it like an apple. I want a pain pill. Why did you tell them you were the oldest?" Cricket asked.

"Show me the kitchen and I'll make her a quick meal," Jennie Sue told Rick and then turned her attention back to Cricket. "I was always the oldest in the class, and you were one of the youngest ones. Didn't we all have to line up according to age in the first grade? We were the brackets. I was jealous of your braids and the freckles across your nose. Frank said that freckles were where angels kissed a person, and I wanted them. I loved your hair, and Mama wouldn't ever let me have braids."

"You remember that?" Cricket asked.

"Yep, now how do you like your omelet?"

"With bacon, tomatoes, peppers, and lots of cheese. And Rick . . ." Tears started down Cricket's cheeks again. "I'm so sorry . . . What are we going to do for real? I can't help with the crops."

"I'll do it." Jennie Sue headed for the kitchen. "When I get off from my other two jobs each evening, I'll help you. I don't have anything to do in the evenings anyway. You just have to pick me up."

"Thank you. I can't pay much, but I can at least give you minimum wages."

"How about I make supper for you both each evening, and what I eat can be my payment?

That way I don't have to buy food, and I have someone to eat with and cook for," Jennie Sue said. "And besides, it's what civil friends do to help out someone who needs it."

"We don't take charity," Cricket said.

"I'm workin' for my supper, and it's you givin' out charity, not me. I'm probably the poorest person in Bloom right now. Are you goin' to let your sister starve?"

"Okay, okay, if it's all right with Rick, we'll accept, but I hope you know how to cook plain food."

"I was trained by Mabel. Now show me the kitchen and I'll get busy."

"You sure about this?" Rick asked.

"Just lead the way," Jennie Sue answered, not sure at all about what she'd just done.

Chapter Nine

"Well, there's my new employee." Amos opened the door and bowed with a flourish when Jennie Sue arrived at the bookstore the next morning.

"Thank you for the welcome. I'm ready to work. What do I do first?" she asked.

"Whatever you want. I'm just glad that I can keep the store open all day on Monday through Wednesday. Half days were killin' me, but I've always helped with the library, and I didn't want to give it up. This store was my sweet wife's, and I just couldn't completely close it up," he said.

She noticed romance, nonfiction, and cookbooks all on the same, most visible shelf. "Looks like we need some organizing."

"That would be great. The office is through that door." He pointed. "Restroom is over there." He swung his finger to the other side of the store. "We're closed from twelve to one for lunch, and now I'm going to a Kiwanis breakfast. Make yourself at home. Paperbacks sell for a quarter of whatever the retail price is on them. Hardbacks sell for five dollars."

"You really don't care if I do some rearranging?" Jennie Sue asked.

"Honey, I'd appreciate anything that you want

to do with the place." Amos waved and left her alone in the bookstore.

She found two big boxes in the back of the store and brought them up front, where she filled them with books from the first set of shelving. She'd recently read that romance sales were a large percentage of the market, so she planned to fill the first row of shelves with that genre—alphabetically according to the author's last name. It would take weeks to organize the whole store, but she'd get a little bit done each day, and before she left town, folks could easily find what they wanted.

Humming as she put the first twenty books on the top shelf, Jennie Sue drifted off into her own little world, remembering how fun it had been to get dirty and sweaty in the huge garden on the Lawson farm. Even if Cricket was cool toward her and at times downright hateful, she'd still enjoyed cooking for three and having someone to eat supper with.

"Besides, I've lived with Charlotte Baker all my life, so Cricket doesn't have a snowball's chance in hell of intimidating me," she muttered. "I kind of like her brutal honesty. Different from the kind of girls I grew up with—or in Percy's world."

Looking back, that first year hadn't been so bad. He'd been busy building up the business he and his partner had bought. A jewelry launch party or something similar filled every weekend. Not to mention the charity events where Percy tried to get new—*female*—clients. She'd been swept into a world that her mother loved and tried very hard to fit into it, but it bored her.

They hadn't been married a month when he'd found water spots on the bathroom faucets and decided that the housekeepers weren't doing it to suit him. When she asked her mother about it, Charlotte had said it was just a test to see how much she loved him.

They never hired another housekeeper after that.

It went downhill from there. He gradually became more and more verbally abusive and demanded more from her. She thought things might change for the better when she told him she was pregnant, but she was wrong.

"You did this on purpose. A baby will ruin our life. I'll make an appointment tomorrow for you to get rid of it," he'd said in a tone so cold it had sent shivers down her spine.

"It was a pure accident. The pill is only ninety-something-percent effective, you know," she argued. "And I'm not having an abortion."

"Yes, you are," he screamed, and threw the bowl of potato salad at the wall.

"I will not, and since you're already angry, I might as well tell you that I've been taking online courses a few at a time to finish up my business degree. I'm hoping to have it completed the semester after the baby is born." She remembered thinking that she'd just spring it all on him at once since he was already angry.

He'd glared at her for a full minute before he stormed into the hall and brought out a blanket and pillow. "I'll sleep in the spare room. I'm finished with you until the abortion is done."

"Then you might as well move on out, because that is not going to happen." She'd gone to the kitchen for cleaning supplies to take care of the mess he'd made.

The squeal of tires right outside the store jerked her out of the past and into the present. She glanced up to see a van coming right at the glass storefront. She took off to the back of the store in a dead run. She'd passed the romance section and the mysteries before she came to a halt. Total silence filled the store. No broken windows or books flying through the air. She turned around when the cowbell above the door jingled. Adrenaline rushed through her body, and her heart was pumping so hard she could scarcely breathe.

"Sorry sumbitch brakes," Nadine fumed as she made her way into the store. "Not a bit more dependable than a Missouri mule. Does Amos have any sweet tea made up? Or has he got some of that elderberry wine that he brews up in the fall hidin' back there under the counter?"

"Nadine Clifford! You don't even have a driver's license. What are you doin' behind the wheel?" Jennie Sue had to steady herself on the bookcase in front of her to keep her trembling legs from collapsing.

Nadine slung her bony body down on the recliner. "Don't fuss at me. Just because I ain't got a license don't mean I can't drive. Them damned brakes is just tough to mash down when you get to be ninety. And if I get caught, then you'll come bail me out of jail. Get us some tea or some wine and let's talk about what happened to Cricket. I swear, that girl is carryin' too much weight on them little bitty feet and that's the reason she's got a bum leg right now. She needs to jerk about forty pounds off her body, and then she could catch a husband."

"Are you drunk, Nadine?" Lettie rushed into the store and popped her hands on her round hips right in front of her sister. "What in the hell do you mean drivin' when you ain't even had a license in ten years? I told you that I'd drive over and get you. When I got there and you was gone, I thought the aliens had finally gotten through on my phone."

Nadine's chin jacked up three inches. "Hell, if they had, they would have let me go in an hour. I'm ninety years old. There ain't nothin' in this old body they'd want to study. And"—she shook her finger under Lettie's nose—"you're too damn slow. I was ready an hour ago, and it's too hot to walk down here. I can drive if I want to. Now stop your bitchin' at me and sit down here." She patted the sofa. "Jennie Sue is going to bring us some tea and tell us about how Cricket hurt her foot. Bless Cricket's heart, she'll shrivel up and die if she can't get out and visit with people."

"Don't change the subject." Lettie plopped down. "Look at my shoes. They don't even match, and it's your fault. When Amos called and said that someone told him you were weaving all over the road, I picked up the first two I could find. If I'd had to go to the hospital like this because you had a wreck, everyone in the county would say I was losin' my mind."

"Well, you are," Nadine said in an icy tone. "Go rushin' around like a madwoman just because I decided to do something on my own and come see my friend Jennie Sue. Maybe I wanted to talk about you and didn't want you here."

Jennie Sue went to Amos's office, found a stack of disposable red plastic cups, and filled three with ice cubes and sweet tea. They were still arguing when she made it back to the front of the store and handed off one to each of them.

"Sit down and talk to us. My heart is pumping so hard it's goin' to break a rib. I swear, Nadine, I ought to shake the shit out of you for scaring us like this," Lettie fussed.

Jennie Sue glanced longingly at the shelves, but

these two old girls needed her. She eased down in a chair across from them. "Let's catch our breath and let the adrenaline settle before we go shaking anyone."

Lettie leaned her head back and put a hand over her eyes. "My blood pressure is at stroke level."

"It's all that fat around your heart that's making it go high today," Nadine said sarcastically.

Lettie sat up straight and glared at Nadine. "Bullshit! It's havin' a crazy sister."

"Let's talk about something else," Jennie Sue said quickly. "I'm rearranging the store so the customers can find what they want easier. Amos told me to do whatever I want, and it could create more sales."

"That's nice. We heard you told the doctor Cricket was your sister. Did she try to scratch your eyes right out of your head? You know she hates you, don't you?" Nadine downed half her tea and said, "It's tough to hate your sister, right, Lettie?"

"Don't ask me that right now. I wouldn't have a bit of trouble scratching her eyes out," Lettie yelled, winding back up.

"Then I'd be blind and I might really hit the storefront." Nadine slapped Lettie on the arm.

Lettie slapped her back. "You don't get to talk right now." Then she turned her attention back to Jennie Sue. "We also heard you were out there at the farm until late."

"I'm going out there every evening to help get in the crops and make supper for them. I get to eat for free, and they get a cook and a field hand. Sounded like a good deal to me." She stood up and went back to working on the books. "And Cricket and I've decided to be civil friends. Emphasis on being civil. I told the lady at the hospital I was her sister just so I could get past the doors into the place where she was."

"You're hoping to change Cricket's mind, aren't you?" Lettie asked.

"We're your friends, but she probably won't never be anything more than this civil-friend thing you said. Sounds kind of crazy to me," Nadine said.

"Not really. We're kind of civil friends with Charlotte. We speak when we have to, don't we?" Lettie said.

"Well, I'm not so sure that Cricket can even do that much with Jennie Sue. She's stubborn like Rick. You know that man ain't set foot in church since he got home?"

"Well, I haven't been in church since I married Percy. God hasn't struck me dead yet."

Lettie laughed out loud. "You are so much like your grandma Baker. She had a wonderful sense of humor. I liked her almost as much as I didn't like your other great-grandma for takin' Gene away from Flora."

"Lettie! You don't need to be draggin' them

old bones out of the closet again." Nadine shot a dirty look her way.

"It's okay. Daddy told me the story at lunch yesterday. Did y'all realize that my mama will be fifty this year? No wonder she's havin' such a meltdown. She's too beautiful to get old." She carried a box through the store, searching for more romance books.

"Charlotte always was gorgeous. You know what she should do? She should start a beauty-treatment business for girls like Cricket," Nadine said.

"There's nothing wrong with Cricket. Some of us are just fluffier than you skinny broads," Lettie huffed. "What Charlotte needs to do is accept age gracefully."

"Like you do with that jet-black hair," Nadine snorted.

"Don't you start on my hair, and I won't say a word about your flat chest," Lettie shot back.

Life was so much fun in Bloom, Texas. Jennie Sue wondered why she'd ever left in the first place. Oh, yes, it had something to do with her mother paying a down-on-his-luck diamond dealer to woo her—did they even use that word anymore? If not, they should, because it was as outdated as a dowry.

She could hear the sisters arguing in the background, but she let her mind wander. Did Percy ever love her? Would it have even made him sad to know that their child had been stillborn? Or would he have been relieved not to have to pay child support?

"Poor Cricket." Nadine clucked like an old hen gathering in her chicks. "She's always been one of them girls who like to be out in the middle of things, not stuck in the house with her foot propped up."

"We'll have to go out and visit with her tomorrow afternoon," Lettie said.

Nadine sipped at her tea. "Take notes."

"Notes?" Jennie Sue asked.

"Honey, at our age, we might forget an important little bit of news, so we'll take notes between now and tomorrow about everything we hear," Lettie explained.

"You mean gossip?"

"It's one and the same," Lettie and Nadine said in unison.

"So now, what's going on with you and Rick?" Nadine leaned forward like she was sharing a secret.

"As in?" Jennie Sue asked.

"Do you like him? Does he like you? Are you going out on a date?" Lettie asked.

"Slow down. Yes, I like Rick as a friend. I don't know if he likes me, and we are definitely not dating. I've only been home a week. That would be moving too fast," Jennie Sue answered.

Nadine clapped her hands. "You lost. You owe me two dollars."

Lettie pulled two rumpled dollar bills from her purse. "I'll win it back by the end of the day."

"Maybe so, but it's mine now."

"Is that real money?" Jennie Sue asked.

"We got about ten of them dollars, and that's our rumor money. We been using the same bills for up near fifty years now," Lettie answered.

Jennie Sue dropped the two books in her hands. "You're kiddin' me, right?"

"Truth." Lettie held up two fingers. "Swear it on my mama's Bible. We wouldn't lie to our friend."

"So I'm your friend even though you've been feuding with the Wilshires for all these years?" Jennie Sue asked.

"Honey, you are a Baker and we loved your grandma Vera, so yes, you are our friend."

"And since you are our friend"—Nadine lowered her voice to a whisper—"when the aliens do figure out a way to get into our business because of that fancy phone you have, we'll protect you. I got a concrete cellar full of canned vegetables and fruit. Got two old bunk beds down there, too, and a thousand rounds of ammo to go with my guns. I reckon we can hold 'em off for a little while."

"Thank you. That eases my fears." Jennie Sue stopped what she was doing and gave them both a hug.

• • •

Even though Rick usually avoided mirrors like the plague, especially when he wasn't wearing a shirt, that morning after his shower he stood in front of one and let the memories of that day rush over him. He and the rest of the Rangers had gotten the mission plan and packed their gear. They were all as superstitious as baseball players and had their own special routines. Rick's was that he had to put all his gear into his go bag and take it out three times to make sure he hadn't forgotten anything. Then he had to zip it, unzip it, and then zip it one more time. After that, he'd check his guns and count the ammo twice. Finally, he'd kiss his dog tags, and then he was ready to go.

He'd done it all that morning, but his mind had been on his dad. He and Cricket had talked on FaceTime the night before, and she'd told him that their father was running out of steam early in the afternoon. The man had worked his whole life in the fields—he was as strong as a bull—so it was a big thing when he couldn't go all day anymore. They found out that he had cancer the same week that Rick lay unconscious in a hospital.

Rick touched the scars on his chest and sides and then turned to see the big one that had made him have to relearn the art of walking. "No woman would ever want something that looks like this," he muttered.

His team had accomplished the mission and had made it to the helicopter, all of them running full-out with gunfire behind them when he'd heard a click. He hadn't had time to make a decision about whether to take another step or not. The next thing he knew he was flying through the air.

Two of his friends grabbed him under the arms and pulled him into the chopper, and then it was lights-out. When he woke up, he knew he wasn't dead because it hurt too much. His best friend had slept in a chair beside him, and when Rick groaned, he awoke with a start and ran for a nurse. The good news was that he was alive. The bad was that he'd spend several months in rehab and he'd never be fit for active duty again.

Cricket's loud voice startled him from the past into reality when she yelled from the living room. "You better get a move on. You need to be at the library to get the bookmobile in exactly fifteen minutes."

"Yes, sir, Sarge," he called out.

"I'm cranky. Don't get cute with me," she hollered back.

He hurriedly threw on a pair of jeans and a T-shirt. After he'd put on his athletic shoes, he grabbed the book he'd been reading. He shoved it down into a backpack with half a dozen bottles of water and the last half dozen peanut butter cookies Cricket had made a few days before.

"You good for the afternoon?" he asked.

"Might as well be. I can't do anything but sit here. I'm just glad it's summer and Elaine can get high school girls to pick up my shifts. She's called twice this morning already to check on me and ask if we needed anything."

"That's great. Keep the ice regimen going, and remember to take the pain meds like the doctor said. Jennie Sue will be here this evening, so you'll have some company then."

He heard her grumbling on his way out.

He drove straight to the library and got the keys, then headed north up to Roby. Fifteen minutes later he arrived at the school parking lot to find several folks already waiting for him. When Rick was sixteen, the big news in the area had been about the forty-two people who each put a ten-dollar bill in a pot to buy lottery tickets. They'd won a forty-six-million-dollar pot and split it, making several citizens of Roby instant millionaires.

"Hey." Claud Brewer stepped inside the second that Rick opened the door. "I heard that your sister done broke her leg, and you hired an old girlfriend to come help out on the farm. Any truth in that?"

"She sprained her ankle, and Jennie Sue Baker agreed to help out since Cricket is her friend." He'd have probably fainted like a girl if Cricket had made that drastic of a change in her actual opinion of Jennie Sue. "Been hot enough for you?" He tried to change the subject.

"That's Dill Baker's daughter, right? The one that married that fancy feller from New York a few years ago?"

"Yep, but she's been divorced for a while now." Rick made another stab at changing the conversation. "I brought the last two John Grisham books with you in mind today."

Claud put his two return books in the bin right inside the door. "I heard he took off with another woman, and the gover'ment is hot on his tail. And I'll take both of the books you brought. Too hot to be outside these days, and my wife yammers about it if I try to cook. Says I mess up too many dishes."

"You like to cook?" Rick found the books for him and had him sign the cards in the back.

"Naw, I just like to piss my wife off." Claud winked. "Retirement isn't all it's cracked up to be. I work on keepin' her blood pressure up. I figure pissin' her off is savin' her life. You might remember that when you get old and that young filly you are seein' down there in Bloom needs a little help with her blood pressure."

Yeah, like that would ever happen. Rick sighed. *She's way too beautiful to ever look at me in any way but as a friend.*

"Evenin', Cricket. Are you bored to death?" Jennie Sue passed through the living room without stopping.

"You don't know the half of it. What is that in your hands?" Cricket groaned.

"Italian bread. I'll make it out into a loaf and let it rise again while I get things prepped for supper."

"What's your angle, Jennie Sue? My brother is off-limits, if that's it." Cricket's tone was edgy.

"I'm sure your brother can do better than a divorced woman who's the talk of the town right now. Why don't you get Rick to drive you into town tomorrow morning and spend the day with me at the bookstore? Folks are comin' in and out all day. There's a recliner back in the office that I can push into the seating area. We can keep up with your ice packs, and it wouldn't be any different than sitting here."

Jennie Sue immediately wished that she could take the words and shove them back into her mouth. Putting up with Cricket all day would be as bad or worse than spending hours with Charlotte. The only difference would be that Cricket wouldn't tell Jennie Sue that she was ten pounds overweight.

Cricket hesitated long enough to leave no doubt in Jennie Sue's mind that she was weighing the pros and cons. She'd have to spend the day with someone she didn't like, but she'd get to be in the middle of things, and folks would drop in to visit when they learned she was there.

Rick poked his head door. “You fit to live with, Cricket?”

“No, I’m even crankier than I was this morning, and now I’m hungry on top of it,” she answered.

“Supper will take care of that.” Jennie Sue set a cast-iron skillet and a steamer pot onto the stove.

Rick followed Jennie Sue into the kitchen. “Looks like we’ve got maybe two hours’ worth of harvesting to do after supper. That’ll give me plenty to do my Tuesday deliveries around town. What’s for supper? Can I help with anything?”

“Alfredo, steamed vegetables, salad, and fresh bread. This won’t take but forty-five minutes to get ready. I’m used to working alone,” she said.

“Sounds great,” Rick said. “If I can’t help, I’m going out to the watermelon field and finding a dozen nice ones for my deliveries in the morning. Cricket, you want me to help you out on the back porch so you can get some fresh air?”

“I’ll just stay put,” Cricket said. “I’m going into town tomorrow and spending the day at the bookstore. Jennie Sue invited me.”

“Thank you,” Rick mouthed as he closed the door behind him.

“You might want to call Nadine and Lettie and let them know your plans. They were planning on driving out here tomorrow afternoon to bring you the news.” Jennie Sue turned around so she could see Cricket.

Cricket's whole expression perked up. "News about what?"

"I have no idea, but they were going to take notes so they didn't forget anything." Jennie Sue shaped the bread dough into a long loaf, cut a couple of slits on the top, and then boned out three chicken breasts.

She peeked around the edge of the refrigerator to see Cricket with her phone to her ear, and, sure enough, the woman looked happy.

Chapter Ten

Amos strutted around like a little rooster in the store. According to him, the place hadn't been this busy since Iris had passed away. He didn't seem to care that most folks weren't buying a book but rather spending time visiting with Cricket.

"Look at her over there holdin' court," he said.

"She does look happy." Jennie Sue was glad that folks didn't want to talk to or about her. "And I'm gettin' a lot of work done."

"Store is beginnin' to look like it did when Iris was here," Amos said. "I love it, but I just don't have the know-how to do what she did."

"I can understand that, but, Amos, I was serious when I told y'all that this is temporary. I need to get busy on résumés next week, and I hope to be gone by fall." She ducked around the end of the next row of shelves and started working on that section.

At noon the place had cleared out, and Amos announced that he was going to the café to buy lunch for all three of them and asked Cricket what she wanted on her burger.

"Mayo, no pickles or onions, and tots instead of fries," she said.

"Same here," Jennie Sue said from the other

side of the first row of shelving. “And I’ll just have sweet tea from the fridge here, so you don’t have to carry so much.”

When Amos was out of the store, Cricket called out, “Thank you, Jennie Sue.”

Jennie Sue rounded the end of the bookshelf and sat down on the sofa. “Did it hurt to say those words? Do you need a pain pill?”

“More than you’ll ever know,” Cricket admitted.

“Why do you hate me?”

“*Hate* is too strong a word for what I feel for you, Jennie Sue.”

“Then what is it?”

Cricket inhaled deeply and let it out slowly. “I don’t know. Maybe I wanted all that acceptance you always had when we were growing up. You fit in and I didn’t.”

“You may have thought so, but I always felt like an outsider with every group,” Jennie Sue said. “Did I ever tell you that I loved it when your mama brought chocolate cupcakes to our class parties? I’d really like to have her recipe for that icing. It was like a layer of fudge resting on the top of the cupcakes.”

Cricket slowly shook her head. “That recipe is in the church cookbook now. They were homemade. I loved the ones that your mama sent to the class. Those ones from the bakery looked so pretty. My mama’s were so plain.”

"But they tasted so much better than the bought ones. Think we'll ever be able to be friends?"

Another shake of the head. "Probably not, but I don't dislike you as much as I did last week."

"I guess that's a step in the right direction," Jennie Sue said.

"Rick says that I'm too blunt."

"He's right," Jennie Sue agreed. "But then there is an upside to that. A person knows where they stand with you."

"Do you always have to say something positive? It makes it real hard to hate you," Cricket sighed.

Before Jennie Sue could answer, Amos backed through the front door with a brown bag. "After we eat, I'm going to drive over to Abilene and visit my brother the rest of today and tonight. I'll leave the keys on the counter, Jennie Sue, so you can lock up and open up in the morning," Amos said. "I'm likin' having someone three days a week. Gives me time to enjoy retirement."

Retirement was something in the far future for Jennie Sue, and only if she could find a job that paid well with good benefits. But change happened and couldn't be helped.

With wet dirt clinging to her feet that evening after supper, Jennie Sue picked green beans from vines that Rick had trained up a trellis. A hot breeze ruffled the leaves on the cornstalks, and carried Rick's humming to her ears. Then suddenly the stalks parted and his face appeared about three feet away.

The setting sun lit up the scar on his jaw, and his hand went to it when he caught her staring.

"It's ugly, I know," he said.

"I don't think so." She took a step forward and touched it.

"Well, you are probably the only one who thinks that way." He stepped out and sat down on a narrow strip of dirt separating the beans and corn. "Let's take a little break. My basket is full and yours is almost overflowing."

She sat down beside him. "Did you hate coming back here to farm?"

He shrugged. "I didn't have a choice."

"Surely there was something else," she said.

"Maybe being a security guard, but even that was iffy with this limp. What about you, Jennie Sue? What are you doing back here?"

"Trying to talk my dad into giving me a job at the company, but I'm not having much luck. Whatever happened ended your career, right?" she asked.

His eyes remained fixed somewhere out there near the sunset. "Yes, it did. I was treated, discharged, and released. I've questioned God for letting that happen to me. Twenty more steps and I'd have been in the helicopter and safe with the rest of the team. But half a step back and I would have been sent home in pieces." He still focused on something far away.

"I've done the same thing, but we both know that it's not God's fault. We just needed someone to blame." She wondered if he was seeing the whole thing again, reliving it, probably not for the first time.

Rick jerked his head around to look at her. "What are you blaming him for?"

"Letting me be sold off like a bag of chicken feed, for one thing."

"What?" Rick frowned.

She told him what her father had told her about Percy and the dowry. "No one knows that, so I'd rather you kept it a secret. It makes me feel cheap and dirty."

Rick reached across the distance and laid a hand on her shoulder. There was that chemistry—electricity, vibes, or whatever folks called it—again.

"You should never feel like that, Jennie Sue." His drawl softened. "You are an amazing woman any guy would be lucky to have beside him. Percy should be shot."

"I really don't care anymore. I'm pretty much indifferent to him. If they catch him, then he can pay the consequences. If they don't, then he'll be looking over his shoulder the rest of his life," she said.

"So have you forgiven your mother?"

"Not yet, but I'm workin' on it. If I can't forgive her, then it'll sit on my heart the rest of my life. I don't want anyone, not even my mother, to have that kind of power over me." She covered his hand with hers. "I'm glad you survived."

"Well, I'm glad that I survived, too." He nodded. "Because I get to sit in this garden with you, and we can be friends." He cocked his head to one side. "What do you really want in life, Jennie Sue?"

"Right now? Tomorrow or five years down the road?" she answered with more questions.

"All of the above," Rick answered.

"Right now, to see if Cricket will snap beans tomorrow at the bookstore. We could sell them in quart bags to whoever comes into the store, and it would make her feel productive. Tomorrow—to phone my mother. Five years down the road? That's too far to think about. What about you?"

"I want a family someday. No hurry, but that's my long-term goal," he said.

"Me, too." She glanced his way to find him staring out across the fields again. She tried to imagine where the rest of his scars were but could only see him as a perfect man in her mind.

"I'll hate to see you leave Bloom, but I understand. Don't worry about all the gossip and rumors. Folks are goin' to talk, and what they think about the way you live your life doesn't matter."

He turned quickly and caught her staring. A blush dotted her cheeks, and she blinked. "It's not a matter of what other people think of me, Rick. It's what I think of myself, and that'll take a while to get over, if I ever do."

His hand went to her shoulder again. "Don't be so tough on yourself. You're a victim."

She slowly lifted her eyes. "What about you? You're a victim, too."

He nodded. "That's what my therapist said in the hospital. But just sayin' it isn't like takin' a pain pill, and it all disappears. I've got scars on the outside, and we both have some on the inside. Maybe God slapped us down together in Bloom, Texas, so we could help each other get through the past and move on to the future."

"I think a good friend is even better than a therapist," she said.

"Me, too, Jennie Sue." He nodded. "It's gettin' pretty dark. Let's call it a night. I've got plenty for the deliveries tomorrow."

"You are the boss."

He stood and stretched out a hand. She put hers in it and imagined him pulling her to his chest, holding her there and maybe even kissing her. The vision made her pulse race a little, but it didn't happen. Once she was on her feet, he let go of her hand, and they picked up their baskets to carry back to the porch.

"What makes you trust me? I could go tell

your secret tomorrow," he asked as he turned the faucet on that stuck out of the back of the house. In seconds a stream shot out from a short hose, and he sprayed off her feet before doing his own.

Oh, honey, she thought. *Compared to the rest of the baggage, you know very little.* She wiggled her toes to air-dry them and then put on her sandals. "Because my heart says I can trust you. I'd ask you the same thing—you just told me things that Cricket doesn't know."

"I feel better for tellin' you. Kind of takes part of the burden off my chest," he answered.

"Me, too, Rick, but you'd better take me home now, or else Miz Lettie will get out the shotgun and insist you make an honest woman out of me," she teased.

"Or Dill Baker will, and believe me, darlin', I'd be more afraid of his aim than Miz Lettie's." He opened the door a crack and yelled inside, "Hey, Cricket, I'm takin' Jennie Sue home now. Anything you want from town?"

"Not a thing," she answered.

A few minutes later, he was pulling into Lettie's driveway. "Thanks for listenin' to me tonight."

"That goes both ways. There's just something about being in a garden—" She paused.

He laid a hand on her arm. "I understand."

"I think you do." Three times—or was it four?—he'd touched her that evening, and every time she'd wanted more. A kiss or even a long hug. "Good night, Rick. See you tomorrow."

"After I park the bookmobile at the library, I'll come down to the bookstore. Maybe I'll get in on the job of snapping beans, or I can help you rearrange the shelves." He put his hand back on the steering wheel. "Thanks for all this, Jennie Sue."

"You are welcome, but I should thank you."

She hopped out of the truck and was on her way through the garage when Lettie hollered from the kitchen door, "I've been lookin' for you. Come on in. We can brew up some hot chocolate and have a cookie. I've got news."

She did an abrupt turnaround and headed toward the porch, carrying her shoes.

"I'm coming right out of the garden, so I might track in some dirt," she called out when she reached the house.

"I've got this really good cleaning lady who'll come around in a couple of days, so I'm not worried. Pull up a chair to the table and let's visit. Lord, I love having you close. It's like you're the granddaughter I never got to have," Lettie said.

A lump popped up in Jennie Sue's throat. "I'd hug you, but I'm too sweaty and dirty."

Lettie patted her on the shoulder. "We'll hug it out later. Hot chocolate is in the slow cooker. I make a batch every couple of weeks and then store it in the refrigerator. It's good with a little whiskey in it on the nights when I can't sleep. Want a little shot in yours?"

Jennie shook her head. "I really don't want anything at all to eat or drink, honest."

"Then tell me how things are going out on the farm."

"Just fine. We got plenty gathered in for Rick's deliveries tomorrow, and it seems like Cricket is coming around. I kind of like her bluntness, to tell the truth. My friends in high school were the Belles' daughters, for the most part, and in college, it was sorority sisters. I always felt like they couldn't wait for me to leave the room so they could bad-mouth me. With Cricket, I don't need to leave the room. If she's got something to say, she says it."

Lettie picked up a cookie. "The secret to good pecan sandies is real butter. Don't never use margarine in pecan sandies." Lettie handed a mug of chocolate that smelled like Irish whiskey to Jennie Sue. "You can have a sip of mine just to see how good it is."

Jennie Sue took a small sip and rolled her eyes. "That is amazing. Next time I'll have a cup with you."

"I can heat you up a cup anytime. Didn't you make friends in New York?"

"A few, but when Percy divorced me, they stopped invitin' me to anything or even callin'. Tell the truth, when I left, I didn't have a single person to tell goodbye except the IRS guy who wanted the keys to the apartment and my car," she said.

"How did you live like that?" Lettie shook her head in disbelief.

"It was just the way things were. You said you had something to tell me," Jennie Sue answered and reached for a cookie. Just one, because anything with real butter and fresh pecans had to be good.

"Yes, I surely do. Your mama and her little Sweetwater bitches are coming home earlier than they'd planned. Remember when we talked about Belinda bein' sick? Well, it ain't got nothing to do with the food at the spa. She's pregnant." Lettie picked up a cookie and dipped it in her Irish coffee.

Jennie Sue wasn't sure that she could utter a word, but when she opened her mouth, they came tumbling out like marbles from a soup can. "Good Lord! How did you find that out? They've got a rule about not telling anything on each other except to the members in the club."

"The rumor pipeline reaches to far places," Lettie laughed. "Take a bite of that cookie and tell me what you think."

Jennie Sue rolled her eyes. "Oh. My. Goodness. This is amazing. Belinda is pregnant? Her girls must both be at least twenty years old."

"Fattenin' as hell, but worth every bite," Lettie

said. "And Belinda's daughters are both over twenty. Thinkin' of mothers and daughters, you need to make up with your mama. If I had a daughter like you, I'd bend over backward to keep her happy. But that ain't Charlotte's way. If it means that you can't clean for me, then I can live with that. But even in this short while, we've become close enough that I don't ever want you to have regrets about bein' my friend."

Jennie Sue laid a hand on Lettie's arm. "I'll talk to Mama, I promise, but I will not have regrets. I'm happier than I've been since I was a little girl and Mabel took care of me."

Lettie dabbed at her eyes with the tail of her apron. "That woman has the kindest heart in the whole world."

"Yes, she does. Thanks for the cookies and chocolate. I should be gettin' up to my place for a shower," Jennie Sue said.

"Refill your cup and take half a dozen cookies with you. You might need a little bedtime snack before you turn in," Lettie said.

She gave Lettie a hug before she left. After a shower, she crawled up in the middle of her bed and replayed the day, the funny moments, the sad ones, but most of all the emotional ones.

"Thank you, Cricket and Rick and Lettie and Nadine." She yawned and pulled back the covers. "Enemies, frenemies, or friends."

Chapter Eleven

When she was a child, Jennie Sue had often wondered if she was even related to her mother. Charlotte was a night owl, staying up until the wee hours of the morning and then sleeping until almost noon every day. Jennie Sue was the opposite. She liked to be in bed by ten and was awake at the crack of dawn. She loved the quietness of the early morning and had missed that in New York, the city that never slept. But what she liked even more in the rural area of Texas was the smell of morning—fresh dew on green grass, maybe the scent of dirt coming from a neighbor plowing a field or a soft breeze blowing across the roses. Those kinds of things couldn't be faked with a scented candle.

That Thursday morning she sat on her tiny little balcony and gazed out across the trees. Three miles away was her folks' place, but it might as well have been eight thousand miles and several time zones.

"Why can't she like me as much as she does her girlfriends? Maybe if she did, she wouldn't feel the need to pay someone to marry me," Jennie Sue whispered and then sighed. "I'll call her tonight. I promise," she vowed to the universe.

"Maybe since she and her little buddies have had a fallin'-out, she'll be a little softer."

She finished off the last of the pecan sandies that Lettie had sent home with her night before last and a second cup of coffee before she got dressed and headed to Nadine's to clean that day. She smelled the bacon half a block away. She crossed her fingers, hoping Nadine had made enough breakfast for an extra person.

She was not disappointed.

Nadine met her at the door and ushered her inside. "I've got bacon and waffles. Got to use up those fresh strawberries that Rick brought me last Friday, so I sliced and sugared them and whipped up some real cream. I haven't eaten yet, either. It's no fun eating alone."

"Thank you. That sounds delicious. What can I do to help?"

"Not one thing, darlin' girl. Just pull up a bar stool, and we'll eat right here. Waffles won't take long to cook. I've already got the iron heated up."

Jennie Sue nodded. "So what's on your agenda today?"

Nadine poured batter into the waffle iron that she'd placed in the middle of the bar. "I'm going to do a little yard work this mornin' while it's cool, and then I'm plannin' to fry apple fritters so I can send some out to the farm when Rick picks you up this evenin'. Cricket is real partial to them. And I got to tell you, she said that you're a real good cook. She loves to bake cookies and cakes and such, but she don't have a lot of imagination when it comes to real cookin'. Y'all ought to go into the cleanin' and caterin' business together." Nadine rattled on while the first batch of waffles cooked.

Yeah, right. I'd rather go into business with the devil himself, Jennie Sue thought as she listened with half an ear. But that idea didn't sound too bad. After seven years of marriage to Percy, she definitely knew how to clean a house and plan a party. If she started up a business of her own, she could live right there in Bloom in Lettie's apartment. She could do events on the weekends, especially in the winter after the farmers' market closed down. She'd have to give up her goal of finding a job in her field for this crazy idea. Or maybe not? She wasn't even thirty yet—she could give the new venture a couple of years and then use her education to run her own business. It would take some serious thought, but maybe it was worth looking into.

"I'd have to have equipment," she mused aloud.

"Oh, honey, between me and Lettie, we've accumulated enough silver and crystal that you wouldn't have to buy a thing. We come from a long line of hoarders when it comes to pretty things." Nadine opened the waffle maker and put the first one on Jennie Sue's plate. "Pile on the strawberries and whipped cream and add some bacon on the side for a little protein. Juice and coffee are on the end of the table."

"Why would you loan me your precious things?" Jennie Sue asked.

"Honey, it's just stuff," Nadine answered.

Ideas bounced around in Jennie Sue's head. In five years she could be using her business degree to run two businesses—a housecleaning one that might employ four or five ladies, and a catering one that could give part-time work to dozens.

But why would I want to stay in Bloom? she asked herself as she finished her waffle.

Because that's where Emily Grace is buried, and your new friends are here, and they care enough about you to offer to let you use their pretty things to start a business and even make you waffles with sugared strawberries without even noticing your weight, the voice in her head said.

"I can see the gears workin' in your head." Nadine refilled her coffee cup. "Well, you just let them keep turnin' while you clean today."

"It's hard to think that I've only been back in Bloom a bit and I'm even entertaining the idea of stayin'. I really wanted to walk into a company and start working my way up the ladder," Jennie Sue said.

Nadine patted her on the arm. "You just think about it, honey. If you decide to go the CEO route, then you could commute to Sweetwater.

It ain't but a fifteen-minute drive, and you could still live in Lettie's apartment."

"Thank you, Nadine," she said, "but one thing is for absolute sure—Cricket Lawson wouldn't be interested in helping me with a business in town, and I'm not sure I'd want her to. It would be like workin' with my mother."

"Lot alike, ain't they?"

"In different ways, but yes."

"And you like Cricket enough to be an almost friend with her and not your mother?" Nadine asked.

"At least Cricket doesn't tell me I'm fat," Jennie Sue answered.

"Charlotte is wrong to do that, but she is your mama. You can have lots of friends, but you only get one mama. So call her and make things right," Nadine said.

"I will. I promise," Jennie Sue vowed for the second time that morning.

She'd worked her way from the bedrooms and the bathroom and had dusted the pictures lining the walls in the hallway. Most of them were of people that she didn't know, but there were a few of three little girls, then three teenagers and three older women that she figured were Flora, Nadine, and Lettie at various stages of their lives. Someday Jennie Sue was going to have a hallway with pictures of her family all lined up pretty in it to make her smile when she dusted them each week. She'd never have a picture of Emily Grace to hang on the wall with the rest of her kids', if she was ever blessed enough to have them, but she'd tell her children about their older sister, for sure.

Leaving the pictures behind, she parked the vacuum in the middle of the living room floor and headed outside to see if the slight wind had dried the sheets hanging on the line. Stepping out in the heat from the cool house almost took her breath, but that was Texas in the summertime. It was unusual that there was even a slight breeze. Mabel said that the wind blows constantly in Texas until the first day of July, and then it's impossible to buy, beg, or borrow enough to flutter the leaves until September.

The sheets still felt damp on the edges, so she crossed the yard to go back inside and dust the living room when she caught a movement in her peripheral vision. Before she could jerk her head around to see what was happening, she heard a thud and a moan. She took a step backward and peeked around the edge of the house to see Nadine lying on her back under the huge pear tree.

"Sweet Lord." Jennie Sue dropped to her knees beside her and touched the artery in her neck to see if she was alive. Her pulse was beating, but not nearly as fast as Jennie Sue's.

Nadine took a huge gulp of air, and her eyes opened wide. "Help me up. Gravity just got more than my boobs and butt. Either that or them damned aliens swooped down and pushed me off that limb."

"You lie perfectly still. Don't even move your fingers," Jennie Sue demanded as she pulled her phone from her pocket and dialed 911. "You could have a fractured back or neck. If you move, it could paralyze or kill you."

"I'm fine," Nadine argued. "I'm not going to die fallin' out of the pear tree. Me and God got a deal. I get to live to be a hundred years old, because that's how long it'll take for Him to forgive me of all my sins. Dammit! My shoulder hurts."

"Don't move." She kept her eyes on Nadine as she talked to the lady on the other end of the line and explained what had happened.

"I'm not payin' for an ambulance. You and Lettie can take me to the doctor here in town," Nadine fussed.

"If you don't be still, I'll tell the aliens to come back and get you," Jennie Sue threatened.

Jennie Sue finished talking on the phone, quickly called Lettie, and then sat down on the grass beside Nadine. "If you don't have the money for an ambulance, then use my cleaning money until you save up enough to pay for it. You'll need a backboard and a neck brace."

"It's not the money. It's the principle. They come less than ten miles and charge out the ass for what? A ride in the back of a crowded van. Hell, I got a van, and I'll even lie in the back seat if you'll let me sit up. Besides, I've got on my oldest panties. I can't go to the hospital with ratty underbritches. What will people say?" Nadine said.

"I won't tell a single soul about your panties, and you know those doctors can't, either." Jennie Sue crossed her heart with her forefinger and then pulled her phone out of her hip pocket to check the time. It startled her so badly when it rang that she dropped it like a hot potato. She hurried to pick it up to answer.

Lettie's voice cracked. "Please tell me she's still alive."

"She's talkin' and breathin' and there's no blood, but I'm not letting her move. She's fightin' with me about an ambulance," she answered.

"I'm on my way over there. Turnin' onto Main Street, I heard the sirens blowin'. We'll follow them to the hospital. I've told her a million times not to climb up in that pear tree to trim it. I swear to God, if she's broken a hip, I'm going to make her go to a nursing home," Lettie yelled into the phone.

The phone went dark and Jennie Sue heard the squeal of tires on the driveway and the sirens coming down the street at the same time. Lettie came around the side of the house, her chubby little legs churning as fast as they would go. She had her right hand over her heart and the forefinger on her left hand wagging before she even plopped down on the grass beside her sister.

Nadine cut her eyes around at Lettie. "Don't start on me. I'm already mad because y'all are makin' me go in the ambulance. You was yellin' so loud on Jennie Sue's phone that I heard what you said. I'm not goin' to no damned nursing home. If my hip was broke, I'd know it. Only thing that hurts is my shoulder. I know how to tuck and roll when I fall. I'm not like you and Cricket. Y'all just sprawl out when you go down."

"What have we got?" Two paramedics jogged around the house with a body board and a neck brace.

"Ninety years old and fell out of a pear tree," Lettie said. "She hates doctors and hospitals, so make her stay for a week to teach her a lesson. And give her shots every day even if she don't need them."

"Don't be a bitch." Nadine shot daggers toward her sister.

"We'll give her a good checkin' out. You want to follow us?"

"Of course I do," Lettie said. "She'll lie out her teeth so you'll let her come home, otherwise."

"Jennie Sue, make her stay here, and when I'm

ready to come home in an hour or so, you can come get me." Nadine winced when they put her on the board. "She'll drive the doctors and nurses crazy with all her questions and carryin' on."

"This time Lettie wins," Jennie Sue said.

"Okay, ladies, we'll see you there." The paramedics each took an end of the board and carried Nadine to the driveway.

"We'll take her van so if they do let her come home, we can bring her," Lettie told Jennie Sue. "She keeps an extra set of keys in the front passenger fender well."

"Dammit!" Nadine huffed. "I was hopin' you'd forget."

"I've got the memory of an elephant."

"And the butt of one," Nadine said as they lifted her into the ambulance.

"At least I'm not crazy enough to climb up in a pear tree like a monkey," Lettie said, and then laid a hand on one paramedic's shoulder. "You take good care of her and don't hit any bumps, you hear me?"

"Yes, ma'am." He nodded with gravity.

Jennie Sue found the key in a little magnetic container with no problem but had to rush back inside the house for her purse. When she returned, Lettie was sitting in the passenger seat. Tears rolled down her cheeks, and she kept pulling tissues from the interior of her big black purse. Jennie Sue took the time to lean across the console and hug her tightly. "It's going to be all right. She might have a busted shoulder. Know what she told me? That the aliens pushed her out of the tree."

"If them sorry bastards ever do find a way to Earth, I'm going to shoot first and ask questions later. I thought for sure she'd be dead," Lettie whimpered. "Next week I'm hiring someone to cut every tree on her place down to the ground."

Jennie Sue started up the engine and backed the van out, drove a couple of blocks to Main Street, and then headed south to Sweetwater. "How did you find out so fast? It hadn't been three minutes since I called 911."

"Someone must've heard it on the scanner and called Amos and he called me. I dropped what I was doin' and pushed the gas pedal to the floor on my old truck. She's so skinny, and she's been clumsy her whole life. If they'll keep her, I can have these trees gone by the time she gets home," Lettie declared.

"Folks are going to say that I'm bad luck. They may tar and feather me and run me out of town," Jennie Sue said.

"Why?" Lettie stopped sniffling and whipped her head around to stare at Jennie Sue. "Did she land on you when she fell? Are you hurt?"

"Of course not. I wouldn't have let her climb up in that tree if I'd known what she was up to. She said she was doing yard work, so I figured she was pullin' weeds out of her flower bed. But think about it, Lettie. First Cricket sprains her ankle, and then Nadine has a bad fall. Am I bad luck?"

Lettie shook her head hard enough that all her chins wiggled. "Stop that kind of nonsense talk. You weren't anywhere near either of them when they fell. Cricket slipped on a wet sidewalk. Besides, she was wearin' them spike heels, and they don't make her look a bit skinnier. Them things is just askin' for trouble. And you sure didn't tell Nadine to climb a tree." She pointed toward the sign that said to turn for the emergency room. "You park right there. If they got a problem with it, I'll straighten them out. And I'll hear no more about you bein' bad luck."

"I hate seeing my friends get hurt." She parked near the emergency doors.

"Everyone does, but that burden ain't yours to carry, child." Lettie undid her seat belt and was out of the vehicle so fast that Jennie Sue had to rush to catch up to her.

Lettie didn't even slow down at the admissions desk, but told the lady to open the doors or she'd kick them in. The doors were already swinging open when Lettie and Jennie Sue reached them.

"Nadine, where are you?" She raised her voice as soon as they entered.

"Lettie, I'm in here," Nadine called out from

the first room on the left. "They're takin' me to X-ray, and I'm not goin' without you."

Jennie Sue followed her as she breezed into the room like a class 5 tornado. No one even bothered to ask if she was related to these two like they had with Cricket.

Lettie went straight to the bedside where Nadine was still on the body board and nodded at the lady waiting to push the bed down the hallway. "You can go now. I'm here and I'm going with her."

"You'll have to sit outside the room," she said.

"Leave it cracked so I can hear her," Lettie informed the woman.

"They can't, sister," Nadine said. "But I'll yell loud enough they'll hear me all the way in Bloom if they hurt me. I don't trust those machines."

"Aliens," Lettie whispered to Jennie Sue. "I swear to God and all the angels that they are workin' their way to Earth through all this damned technology crap."

"Don't be givin' away our information. That's classified," Nadine whispered.

The lady rolled her eyes and pushed Nadine out of the room. Jennie Sue sank down in an uncomfortable chair and tried to remember if she'd locked the door on her way out of the house. And if she had, did either of the sisters have a key to get back in? While she was pondering on that and sending up prayers that Nadine hadn't broken her neck or her back, her phone rang. She didn't recognize the caller ID, but she answered it anyway.

"What's happened to Nadine? Did she die? Please tell me she didn't die. I'm not sure Lettie would live a month without Nadine," Cricket said at Jennie Sue's greeting.

"She's in X-ray, but they don't think anything is broken right now," Jennie Sue said. "She fell out of that big pear tree in her backyard."

"Holy cow. I'll call back later for more news. I've got to make half a dozen calls right now so folks will know that she's not dead. The ladies at the church are already tryin' to decide whether to start thinkin' about a funeral lunch for the family and friends. And Elaine said that the flower shop has had a dozen calls wantin' to know if she'll be at the local funeral home or the one in Sweetwater," Cricket said. "You've got my number, so if you hear anything, call me and I'll pass it on."

"Small towns!" Jennie Sue groaned.

She'd begun to think that the hospital had swallowed both of her new friends and had started to pace around the small emergency room when she heard Nadine and Lettie arguing loudly.

"You cut down one of my trees, and I'll set fire to your house and blame it on them damned little bald-headed fellows from outer space." Nadine's tone was high and squeaky.

"You have to promise me with one hand on Mama's Bible and the other raised to God that you will never climb up in one of those trees again or I'll do it," Lettie said. "You're lucky this time, but next time you might kill your fool self. If the trees need trimmin' or pears need pickin', you can hire the work done. You're not poor, for God's sake."

"Waste not, want not!" Nadine continued to argue.

"I'll pay for it if you are that tight," Lettie said.

The lady bringing Nadine back rolled her eyes and escaped as the doctor entered the room. He stuck the big negatives up on a screen and shook his head. "By all reasons, you should have broken every bone in your body, Miz Clifford. What on earth were you doin' in a tree?"

"Trimmin' it, and I don't want to hear a lecture. Lettie's already bitched at me enough. Just get me out of this thing and let me go home," Nadine told him.

"I should do an MRI for precautionary reasons. You might have scrambled your brain," he said.

"No!" Nadine squealed. "I'm not gettin' in no tube."

"You'll have to sign a form saying that you refused the test," he said.

Nadine held out a hand. "Give me a pen. It knocked the wind out of me and that's all. I was on the lowest limb on my way down when my foot slipped, and I tucked and rolled. My brain is fine."

"Might have even knocked some sense into her," Lettie snorted. "Anyone as cantankerous as she is right now can't be hurt too bad. And I'm not goin' to feel sorry for you one bit because you have to wear a hospital gown home."

Nadine shook a finger at the doctor. "Don't you charge me for this ugly thing. I'll wash it and bring it back to you, but when I see my itemized bill, this better not be on it."

Jennie Sue could imagine the argument if they charged Nadine for the faded gown and hoped that she was around when the bill came.

Chapter Twelve

How's Nadine?" Cricket asked first thing that Friday night when Jennie Sue and Rick entered the house. "I've talked to her twice today, and she says she's sore and got a bruise on her shoulder—and that aliens pushed her out of the tree. Did it do something to her brain?"

"Same thing she tells me and Lettie. She hasn't told you about the aliens before now?" Jennie Sue kicked off her shoes at the door.

"No, what's she talkin' about?" Cricket straightened up and leaned forward.

"She and Lettie think that outer-space people can listen in on our technology." Jennie Sue grinned. "Like on cell phones and X-ray machines." She headed to the kitchen to make supper. After a week, she'd pretty much gotten things set into a routine. She kept it fairly simple so she and Rick could get out to the garden early enough to harvest the crops for a few hours before dark.

"Just because we're barely friends doesn't mean you should know stuff about Lettie and Nadine that I don't." Cricket picked up her crutches and went to the kitchen with Jennie Sue.

"I'm surprised that you didn't already know," Jennie Sue said.

Rick pulled out two chairs—one for Cricket to sit in, the other to prop her foot on. "Lettie told me to tell you that the ladies at the church meetin' missed you yesterday and they were prayin' for you."

"Aw, that's so sweet," Cricket said. "If I promise to keep my foot propped up, can I go to the farmers' market tomorrow?"

Well, praise the Lord and kiss the angels! Cricket was showing a kind side to her personality.

Jennie Sue glanced over at Rick. She'd loved going with him the week before and had looked forward to Saturday all week, but Cricket could take money and make change while sitting. It had helped her to go to the bookstore, but not nearly as many people came in after that first day, and it would give her an outing.

"I think that would be a great idea," Jennie Sue agreed. "I've been procrastinating about going to see Mama, and it will be a good day to do that."

"Rick?" Cricket looked past Jennie Sue at her brother.

"Don't see why not, if you keep your foot iced and propped up," he answered. "Right now I'm going out to the melon field and get what we need to take to the market. Be back by the time supper is ready."

He'd barely cleared the door when Cricket blurted out, "Everyone thinks you are some kind of angel with a halo and wings, but I know better, Jennie Sue Baker. You've got to have an angle in all this."

"All what? And why would I have an angle in anything at all? I'm not that kind of person."

"Bein' nice to Lettie and Nadine when they're your mama's enemies. Bein' nice to me and Rick when we aren't anywhere near your league. People are talkin' even worse than when you came home and word got out that Percy left you. They've got bets goin'."

"Bets on what? That I'm stayin' or goin'? And what are you betting, Cricket?"

"That you're using the whole bunch of us to make your daddy give you a job in his oil company. Charlotte is mortified, and she'll do anything to get things right in her fancy world again. So when she comes home, she'll fall all over herself to let you have your way about a job, and you'll never speak to any of us again," Cricket answered. "As for me, I don't care, because I'm not believin' one bit of this, but I hate to see Rick hurt. Not to mention Lettie and Nadine."

"You really think I'm that kind of person?" Jennie Sue set a skillet on the stove and added oil to fry okra. "And why would Rick be hurt? Even if I did go to work, it wouldn't mean that I wouldn't remain friends with him or with Lettie and Nadine. And maybe barely friends with you."

"I thought we were civil friends," Cricket argued.

Jennie Sue came back with, "You're the one who just used the term *barely friends,* not me."

"Well, it just slipped out. 'Civil friends' sounds kind of silly, doesn't it? But you were one person in high school, and now you are pretending to be another altogether."

"Maybe I was *pretending* in high school, trying to fit into the mold that I'd been given from birth. Maybe I didn't like that world or the one I got when I got married. And maybe I like this world a lot better," she said as she kept working. "How are Lettie and Nadine betting?"

"They both think you have glitter on your wings, but they're old," Cricket said.

"You better not let either of them hear that." At least her two sweet friends didn't think she was using them.

"And before you ask," Cricket went on, "Rick won't listen to rumors. I don't know where he stands."

Jennie Sue sautéed bell peppers and onions in a second skillet to make meatballs for supper. Served over rice and with okra, sliced tomatoes, and cucumbers, it was one of Percy's favorite meals. The idea of him coming home to their fancy apartment, expecting the table to be set perfectly and his food ready to serve, made her think again of the friends they'd had in New York. Ladies she'd served on fund-raising committees with, those she'd gone shopping with or out to lunch with. They'd all forsaken her when he got into trouble and fled with his new girlfriend. So three friends who believed in her in spite of her past seemed like a pretty big blessing to her that evening.

"You don't have anything to say?" Cricket asked.

Jennie Sue shook her head. "All the talk in the world won't change your mind or the minds of people in town, so no, I don't have anything to say. What would you say if our roles were reversed and you were in my shoes?"

"I'd damn sure say something. What people think of you can have a big bearing on the way your life turns out."

"Oh, really? People thought I was a privileged person, and look what I'm doin' for a livin'," Jennie Sue said. "I'm cleanin' houses, reorganizing a used-book store, pickin' vegetables in the evening, and puttin' up with a barely friend. And if that's not bad enough, I'm doin' my own hair and fingernails, and I only have one color of polish."

Cricket glanced down at her bare feet, and Jennie Sue followed her gaze.

"Your toenails look like crap, but Mama would stroke out if she could see mine. Want me to do them for you after we get done with the harvest tonight?"

Cricket fiddled with her bandage and bit at her lower lip. "Are you crazy? Why would you do that after what I just told you?"

"What you said has nothing to do with your nails, does it?" Jennie Sue asked.

She looked down at her feet. "They are in a mess."

"Then let's take care of them. Do you have a file and polish and maybe some decent lotion?"

Cricket pointed toward a closed door. "In a shoe box on the shelf in my closet."

"Good. Then we'll make them pretty after I get done with the crops." She handed Cricket a knife and a small bowl of washed vegetables. "Make yourself useful instead of bitchin' about everything. You can slice tomatoes and cucumbers while you are sitting there."

Cricket raised an eyebrow. "Are you going to trust me with a knife?"

"I can run faster than you can," Jennie Sue said.

If someone had told her ten years ago that Jennie Sue Baker would ever be sitting in her house doing her toenails, Cricket would have asked them what they'd been drinking. But there she was on the floor with a pan of warm water, towels, and a shoe box full of Cricket's nail supplies.

Jennie Sue handed her the small box. "Pick your color while I get them trimmed and the cuticles in shape. I can also do french nails if you want those."

"Do I get to pick a color for my toenails when you get hers done?" Rick asked.

Jennie Sue nodded seriously. "Red would be real nice on you."

Good Lord, were they flirting? Cricket rolled her eyes.

"No, thank you," Rick said.

"Ah, come on. Be adventurous." Jennie Sue wrapped Cricket's bum foot in a hot, wet towel.

"No, thank you. All the other guys in town would be jealous. You'd have a line from one end of Main Street to the other of men wanting their nails done," Rick told her.

"I've still got Sunday afternoons fairly free. I could do nails then." Jennie Sue grinned.

Yes, they were definitely flirting. Cricket sighed. But she wouldn't think about that now, not when Jennie Sue was giving her an amazing mani-pedi. This might raise her status to a barely friend for sure.

After a couple of minutes, Jennie Sue removed the towel and dropped it into the hot water, then she started to work on Cricket's toenails. "Do you like them square or rounded?"

"Round," Cricket answered.

"Me, too. Never could get used to those square things," Jennie Sue said.

A memory of Percy telling her that her nails

looked like an old lady's flashed through her mind. She'd come home from the salon, where she'd had them painted a pale pink to go with a dress she planned to wear to a party that evening.

"Modern women wear bright colors and square nails. And good God, Jennifer"—he'd never called her Jennie Sue because that sounded too redneck for him—"whoever did that horrible job left a dab of polish on your big toe. That's unacceptable."

She'd learned to do her own nails from then on. *Unacceptable* in his world was the worst thing in the whole universe.

When she finished with that foot, she stood up. "Now scoot forward while I go get more warm water. The polish should be dry enough so that it won't smear."

"Looks like you've done this before," Rick said.

"Lots of times," she said.

"Why didn't you have yours done professionally?" Cricket asked.

"I did for a while," Jennie Sue said. "By doing them myself I didn't have to smell all those awful chemicals."

"Amen to that," Cricket said. "So you definitely aren't leaving Bloom to go into the nail business."

"Nope, hopefully I'm leaving to get a start somewhere on the bottom rung of a corporate ladder if I'm lucky," she answered.

"And if not?"

"Then as a glorified secretary in a used-car dealership," Jennie Sue answered. "What about you, Cricket? If you could be anything in life, what would it be?"

"What I really want to be . . ." Cricket paused.

"She wants to be a gossip columnist. If you can make that happen, then I'd like for you to invent a time machine so I can go back and sidestep the bomb that turned me into a disabled veteran," Rick said. "That way I'd still be a whole man doin' what I love in the military."

"I want to someday make cupcakes for my kids like my mama did for us. We always had something homemade for an after-school snack," Cricket blurted out.

Jennie Sue was shocked that Cricket would admit that much in front of her. "I could go for one of your mama's cupcakes right now, maybe even two or three."

"To have kids, I'll need a husband. Rick says I'll never find anyone who can put up with my bluntness," Cricket said.

Jennie Sue jerked her head around to face Cricket. "What's the matter with that? At least people know where they stand with you and that you won't turn your back on them."

"Speakin' from experience?" Cricket asked.

"More than once." Jennie Sue nodded. "Now prop your foot up here on my knee and we'll get this one done and go on to your fingernails."

• • •

It was almost ten o'clock when Cricket said, "Thank you for everything, Jennie Sue. It's past time for Rick to take you home. The news tomorrow will be that you've stayed out here later than usual and that he might have to make an honest woman out of you."

Rick felt the heat start on his neck and climb all the way to his cheeks. "What a time to find out my sister has a sense of humor."

"I reckon my reputation can handle another black mark," Jennie Sue said.

"But mine can't. Someone might think I was changing my mind about you," Cricket said with her usual sarcasm as she tucked her crutches under her arms. "See you bright and early in the morning, Rick. I'm lookin' forward to going to the market and seeing all the people."

"Well, honey"—Jennie Sue's tone was saccharine sweet—"when they find out that we spent the evening doing your nails, they're going to know that we're friends."

"I'm not tellin' anyone that, and if you do, I'll take back the barely friends promotion," Cricket said.

Rick couldn't tell if she was teasing or not and didn't want get into it with her. He turned to Jennie Sue and said, "Thanks for what you do for us. You ready to go home?"

"Not just yet. I'd like a glass of sweet tea."

Jennie Sue took down her ponytail and raked her fingers through her long, blonde hair.

Mesmerized by her actions, Rick wished that his hands were the ones tangled up in her hair. He blinked half a dozen times and finally got to his feet. "I'll take care of the tea while you dump the water."

She was sitting on the end of the sofa when he returned. He handed her a full glass of sweet tea and sat down on the other end. "I was surprised to hear Cricket admit that she wanted to be a wife and mother. She's always told me that she wanted to be a gossip columnist."

"Dreams change with age." She took a long drink of her tea.

Rick set his glass on the end table, picked up her feet, and put them in his lap. He started massaging her left foot, digging deep into the heel.

"You've missed your callin'," she groaned. "You should be a masseur."

He finished with that foot and picked up the right one. "It was really nice of you to step back and let Cricket go to the market with me tomorrow after you'd already made plans to go. I'd offer to take both of you, but one would have to ride in the back of the truck with the produce."

She nodded toward the other side of the room. "You could put that rockin' chair over there in the bed of the truck, and everyone could say I was Granny Clampett from *The Beverly Hillbillies*."

Rick laughed out loud. "Well, you do have the fancy house. Do you have possums and raccoons livin' out there?"

"Yes, I do." Her blue eyes glimmered. "But don't tell Mama. Mabel and I've kept it a secret for years."

He raked his fingers through his hair. "I can just see Charlotte Baker if she found a possum in her living room."

"We keep them in the garage." Jennie Sue continued the joke as she laid her head back on the sofa and shut her eyes. "Frank feeds them." She yawned and her eyes fluttered shut.

He stared at her for a long time, not wanting to wake her and yet knowing that he should. He wanted to look at her a little longer, so he moved to a recliner and carefully popped up the footrest. Several hours later he awoke to find Cricket glaring at him with a hand on her hip.

"What in the hell is going on in here? Don't you have a lick of sense, Rick? People are going to see you takin' her home at daybreak. She's going to make a complete fool out of you." Her voice was so shrill and loud that no one could ever sleep through it.

"That's enough," Rick said calmly. "Nothing happened. We fell asleep, and if you'll stop worryin' about what people think or talk about, you'd notice that we are both fully dressed and that she's on the sofa and I'm in a chair."

Jennie Sue sat up and put her hand over a yawn. "Is that sin so big it'll keep me out of heaven? Is it really mornin'?"

"And if something did happen, which it didn't"—Rick popped the footrest down on the recliner—"we are two consenting adults, and it wouldn't be a bit of anyone's business."

Cricket tried to stomp her good foot and almost fell before she got her balance back. "It's my business. I live here in this house, too. And for your information, brother, I was the one who stayed here and helped out while you went off to your precious military and secret missions. I picked beans with Daddy and kept house and held down a job," she said.

Rick stood and headed toward the bathroom. "Yes, you did. Where shall I send the gold medal? Or would you prefer platinum?"

"Don't you leave when I'm talkin' to you," Cricket shouted.

Jennie Sue sat up and put on her shoes.

Cricket turned on her. "Where are you going?"

"If I want to listen to bitchin' and yellin', I can move back in with my mother," Jennie Sue answered. "I'm going out to the truck. When y'all get through with this fight, I'd appreciate a ride home."

"Why did you have to drag us into your messy

life? We were doin' just fine without you in town," Cricket groaned.

"Cricket, I'd love to be your friend, but it looks like that's impossible. Since I've embarrassed you so badly that you rant at your brother like that, I won't be coming back out here. I never want to be the cause of such mean things being said to Rick," Jennie Sue said.

"I'm so sorry." Rick came out of the bathroom. "I could hear everything. Let's get you home. Thanks for all you've done. It would have been a tough week without you."

He tried several times to start a conversation on the drive from the farm to Lettie's place, but he had no idea how to even begin. Jennie Sue probably hated him for not waking her and for getting so personal with that foot massage. And if that wasn't enough, Cricket had been horrible. When they finally arrived, and he'd parked outside the garage, he turned to face her.

"I'm so sorry," he said.

"No need for you to apologize. You did nothing wrong." She opened the door. "Let's—" she started.

"Let's not let my sister spoil what we have," he finished for her. "I really like spending time with you."

"I would never knowingly cause trouble between y'all," she said.

He rested a hand on her shoulder. "I know that.

You've got a good heart, Jennie Sue. I'll call you this evening."

She nodded and was gone before he could say anything else.

He slapped the steering wheel of the old truck. "Dammit! Why did we have to be born on opposite sides of the tracks? If she'd been in the same social class as me, this wouldn't be a problem at all."

He backed the produce truck out of the driveway and sat for a full minute at the stop sign before turning onto Main Street. There wasn't a single car in sight, but he couldn't make himself turn north toward the farm and his sister.

Finally, he turned south toward Sweetwater, glad that he'd loaded the truck the night before. It would do Cricket good to stew in her own anger for the whole day. He'd have to do double duty at the market, keeping the display on the table and taking money both, but it would be worth it.

By the time he arrived at the market, Cricket had called three times and sent four text messages. He waited until he got his display set up and had waited on two customers before he returned her call.

"Where in the hell are you?" she asked.

"I'm at the market," he answered.

"Did you take Jennie Sue with you?"

"I did not."

"Then you are punishing me, right?"

He thought about her question for a few seconds before he answered. “No, I’m not. I just don’t want to be around you today. Not after that fit you threw. I think it’s best if we spend the day away from each other.”

“I knew I was right not to trust her. She’s causing problems in our family now.” Cricket’s tone was icy.

“Back up, sister, and do some serious thinkin’ today. It’s not Jennie Sue causing the problems between me and you.” He hit the “End” button.

Chapter Thirteen

Jennie Sue had just gotten out of the shower and was drying her hair when someone knocked on her door. She quickly grabbed a robe, belted it around her waist, and peeked out the peephole before she threw open the door and motioned for Lettie to come inside.

"Sit down. Good grief! You are pale. Why did you climb the stairs?" Jennie Sue asked. "You should've called. I'd have come down to see what you needed."

"Just need a glass of water and I'll be fine. Not as young as I thought I was," Lettie panted.

Jennie Sue rushed to her tiny kitchen and grabbed a water bottle from the refrigerator. She handed it to Lettie and led her to the sofa. "Is something wrong with Nadine?"

"No, she's fine. She could probably climb those stairs two at a time, even now." Lettie's color returned after a couple of sips. "News is that you spent the night at Rick and Cricket's place."

"Yes, ma'am, I did. After we harvested the crops for the market today, I gave Cricket a mani-pedi. I thought it might help her feel better, and then Rick and I fell asleep with me on the sofa and him in a recliner," Jennie Sue explained, "with all our clothing on. We did not have sex or even have a kiss."

"Well, that's a damn shame," Lettie laughed. "Did Cricket pass gold bricks when she found out?"

"Almost. I won't be going back out there. No sense in upsetting her like that again," Jennie Sue answered.

Lettie sipped at the water again. "So what are you doin' today? Evidently you aren't going to the market with Rick."

"I'm going to see Mama," she said with a long sigh. "You are right. It's time to have a visit with her and make things as right as possible."

"Mabel's been fussin' all week that she hasn't seen you in a while. Take my truck and keep it as long as you want. I don't need it today," Lettie said.

"Thanks for believing in me."

Lettie set her mouth in a firm line. "You've been nothing but honest with us, child. Nadine and I just dare anyone to say a bad word about you. We'll put them straight in a hurry. Right now, I'm going to go get the truck keys for you."

"No, you sit right here until I get dressed, and I'll help you down those stairs. If you were to fall, Nadine would never let you live it down after the fit we both threw over her tumble." Jennie Sue rushed into the bathroom and dressed in her best skinny jeans and a sleeveless, light-blue button-up shirt.

"Ain't that the truth," Lettie agreed. "If you get back in time from your mama's, I'd be willin' to pay you same as I pay the nail salon to do my nails this evenin'."

"I'll make it a point to be back in time. Tell Nadine that I'll pick her up on the way, and we'll make it a girls' evenin'. I didn't bring any polish with me when I packed to come home. Should I stop by the dollar store and pick some up on my way back?" Jennie Sue asked.

"Might ought to. I like bright red and Nadine likes a pale pink," Lettie answered. "I got clippers and files and such, but whatever polish I've got is probably a chunk of concrete in the bottle. I'll make brownies, and we'll pop the cork on a bottle of wine."

"I'm nervous about goin' home, Lettie. Mama is so critical. How do I look?" Jennie Sue twirled around twice.

"Beautiful, but then you'd look good in a burlap bag tied up at the waist with a length of balin' twine," Lettie said. "Only thing is that you need to have your toenails and fingernails done, too."

"I don't believe that for a minute. And I'll do my nails after we get y'all's all finished. Just don't let me drink too much wine," Jennie Sue said.

"It's a deal. Now help this old woman down

the stairs, and don't ever tell Nadine that I got winded gettin' up here," she said.

"My lips are sealed." Jennie Sue held on to her arm, and together they slowly made their way down the steps.

Once Lettie was inside the house, Jennie Sue got into the truck, fired up the engine, and backed out into the street. She hadn't even made it to the stop sign at the corner of the street when she began to have doubts. Maybe she should let Charlotte be the one to reach out to her. If she showed up unannounced, it could put her mother on the defensive again, whereas if she gave it a little more time . . . Her palms moistened against the steering wheel.

Sure, she'd stood her ground with Cricket. Yet she'd feel like she'd really accomplished something if just once Charlotte would be proud of her. Even on her wedding day, the woman had been more interested in being beautiful when one of the ushers walked her down the aisle than she was in Jennie Sue.

When the photographer snapped Charlotte putting the veil on Jennie Sue, she'd told him to take several shots so that she could choose the best one for the album. And then as she left the room, she'd looked over her shoulder and sighed. "I liked the other dress better, but then it's your wedding. I wish the Wilshire blood would have come out more in you," she'd said.

When Charlotte was upset with her, she'd always made a remark about either the lack of Wilshire blood or her grandmother Vera Baker, and it was never a good thing. So on her wedding day, Jennie Sue had felt like an ugly duckling the entire ceremony, much like she felt right then. She drove on, slowly, and lingered at every stop sign or corner.

At the city-limits sign, she stopped and pulled over to the side, laid her head on the steering wheel, and literally prayed for a sign to tell her whether to turn around and go back to her apartment or to go out to the house. When she opened her eyes, a big black bird sat on the side mirror of the truck and fussed at her.

"I don't know if it's a sign, but I think he's tellin' me not to look back." She took a long breath and pulled back out onto the highway. The bird stayed with her for a few hundred yards and then flew off. "And there's my second sign," she said when she saw her mother's vehicle in the multicar garage. She pulled the truck into one of the empty places and parked.

Frank grabbed her in a bear hug when she got out of the truck, and Mabel rushed out of the kitchen door into the garage to make it a group hug.

"Would you look at her, Mabel?" Frank grinned as he released them. "She's got some color in her skin. I bet that comes from workin' outside."

"She always did love the garden when we had one here. And I just love knowin' that she might've picked the tomatoes or the beans that I get from Rick. Makes them extra special. Come on in the house, darlin' girl, and tell me all the news." Mabel pulled her away from Frank.

Frank pretended to pout. "No fair. You always get to spend more time with her than I do."

"I'll remember every word she says for you," Mabel promised. "Now tell me about this argument you had with Cricket because you fell asleep in the same room with Rick last night."

"That didn't take long to make it all over town, did it?" Jennie Sue grinned. "But sleep was all we did, honest. I was on the sofa and he was in a recliner. It's not like we were in the bedroom or even together on the sofa."

"Honey, if we had to vote on the best juicy bits of the past decade, these past few weeks would win the contest, hands down. You should buy stock in whatever company is offerin' the most data on those cell phones, because folks are sure usin' up a lot of it since you got into town. Now sit down at the table, and I'll make you some breakfast. What do you want? You look thin. Have you been workin' too hard and not eatin' enough?" Mabel fussed.

"You do look like you've lost a few pounds," Charlotte said as she breezed into the kitchen, leaving the scent of expensive perfume in her wake. As usual, her makeup was perfect and every hair was in place, prompting the ugly-duckling feeling to wash over Jennie Sue again.

"Good mornin', Mama." If she was going to act like nothing had happened, then Jennie Sue would follow her lead.

"I don't suppose a fattening breakfast would hurt you this one time." Everybody in Bloom had better bend over, grab their ankles firmly, and kiss their ass goodbye, because the apocalypse was about to be a reality. Either that or one of Lettie and Nadine's aliens had entered her mother's body.

"Thank you. Want me to make enough for both of us?" Jennie Sue asked.

"Nothin' doin'!" Mabel said. "I'll make the breakfast this mornin', and you two can eat on the porch. It's still cool enough that you won't break a sweat. Just go on out there and get comfortable."

"Thank you, Mabel." Charlotte motioned toward the door. "I'll have an egg-white omelet with mushrooms and tomatoes and low-fat cheese, dry toast, and a cup of lemon tea."

"Yes, ma'am, and you, Jennie Sue?" Mabel asked.

"A whole-egg omelet with bacon, mushrooms, and tomatoes and double cheese, two pieces of buttered toast, a glass of milk, and one of those blueberry muffins you've got hidin' under the glass dome," Jennie Sue answered.

She expected at least a sigh from Charlotte, but she got nothing, which was downright scary. Much more of this and she'd believe in the aliens instead of teasing about them, but, like a dutiful daughter, she followed her mother to the screened porch.

"Don't look at my toenails. Garden work is tough on them, but I'm going to give myself a pedicure tonight," she said before her mother could make a nasty comment about them.

Charlotte waved the comment away with the flick of a wrist, but she did wince slightly when she glanced at her daughter's feet. "When you lived in New York, even when you were pregnant, you took better care of yourself. Since you came back to Bloom, you've become—" Charlotte struggled with the words.

"What, Mama? What have I become?" Jennie Sue was almost glad to be back on argumentative ground, despite her mission of peace.

"White trash," Charlotte spit out.

"And what makes me white trash?" Jennie Sue asked. What would come out of Charlotte Baker's mouth now?

"Runnin' with those low-class farmers and cleaning houses," Charlotte answered without a moment's hesitation.

"People like James?" Jennie Sue asked.

"Where did you hear that name? No, don't answer. Those wicked Clifford women have been spreading gossip." Charlotte laid the back of her hand over her forehead in a dramatic gesture as she stretched out on the lounge.

"Who cares who told me what? You should have told me rather than letting me hate Daddy all these years for his affairs. You were both doing the same thing," Jennie Sue said. It didn't look like a truce was going to happen today. If she didn't eat the breakfast Mabel was fixing, it would hurt her feelings.

"Sure thing," Charlotte hissed. "I could tell my five-year-old daughter that I was in love with another man, and I couldn't leave her father, because if I did, then I'd sully my mama and grandmama's names. There was never a divorce in the Wilshire family until *you* got one, so that dirty mess is on you."

"I'm not feelin' guilty about it or any of my other decisions. Can we leave the past alone and move on to the future? I should've already been putting out résumés, but I keep hoping you and Daddy will change your minds and let me work for the family company. If I'm going to inherit it someday, it stands to reason I should be busy getting to know it from the ground up," she said.

Charlotte dropped her hand and sat up straight. "It will not happen."

"Why?"

Charlotte sighed. "I'll make a deal with you. I'll tell Dill to give you a job if you move back home, go to the Belles meetings and parties with me, never speak to those Clifford women again, and break it off with Rick Lawson. And also his sister, Cricket. I never did like that girl. She's nothing but a gossip."

"No, thank you." Jennie Sue shook her head.

"I'm willing to compromise. You can keep Rick if he's that good in bed, but only on the sly. I don't want him in this house except to deliver vegetables to Mabel," Charlotte said.

"No, thank you," Jennie Sue repeated. "I can get a job somewhere else. Mama, I don't know if Rick is anything but a very good friend. I'm not sayin' that there are no possibilities with him. He's a good man and I do like him a lot, and he could turn out to be 'the one.' " She made air quotes around the last two words. "But let's get something straight—I don't give a damn about the Wilshire name. I'll never marry another man that you can pay to marry me." She stopped for a breath. "Don't look at me like that. I know what you did. Any man that can be bought ain't worth havin'."

"Isn't," Charlotte corrected. "You've been hangin' around the lower classes too much. You're beginnin' to sound like them."

"Thank you," Jennie Sue said. "I consider that a compliment."

"I admire you," Charlotte said.

"Would you repeat that?" Jennie Sue shook

her head. Surely she'd heard her mother wrong. Charlotte fussed at her, tried to control her, wanted to fit her into a mold, but she'd never given out compliments.

"I wish I'd had the courage to tell my mother to go to hell, that I was going to marry James and go off to wherever the military stationed us," she said wistfully. "But I didn't."

"Why didn't you get a divorce and marry him when he came home?" Jennie Sue asked.

"Wilshires didn't do that. Besides, I had a child by then, and it was my duty to make sure you had a proper home."

"A Wilshire home?" Maybe if she'd been raised a military brat, her mother would have at least made her feel loved.

"Okay, I'll admit it. James couldn't give me the living I was used to, and my mama had to give me the same talkin'-to I'm givin' you today," Charlotte told her. "Why didn't you ever ask me why I wanted to keep your baby a secret?"

Mabel brought out food on a tray and left it on the table between them. "Y'all need anything else?"

Charlotte waved her away with a flick of her wrist. "We're fine. Thank you, Mabel."

Jennie Sue sat in stunned silence for several minutes. "So my grandmother knew about James?" she finally asked.

"Of course. The whole town knew. You can't

hide anything in Bloom, Texas." Charlotte's laughter was brittle. "Rumors will run rampant, darlin'. According to talk, I'm sure that you are pregnant with Rick's baby already. But a lady simply holds her head up and pretends that she's done nothing."

Jennie Sue downed part of a glass of water to keep from choking on a bite of omelet. "I didn't sleep with him in the biblical sense of the word. And I want to hear about why you were so insistent about keeping Emily Grace a big secret. Why isn't there a tombstone on her grave?"

"I was looking out for you. I knew the day would arrive when you'd come home and start a new life with someone local. I wanted you to be able to do that without all the drama and genetic issues getting in the way over losing a baby."

"A local man?" Jennie Sue asked.

"There are some really nice guys in the company that I will introduce you to. Dill is grooming at least three of them to step up into the CEO position in a few years," Charlotte said.

"No, thank you," Jennie Sue told her with a shake of the head.

"You'll change your mind. And speakin' of being the wife of the future CEO, we really do need to shop for you when you get enough of diggin' in the garden with that scarred-up soldier and come home where you belong." Charlotte toyed with her food, taking only a few small bites.

"Did Daddy's affairs begin before or after James?" Jennie Sue asked bluntly.

"Bless your heart, honey, you shouldn't listen to gossip or worry your pretty little head about things like that."

Jennie Sue recognized that fake smile on her mother's face. It meant that they should move on to another subject, but she wasn't going to let it go.

"I really want to know, Mama," she pressured.

"After," Charlotte admitted. "He confronted me, and we came to an understanding. I wouldn't divorce him and take the company from him if he'd let me have James."

"And how did James feel about all this?" Jennie Sue couldn't imagine that he was happy when the love of his life wouldn't leave her husband.

"He loved me enough to take me any way that he could have me," Charlotte said. "Now can we change the subject and go on to shoes or the weather?"

"Daddy still loves you," Jennie Sue said.

"And I've always loved Dill. He's a good man and he's done wonders with the company. The trouble was that I wasn't *in* love with him. That's what the therapist told me after James died. It makes sense." She sighed. "Come on. Let's put this behind us now that you know the details and do some serious shopping this afternoon. I'm going with the Belles whether you come along or not."

Jennie Sue shook her head. “I can’t afford to shop for new clothing or shoes. Maybe I’ll borrow one of the extra swimsuits in the bathhouse and spend some time in the pool, if that’s okay.”

Neither of them had worn the other one down, so it was a standoff. “Make yourself at home. A couple of the Belles should be arriving”—Charlotte was interrupted by the doorbell—“right now.”

Both women were dressed in cute little capri-length pants and sandals. Underdressed for a day of shopping, and yet there was no doubt that what they were wearing would cost more than Jennie Sue made in a month at her two jobs.

“Jennie Sue, darlin’!” Aunt Sugar rushed to her side and kissed her on the forehead. “We told Charlotte that you’d get enough of that crazy notion that you want to be independent and come home.”

Aunt Mary Lou pushed her out of the way and bent to hug Jennie Sue. “But, honey, you have to be more discreet with the boyfriend. He may be delicious in bed, but after today, you’ve got to keep it on the down low. We’re all disappointed in Percy, but don’t worry, we’ve already got feelers out for the next Mr. Wilshire.” She headed toward the bar. “It’s still mornin’, so a mimosa is in order. How many shall I make? Did y’all hear that Belinda has gotten religion? If she's atoning for her sins, it's more than twenty years too late. And I don't mean she's just goin' to church—hell, we all do that—but she's all up in the food bank and the free clothing for the poor. We might have to have an intervention if she doesn't straighten up. It'll give the Belles a bad name."

Oh, no! Jennie Sue wanted to slap her hands over her cheeks and make a perfect little *O* with her mouth. The first thing Nadine's aliens would have to learn if they ever came to earth was that they couldn't do anything that would give the Sweetwater Belles a bad name.

"No mimosa for me," Aunt Sugar said. "I'm driving today."

"None for me. Too many carbs," Charlotte answered.

"Jennie Sue?" Mary Lou asked.

"No, thank you. And just to be clear, I'm only here to see Mama. I'm not moving back into the house," Jennie Sue said.

The bottle of champagne hit the ground and splattered everywhere. "Sweet God in heaven. Girl, are you insane?" Aunt Mary Lou gasped. "Do the Belles need to have an intervention for *you?* You are, after all, a future member."

"Charlotte, do we need to commit her to a rehab?" Aunt Sugar gasped.

Mabel must've heard the glass breaking, because she was there in an instant. She caught

Jennie Sue's eye as she entered the room and raised an eyebrow.

"Aunt Mary Lou dropped a bottle of champagne," Jennie Sue said. "She'll probably need to go home and change her shoes before y'all go shopping."

"I'll clean it up," Mabel said.

Jennie Sue pushed up off the lounge, popped the last piece of bacon in her mouth, and said, "I'll help you."

Aunt Sugar gasped. "Oh, Charlotte, we were so wrong. We'll definitely take care of this child after your birthday is over."

"She's like her grandmother Baker. That woman was a force. She'll have to learn her lessons the hard way." Charlotte stood up and patted Jennie Sue on the cheek. "Call me when you come to your senses, and we'll do lunch. Even if you are bein' a brat, we need to discuss your daddy's birthday."

"I rather enjoy bein' like Grandma Vera. I'll call you about Daddy's birthday in the next few days, Mama." She stood up and blew a kiss toward her mother as she left.

Jennie Sue did a dive from the side of the pool, swam a dozen laps, and then stretched out on the lounge. The whole conversation with her mother was surreal in too many ways to count. Were all the Wilshire women so devious? Did they all have lovers outside their marriages?

"And why weren't there ever any sons born to carry on the name? Mama wasn't a Wilshire. She was an Alexander by last name before she married Daddy. How did it make Grandpa or any of the men in the family feel for their wives and daughters to still be referred to as Wilshires?" she said aloud.

"Don't know." Frank startled her when he spoke. "It's always seemed a little bit odd to me and Mabel, too."

Jennie Sue pointed to the chair beside her. "Sit down and talk to me. Can I get you something to drink?"

He shook his head. "Thanks, but I just had a glass of tea a little bit ago, and I don't have time to talk. Mabel sent me out here to ask if you'll have lunch with us in the kitchen in about fifteen minutes." Frank patted her on the head like he had when she was a child. "Honey, don't fret over the past. Just look to the future and forget all those old stories. Only person we're responsible to make happy is ourselves, and you're doin' a fine job of it."

"Thank you. Did you know my grandparents well?" She hoped to get him talking so he'd stay with her for a while.

"Worked for them until your mama married, and then they transferred us over here to work for her after she'd fired at least half a dozen housekeepers. We been here ever since. It's time that this thing with the Wilshire women stopped." He turned around. "See you in the house in a few minutes. Mabel made broccoli-cheese soup and chicken-salad sandwiches because that's your favorites."

"I love y'all," Jennie Sue said.

Frank's crooked grin lit up his eyes. "We love you."

When he'd left, she dived into the water from the side of the pool and did two laps, then hopped out, hurried to the bathhouse, and changed into her clothing. That done, she braided her wet hair into one long rope that hung over her shoulder and padded barefoot into the house.

When she reached the kitchen, Mabel motioned toward the table. A steaming tureen of soup sat in the middle with a plate of sandwiches to one side—crust left on because that's the way Jennie Sue liked it. A plate of fresh fruit and a big loaf of fresh bread were right beside it.

"Where's Frank?" Jennie Sue asked.

"Right here." He rushed in from the hall. "Mabel has a rule about me washin' my greasy hands in her kitchen sink. Man, don't this look good today?"

"It don't get no better than this—food and company," Jennie Sue agreed.

Mabel sat down across from Jennie Sue, leaving the place at the head of the table for Frank. She laid a hand on his and said, "You say grace, but don't make it too long. The bread needs to be hot enough to melt butter."

When he finished, Jennie Sue and Mabel said amen at the same time. Mabel dipped out bowls of soup while Jennie Sue passed the sandwiches and thick slices of bread to Frank.

"I'll miss y'all when you ever retire," she said.

"Honey, retirement is when we die," Frank said with a bit of wistfulness in his tone. "We've saved through the years, but it wouldn't be enough to keep us if things ever got bad and we had to go to a nursing home, so we'll be working until we drop."

"But don't you go worryin' about that," Mabel said quickly. "We're happy doin' what we do, and we've been lucky that we get to work together all these years. Plus, what would we do if we did retire?"

They'd done so much and been such an integral part of her raising that Jennie Sue wished that she could do something to help them. They should have a few years to travel or just sit on the porch or even garden again if they wanted to. Truth was, after putting up with what went on in the Baker house, they should be given a million-dollar retirement package with benefits. She pretended to wipe butter from her lip with her napkin and brushed a tear from her eye.

She popped a piece of bread into her mouth. "Mmm, this is so good. Maybe if you retired, you could enjoy not having to get up in the morning if you didn't want to, and never have to worry about anyone but yourselves."

Frank slowly shook his head in disagreement. "If we retired, we'd never get to see you again. We don't get to spend nearly enough time with you as it is. Thank goodness for unlimited long-distance phone calls in between your visits home."

"I'd still come to see you, maybe for supper on Sunday evenings, and you could come see me. I'm sorry I didn't call more often. School and studies took up so much time, and Mama didn't want anyone to know about the divorce, or later that Percy was on the run. It was hard not to blurt it all out," she said.

"No worries." Mabel reached across the table and patted her arm. "You're home where you belong now. I hear you are doing fingernails and toenails tonight at Lettie's place. I thought after we get off work, I might join y'all."

"That would be great." Jennie Sue beamed.

"I can't remember the last time I had an evenin' out just for fun, and"—she lowered her voice—"Lettie says there will be wine."

"I might have to drive you and Nadine both home," Jennie Sue whispered.

Mabel nodded. "You just might at that."

Mabel and Lettie sat on either end of the sofa that evening, and Nadine chose the recliner. One at a time Jennie Sue brought three basins of warm water with bath salts dissolved in it for them to soak their feet. Then she sat down on the floor and started to work on Mabel's feet first.

They'd finished their first glass of wine when she moved down the line to do Lettie's toenails. And they were working on their third when she started Nadine's. No one could ever accuse these old gals of not being able to hold their liquor. It wasn't until she'd finished and had started back around to do Lettie's fingernails that they got happy and started slurring their words.

Mabel tapped Lettie on the shoulder. "Did you hear that the almighty Belinda Anderson has gotten religion?"

Nadine guffawed. "After all them wild oats she's sowed, it'll take more than workin' in the clothes closet for the poor to redeem her. She'd do better to join a convent."

"Man, that must've been a shock to Belinda," Jennie Sue said.

"They say karma will sneak up on a person and bite them on the butt. Well, this is Belinda's time to get bit. Neither of her daughters belong to her husband, and all her diamonds are fake," Lettie whispered.

"No! She could be forgiven for sleeping around, but to wear fake diamonds? She might not ever get into heaven for a stunt like that.

What happened to her real jewelry? Did your aliens steal them, Nadine?" Jennie Sue joked.

Nadine shot a mean look her way. "Don't you tease about that, girl. Them things might be real, and you might make them mad if they hear you accusin' them of stealin' diamonds. I heard that she hocked most of her fancy jewels to pay off a blackmailer who threatened to tell her husband about the girls," Nadine said.

"Does he know now?" Jennie Sue didn't think anything could shock her, but they'd proven her wrong.

"Hell, no," Lettie answered. "That man's head is buried in the sand when it comes to Belinda. He has no idea that she had her good stones taken out of her jewelry and fake ones set in their place. She'll be the talk of the town the whole time she's carryin' that baby. And chances are, this time it's poor old Lonnie's kid."

"Why poor old Lonnie?" Jennie Sue asked.

"He's declarin' that they are too old to have another baby and wantin' her to get an abortion. They are both forty-five years old, and she thought at first she was goin' through menopause and had a case of the flu," Nadine said.

"I used to babysit her girls. They were five or six years younger than me. I feel sorry for them," Jennie Sue said. "Poor Lonnie. Is someone going to tell him?"

"Who knows," Mabel said. "Belinda would be

wise if she just came clean and quit trying to get absolution by doing extra duty at church."

"Sometimes that's a lot easier said than done," Jennie Sue said.

Chapter Fourteen

After all the talk about Belinda and a new baby at the end of the previous week, Jennie Sue borrowed the truck on Monday and drove straight to the cemetery before work. The sun was an orange ball on the horizon, and a nice breeze fluttered the old oak trees clustered around the Baker plot. Twice she opened the door and slammed it again, but the third time she made it all the way to the grave site and sat down in front of where Emily Grace was buried.

"I'm so sorry," she whispered as she pulled a few weeds growing up in the plot. "I wanted you, sweet little girl." Tears flooded her cheeks as she laid her hands on the grass covering the spot where her baby was. She wanted closure, but she couldn't find it—not that day.

"I need something to help me decide what to do," she said. "Do I stay in Bloom? Do I go? Do I tell everyone that I had a beautiful baby girl? Oh, my sweet child, I wish we could have had years and years together. Even with family and all my new friends, I feel so alone sometimes."

She felt better when she stood up and went back to the truck, but she was still weeping when she started driving. She was so immersed in her thoughts that she blew right through a four-way stop sign and almost collided with a car. She slammed on the brakes and covered her eyes. When she opened them, Rick was tapping on her window. She rolled it down and hoped that he wouldn't notice that she'd been crying.

"I'm so sorry. What're the odds?" He attempted a grin, but his voice was shaky. "That was totally my fault. I was thinking about something else, and I ran right through that sign. What are you doin' out this early? Are Lettie and Nadine okay?"

This was totally surreal. Was it all a dream? Had she really gone to the cemetery? She reached through the window and touched his face to be sure. He grabbed her hand and held it there.

"Are you okay?" he asked.

The touch of his hand on hers steadied her nerves. "I'm fine, Rick. And Lettie and Nadine are fine." Her voice notched a little higher than usual, and her heart pumped a little faster.

"I had an early-morning delivery, and now I'm on the way home. We'd better both keep our minds on driving, right?" He removed her hand and kissed the palm. "Have a great day, Jennie Sue."

Is that a sign I should stay here? she asked herself as she checked her hand to see if his lips had left a warm imprint. Surprisingly, it didn't look any different than it had before.

• • •

Rick ran a hand over his lips several times as he drove home. His pulse was still racing when he got back to the house. Thank goodness Cricket was still in her room, because he didn't want to talk to anyone who would spoil the mood.

He made himself breakfast and left thirty minutes earlier than necessary. It was Monday, so he would be driving the bookmobile to Roby. He drove slowly past the bookstore, but it was still closed.

This is pretty close to stalking, the voice in his head said.

"No, it's not," he argued, but the idea stayed with him all day. That evening when he got back to town, he dropped off the keys and went straight home.

When he arrived, he made a pass through the house and started for the garden when he saw a note on the kitchen table from Cricket saying that she wouldn't be home until bedtime. So he pulled out a chair and called Jennie Sue. He had to get this heavy feeling about stalking her off his mind, and if she thought he was, then he'd apologize.

She was out of breath when she answered on the fourth ring. "Hello, Rick. I'm sorry it took so long. I'm working late at the bookstore, and I was carrying a box of books from one place to the other. I couldn't get to my phone. What's up? Is Cricket all right?"

"She's fine. I haven't talked to her today. I'm not stalkin' you, I promise," he blurted out.

"What brought that on?" she asked.

"I've been feelin' something between us for a while, and I've found myself . . . You're going to think I am stalkin' you," he said.

"I do not think that. I watch for the bookmobile to drive through town when I'm in the bookstore. I like you, Rick," she said.

"I just wanted to be up-front and honest with you." Had she really said that she liked him? "You never know what the talk might be."

"Ain't that the truth. So how was your day at the market Saturday?" Jennie Sue asked.

"Very busy, but I sold everything I took. And I didn't take Cricket with me." He'd figured that she might hang up on him or tell him that they couldn't be friends because of Cricket.

"Oh, Rick, I really don't want to cause trouble," she whispered.

"You didn't. I just thought it would be best if my sister and I had a day apart. It's turned into three days apart. She left a note on the table this evening sayin' that Lettie had picked her up for supper, and it would be late when she got home tonight. So how was your Saturday?"

"Productive. I had a visit with my mother, and then that evening I gave Lettie, Nadine, and Mabel mani-pedis," she said. "Those old darlin's kept me laughing at their stories all evening."

He shut his eyes and imagined the glimmer in her blue ones that went along with the laughter. Listening to her voice when she was happy was like seeing a gorgeous sunrise bringing the promise of a new day.

She went on, "Those three can flat-out hold their wine. They drank two bottles between them, and other than a little girlish giggling and slight slurring of words, they were steady as a rock."

"And I bet they all had headaches on Sunday morning when they went to church," he said. "Want to go for a drive with me? I haven't had supper. It's half-price burger night at Sonic."

"I'd rather go out to the farm and help you gather tomorrow's deliveries, since Cricket isn't there to fuss at us," she said. "We could pick up burgers and eat them on the way."

"So you missed me?"

"I missed green beans and squash and corn."

He imagined her closing one eye in a sly wink. "And you don't want to go home to your apartment because you know that Lettie will holler at you to come in her house, and Cricket will be there, right? Oh, I do feel used," he said, but his tone said that he was getting a big kick out of this.

"Not you," she said sweetly. "I would never use you to escape going home. But I would use your garden to stay away from Cricket a few more days."

"I'll pick up the burgers on the way and be there in ten minutes."

"Mustard and no onions," she said.

She was sitting on the outside bench when he arrived. She waved and didn't wait for him to get out to open the door for her, but dived right in and grabbed the brown bag. "These smell so good. Man, I missed good old greasy burgers when I was in New York. They just don't taste the same out there." She bit into hers before she got his out of the bag and handed it to him.

"Do you ever have a negative thought in your head?" Rick asked.

"Used to, then I figured out that positive can't survive in a negative atmosphere, so I have a mental 'Delete' button that I press real often. Do you have bad thoughts?" she asked.

Rick chewed fast and swallowed. "I did for a long time, but a therapist in the hospital finally got through my thick skull—negative and positive don't survive together."

She was halfway through her burger when they reached the farm, so he turned off the engine and rolled down the windows. "Let's finish before we hit the garden."

"Thank you. I want to enjoy every bite of this." She kicked off her shoes and slowly ate the rest of her food before she opened the door and said, "I'll grab a basket and meet you in the peas."

He nodded and followed her to the back porch

with both of their drinks in his hands. "You forgot this."

She took a long draw from the straw and set it on the porch. "I missed this the past few days, Rick. It's so peaceful out here—especially with the smell of fresh dirt and creek water. Two more things I missed in New York."

"There's a shallow creek at the back of the place with a big old scrub oak shade tree at the edge. We could go there for a little while when we finish up here," he said.

"Yes," she said without hesitation. "But first, let's get the stuff gathered up for your deliveries tomorrow morning."

They were finished in less than an hour, and once they'd washed off their bare feet and gotten their shoes back on, he led the way down a path with weeds growing up in the middle of two ruts.

"I can hear it already," she said before they made the final bend in the path.

"When Cricket and I were little kids, several times a year we'd have a tailgate picnic at the creek, and then Mama and Daddy would let us splash around in the water," he said.

"Oh, it's beautiful. Look at that big old shady tree. I love it, Rick," she said. "Can we wade in it?"

"It's spring fed, so it's pretty cold, but you can if you want," he answered as he sat down under the huge scrub oak tree.

“I’d rather go skinny-dippin’,” she whispered.

“Would you repeat that?” He could feel a blush heating up his cheeks.

She clamped a hand over her mouth. “Did I say that out loud?”

“I believe you did.” He grinned.

“I was thinkin’ it, but I didn’t mean to say it.” She was downright cute with two bright-red spots dotting her cheeks. “And it would be fun, because I’ve never done that before.”

“I don’t think it would be a good idea. I swear in this area even the blackbirds in the trees carry gossip. You can’t even imagine what one little skinny-dippin’ night would have created by this time tomorrow,” he said.

“It could be one of those ‘used rumors.’ ” She put air quotes around the words. “Those that we file away to sell to a town that’s just gettin’ into the rumor business.”

“We could sell that one pretty high.”

She sat down and nudged him with her shoulder. “We could give classes to towns that don’t have the experience Bloom does. Cricket could work up a syllabus and help teach it. Did your mama like gossip, too?”

“No, ma’am,” he said quickly.

“Then you must be more like her.”

“Pretty much, but sometimes Dad comes out in my attitude if I’m brooding about something. What about you?” He couldn’t see much of either of her parents in her. Not the uppity Charlotte or the philandering Dill. He drew his eyebrows down into a frown, wondering exactly how those two ever made a child so different from them both.

"They say I'm like Granny Baker. She was gone before I was born, but I get told that I'm like her pretty often, mostly when Mama is scolding me about something." She stood up and walked across the green grass to the edge of the water and stuck a bare toe in it. "Man, it is cold, but it feels so good. I'm going to come out here someday and go skinny-dippin'. I'll tell you beforehand so you can guard it for me."

"What makes you think I'll stand guard? I might sit right here and enjoy the sight." Immediately he wondered if *he'd* been guilty of saying words out loud that he shouldn't have even thought.

"Are you flirting with me, Rick Lawson?" she asked.

"Maybe. Probably. Is that okay?"

"Well, when you make up your mind, I'd like to know." She stuck her whole foot into the water and then the other one, only sucking air a little bit. Then she waded out ankle-deep and inhaled. "It smells wonderful. So fresh and clean, and there's little minnows in here, Rick. If I owned this place, I'd build a house right there where you are sitting, and I'd never leave. If I needed anything other than what is grown here, I'd pay someone to deliver it."

He walked out to the edge of the water and extended a hand. "It gets slippery right at the edge."

She put hers in his, but when she took that final step, she faltered and started down into the icy water. To prevent that, he grabbed both her arms and jerked her toward him. He ended up flat on his back with her on top of him. From the waist up, they were on dry ground, while below, the cold water rushed around and over them. Thank God for the cold water or else she would have known exactly how much she affected him right then.

"Are you all right?" he panted.

"I think so. Did I break your back?"

He should sit up and help her, but he liked the way her body felt. "I don't think so." His hands went up to cup her cheeks. "I'm flirting now."

"Okay," she whispered when she realized he was about to kiss her.

Then their lips met, and the whole earth stood still. Maybe he had died, and this was his first taste of heaven. As suddenly as it started, it was over. She rolled off him and lay on the grass, staring up at the limbs of the old oak tree.

"Rick, I've had boyfriends. I've had a husband. I like you better than any of them, and I'd never ruin what we've got for a fling," she told him.

"Who says it's a fling?" he said.

She sat up. "You make me feel special, but you don't know everything about me."

He pulled himself up to stand above her and offer his hand. "You *are* very special, Jennie Sue."

She put her hand in his, and warmth filled his whole body.

"Thank you. Oh, no!" She squeezed his hand.

"What? Did you break something after all? Are you hurt?"

She pointed toward the house. "I hear a vehicle. Cricket must be home. I'm serious, Rick. I don't want to cause problems."

He kept her hand in his as they started walking toward the house. "It's okay. Don't worry about it—I don't need Cricket's blessing to flirt with you."

Her eyes searched his for several seconds. "Are you sure?"

"Absolutely." He bent slightly and kissed her on the tip of the nose.

When they rounded the bend, they could see the silhouettes of two people on the back porch. There was no doubt that the one with crutches was Cricket, and the other one had to be Lettie.

Rick waved when they drew closer as if it was completely normal for him to be holding Jennie Sue Baker's hand. When they were close enough that he could actually see his sister's expression, he had no doubt that Cricket was about to explode.

"I've been wading in the most amazing little creek," Jennie Sue said, but she didn't let go of his hand even when they were at the porch. "It's cold as ice and clear as glass. I helped Rick bring in tomorrow's deliveries, so Cricket doesn't have to feel guilty about not being able to help. Could you take me home, Lettie? That way Rick won't have to drive back into town."

"You said you wouldn't come back out here." Cricket ignored her statement.

"Changed my mind. Women do that sometimes. Besides, you weren't here, so?" Jennie Sue said just as frankly.

"I don't want you here," Cricket said.

"That is enough," Rick said. "This is my home, too, and if I want to spend time with Jennie Sue, then I can invite her here. You bring your church ladies out here and they drive me crazy, but I don't tell you that you can't host meetings here."

"This is different," Cricket said.

"This is clearly something that Jennie Sue and I don't need to be in the middle of. Y'all can straighten it out without us." Lettie turned toward Jennie Sue. "You can drive. Rick, I could use a bushel of cucumbers this week. I'd like to make some bread-and-butter pickles before the end of the season. They make wonderful Christmas presents."

"Sure thing. How about tomorrow mornin'?" Rick tried to keep his voice completely normal as he let go of Jennie Sue's hand, but it wasn't easy. "I'll call you, Jennie Sue."

"I'll be at the bookstore. Stop by if you have time." She rolled up on her toes and brushed a kiss across his cheek. "And thanks again for saving my life."

"You can't drown in a foot of water," he told her.

"If I hit my head on a rock and landed facedown, I might," she argued. "See y'all later." Jennie Sue followed Lettie around the house to the front yard, where her truck was parked.

"Okay, young lady, you are glowing," Lettie said as she got in and fastened the seat belt. "What happened here today?"

"I slipped as I got out of the creek, and wound up on top of Rick, and he kissed me," she said. "I liked it, Lettie—a lot. But I like him too much to ruin a friendship with a fling, and I told him so."

Lettie clucked like an old hen calling in her chickens. "Rick Lawson is the salt of the earth. He'll do right by you in any relationship."

Jennie Sue had no doubt that Lettie was speaking the absolute truth.

Chapter Fifteen

Jennie Sue shook out her umbrella and took a deep breath, sucking in the aroma of fresh rain one more time before she went inside the bookstore. With the rain and it being Wednesday, she didn't figure there'd be many people out and about today, which was fine with her—then she could get the store in shape. Already her efforts were paying off, because they'd sold a lot of romance novels last week.

She used her key to open the door and went straight to the thermostat to adjust it to a cooler temperature before she flipped on the lights and headed to the office to start the coffee and hot water for tea. Once that was done, she started to work on the mystery section, arranging the authors alphabetically by name. She'd only gotten the first shelf cleared off and dusted when she heard the bell above the door.

"Good mornin'." Nadine's voice carried through the store. "Where are you? Is there coffee? I brought doughnuts from the café to share with you."

"Good mornin' to you. Come on in out of the rain. Coffee should be ready. Thanks for bringin' doughnuts. I only took time for a glass of milk and a cookie this morning," Jennie Sue said.

"I'll drag a chair back here so we can visit while you work. You get the coffee," Nadine said.

Nadine had found an old metal folding chair and set the box of pastries on the empty shelf when Jennie Sue returned from the office/kitchen. She had a huge apple fritter in one hand and reached out for her cup of coffee with the other from her rickety seat.

"Look at us. We're dressed alike except that you don't have Minnie Mouse on your T-shirt." Nadine pointed at Jennie Sue's plain dark-blue T-shirt and jeans. "Does that make you old or me young?"

"Might make us the same age," Jennie Sue answered without mentioning that her skinny jeans fit a lot better than Nadine's loose ones. "Please tell me that you didn't drive." The window was too fogged up for her to see if Nadine's van was parked by the curb.

"Nope, caught a ride with Rick when he brought me a gallon of strawberries. I'm makin' jam this afternoon. He was takin' produce to the café, so I got a box of goodies, and he dropped me here. Lettie is comin' down in a little while, and she can take me home," Nadine answered. "Where's Amos?"

"He called last night and said he was going to Sweetwater this mornin'. Something about flowers for Iris's grave." Jennie Sue reached inside the box and chose a doughnut with chocolate icing and sprinkles.

"He needs to sell this place. It was Iris's dream store, not his."

Jennie Sue devoured the first doughnut and reached for one with maple icing. "It's probably hard to let it go—it reminds him of good times with her."

"She's been gone now for years, and the place looks like crap. When she was alive, she kept it all dusted and in some kind of order. If I wanted a Sue Grafton book or a Mary Burton, all I had to do was ask Iris, and she'd take me right to them. Amos just puts books any old place." She reached for her second pastry. "You're doin' a good thing here. I can feel Iris smilin' over my shoulder."

Jennie Sue licked the sticky sweetness from her fingers, finished off her coffee, and went back to work. "Thank you, Nadine, I appreciate that."

"Well." Nadine pursed her lips in a gesture that Jennie Sue recognized as her bearer-of-bad-news expression. "I heard that Cricket was pretty mad last night. She called Elaine and said that Rick wouldn't even listen to her, that he went to his room with an armload of books and slammed the door."

"I hate that," Jennie Sue groaned. "I just wanted to help him pick vegetables, not create another problem. I should've had him bring me home earlier."

"Cricket has a burr in her underbritches and needs to get over it. Jealousy is an ugly thing. Lettie and I had a long talk with her yesterday, but I guess it didn't take as good as we wanted. Some folks have to learn things the hard way," Nadine said. "Now let's talk about what you and Rick were doin' down at the creek. Lettie said he kissed you."

A vision of his deep-green eyes as they fluttered shut, leaving his dark lashes to rest on high cheekbones, flashed through her mind. She blinked away the image and nodded. "Yes, he did, but it was the moment." She went on to tell Nadine about wading and her foot slipping.

"Sounds to me like fate. I've learned that you should never argue with fate." Nadine took out another doughnut and shut the box. "If it's open, I'll eat them until it's empty."

"Hey, where all you at?" Lettie called out at the same time the bell above the door rang. "I brought brownies."

Nadine grabbed the box of doughnuts and hurried toward the office with them. "We're over here in the new mystery section. I'll get you a mug of coffee. Bring a chair with you."

Lettie must've gotten a chair with no rubber caps on the legs. Jennie Sue covered both ears, and Nadine yelled, "For God's sake, Lettie, pick that chair up. That sounds like fingernails scraping against a blackboard."

"Oh, hush," Lettie hollered. "Nothing is that bad."

The mention of blackboards made Jennie Sue think of school. "Maybe I should've studied education. Texas is always needing teachers. I wonder, if I got my education credential, if I could get a job right here in Bloom teaching high school."

"Why would you do that? Kids today are all about entertainment, not learnin'." Lettie popped the chair out, sat down, and put a plate of warm brownies in the exact spot where the doughnuts had been. "Havc one while they're hot. Nadine, you goin' to take all day with that coffee?"

"I'm right here. You don't have to yell at me. And I'd be for anything that would keep you in Bloom. I'd even be willin' to pay for your education and put in a word for you at the school." She put a cup in her sister's hands and reached for a brownie. "Now what did you hear about Belinda this mornin'?"

Just like that, another avenue opened up to Jennie Sue that would keep her in Bloom. Classes would start in the fall if she wanted to go that route. She could probably get what she needed in a year, and then she'd be ready to start teaching. She'd wanted something to help her make the decision about what to do . . . Was this the answer?

"Where are you woolgatherin' at?" Nadine touched her on the arm.

"My future. I'm havin' a lot of trouble making the decision about whether to stay in Bloom or not," Jennie Sue answered, knowing the sisters deserved her honesty.

"We want you to stay, and we'll do whatever we can to help you, but, honey, the final decision has to be yours or you'll always wonder if you made the right one," Lettie said.

"Thank you both. I think we were talkin' about Aunt Belinda."

Lettie and Nadine both cocked their heads to the right at the same time.

"It's a Sweetwater Belle thing that I have trouble shaking. All of us kids were encouraged to call them 'aunt,' since they referred to themselves as sorority sisters," she explained. "Go on about Belinda."

"She's keepin' the baby," Lettie said. "Lonnie wanted her to end the pregnancy at first because he said that there would be a big chance something might be wrong with it. She said that she couldn't ever end the life of a little baby. The doctors did some kind of newfangled test to be sure it didn't have problems, and it's a boy. So Lonnie is struttin' around like he's the cock of the walk now."

"Did she tell him about the two daughters?" Nadine whispered.

"Don't know, but since we didn't hear an explosion, I guess not. But I did hear that the daughters aren't too happy about it. After all, one is twenty-two and gettin' married at Christmas. The other one is twenty-one and just got engaged. Think about it—they'll probably have children not much younger than their brother." Lettie sipped her coffee.

Jennie Sue finished what she was doing and picked up a box to go searching for mystery books scattered about the store. She grabbed a brownie on her way past the plate and winked at Nadine.

"These are fabulous, Lettie. Do you give out your recipe?" she asked.

"Honey, it's on the back of the cocoa box. The secret is not to overcook them. Brownies should be gooey, not dry and stiff," Lettie answered.

"Sounds like good sex," Nadine said.

Lettie slapped her on the knee. "Watch your mouth. I swear to the Lord, you go to church on Sunday and do all kinds of work up there and then come home and talk about sex."

"Do you think Adam and Eve had them kids of theirs by immaculate conception?" Nadine got another brownie. "Hell, no, they did not! And they enjoyed the sex, too, I'd be willin' to bet you."

Jennie Sue ducked behind a row of books and held her hand over her mouth to keep from giggling out loud. A new vision replaced the one concerning the kiss. This one had her and Rick tangled up in cotton sheets with a ceiling fan blowing down on them after an afternoon in bed.

A deep crimson blush dotted her cheeks as she shook the picture away and went back to filling the box with books. Listening to the two sisters bantering made her wish again that she had a sibling in her life to grow old with.

Charlotte arrived just as Nadine and Lettie were leaving at noon. She drew her shoulders back and said, "Ladies," with a nod as she set her wet umbrella just inside the shop.

"Charlotte," they said in unison and left with their chins jacked up an extra inch or two.

Now that was a prime example of civil friends, Jennie Sue thought as she crossed the room to hug her mother. "Mama, what brings you to town?"

Charlotte returned the hug, but only briefly, before she took a step back. "You smell like old books and sweat, and you look like crap."

"Well, thank you for that, Mother." Jennie Sue dragged out the last word into several syllables. "I've been working all morning, like most people in town. Want a cup of coffee or a glass of sweet tea?" She had to bite her tongue to keep any more sarcasm from sneaking out of her mouth.

"No, thank you. I thought maybe we could have lunch together," Charlotte answered.

Oh, goody! A whole hour of listening to

belittling remarks about how she looked, talked, or just her life in general.

"I'd love to. The café is only a few doors down the street, so let's go there. They make a mean burger." She'd get chastised for the fat grams in a burger and fries for sure, but that's what she planned on having.

"I haven't been in there in years. Do they have decent salads?" Charlotte asked as Jennie Sue got her purse and umbrella.

"Just enjoy something fattening, Mama. One time won't even add a pound to your skinny frame." She led the way out of the store, flipped the sign that said she'd be back in an hour, and locked up. "Let's not fuss today."

"I'll try," Charlotte sighed.

It might not be a guarantee, but it was a start. One baby step at a time—at least today she was going to lunch with her at a simple little café. That was a big thing in Charlotte's world.

Though the place was more than half-full, conversation ceased when the two Baker women walked inside. Everyone stared at them as if two of Nadine and Lettie's aliens had dropped out of the sky and hit the café first.

"What's happening?" Charlotte whispered.

"You know us—we're the movie stars in Bloom. The paparazzi will arrive any minute and start flashing pictures of us. Tomorrow we'll be on the cover of all the gossip papers in the whole state—the ones that you buy right next to the grocery-store checkout counter." Jennie Sue chose a booth and motioned for her mother to sit across from her. "Turn your best side toward me. I see phones takin' our pictures."

"Oh, hush! I shouldn't have even come today, but I wanted to see you before your dad and I leave town for my birthday. We're flying to Las Vegas for a few days," Charlotte said.

"Good, because by next week, our picture will be pasted on the front, and the headline will be, 'The Wilshire Women. Mother Still Beautiful. Daughter Looks Like Shit.' "

"Stop it." Charlotte slapped at her and then giggled.

Jennie Sue hadn't heard sincere laughter from her mother in years. It warmed her heart. "Why? I made you laugh and that erases wrinkles. Greasy hamburgers do the same thing. You know, at a certain age, you got to choose between your rear end and your face," Jennie Sue whispered. "Look, everyone is talking again. They're tryin' to figure out what I'm sayin' right now so they can go home and gossip about us."

Charlotte leaned forward and lowered her voice. "I'm going to eat a burger with you, and if I lose a single wrinkle, I'll pay for a patent."

"It's a deal." Jennie Sue stuck out her hand.

Her mother shook it, and Elaine appeared at the table with two menus and a couple of glasses of water. "Good to see you, Charlotte. What can I get you ladies today?"

"Two burger baskets. No onions on either, and mustard. Fries and two Cokes, not diet. And save us a slice of chocolate cream pie. We'll share it to save on fat grams," Jennie Sue ordered.

"Are you insane?" Charlotte asked as soon as Elaine moved away from the booth.

"Maybe so." Jennie Sue nodded. "After all, what sane woman would leave a virtual mansion to live in a garage apartment, clean houses, and work in a bookstore for a living when she could be living in luxury?"

"Why are you doin' it, then?" Charlotte asked.

"Because it makes me happy," she said. "I like having friends that are real and who don't turn their backs on me."

"Like Cricket? Are you callin' that woman a real friend?" Charlotte's mouth set into a firm line.

"She's not my friend yet, but she's honest. Whatever she's got to say comes right out—to my face." At least they'd made a couple of fun memories before the aliens decided Charlotte Baker was much too complicated for them to do anything with.

Charlotte pulled a paper napkin from the dispenser and laid it in her lap. "You're sayin' that my friends talk about me behind my back?"

"Let's discuss Belinda and this new thing with

her and the church. Do you honestly think that the whole town doesn't know that she's pregnant and that her two daughters do not belong to Lonnie? You can't tell me that the Belles haven't been talkin' about her. Don't you think that when she's in the room, you become the headline of the day instead?"

"They wouldn't do that. How did you know about Belinda?" Charlotte asked.

"Yes, they would, and everyone knows. Come on, Mama, do you have real friends?" Jennie Sue asked.

"Maybe not, but I'm comfortable in my world, no matter how mixed-up and crazy it is." Charlotte caught someone actually taking a picture of her with a phone and waved. "You really think we might show up on a magazine cover?"

"Hell, no!" Jennie Sue sputtered. "We, and by that I mean you, are just a big fish in a mud puddle. You've got to be a whale in an ocean for anyone outside West Texas to give a damn about what or who you do."

"I might learn to like this new daughter you are becoming," Charlotte said. "The Wilshire women are probably turning over in their graves, but I like your frankness."

"Thank you." She wished she had that huge compliment from her mother written in calligraphy on fancy paper so she could frame it. Or better yet, engraved on stone to display proudly on a marble pedestal in her little apartment.

Charlotte only ate half a hamburger and two french fries, but that was a lot for her, so Jennie Sue didn't push the issue. When they'd finished, the sun had pushed the dark clouds away and was shining brightly.

"Don't you love the smell of fresh rain?" Jennie Sue said as they walked back to the bookstore.

"It's so muggy that I'm sweating off my makeup," Charlotte answered. "I'm not coming inside. I've got a committee meeting for a fund-raiser this afternoon. We are raising money for the next annual tea for the senior girls at the high school. I remember when you went to that tea. Your lovely blue dress may still be in your closet at home."

"That was a long time ago." Jennie Sue gave her mother a quick side hug. "Have a great afternoon and, Mama, I love you."

"Love you, too." Charlotte got into her car.

Jennie Sue was stunned speechless by the response. Charlotte had only said that a few times, and those had been when Jennie Sue was a little girl. She waved until the Cadillac turned three blocks down Main Street, and then she opened the store door and flipped the sign. She sank down on the sofa and shut her eyes, replaying her mother's words several more times before she made herself get up and go back to work.

A bright ray of light showed how dirty the two front display windows were. A cute little bistro table with two chairs and a selection of books scattered on top sat in one bay window. At one time the other one had held a wingback chair with a book lying on it, but now it was a jumbled mess of boxes and books.

"I should have started there first," she said. "The windows should invite people inside the store, not make them wonder if we're having a garage sale in here."

She started for some cleaning supplies but hadn't gone two steps when Dill poked his head inside the store. "Who's having a garage sale, and who are you talking to?"

Good Lord! Both her parents in the same day, and one right on the heels of the other—this had to be a sign of some kind. Jennie Sue crossed the distance between them and hugged him tightly. "I'm thinkin' out loud. Come in, Daddy. Can I get you a cup of coffee or a glass of sweet tea?"

"Don't need a thing except to see my baby girl." He took a step back. "How are things going? I heard you've been out at the Lawson farm messin' around with Rick."

She pulled him over to the worn sofa and made him sit beside her. "Did you come to fuss at me for falling in love with a farmer? Not that I have or will. It was just one kiss on the lips and one on the nose. I did kiss him on the cheek when I left, but that doesn't count, either."

"No, honey, I did not. I wouldn't stand in your way no matter who you fall in love with. Just be sure it's love and not rebellion. You never did go through that thing that other kids do when they're teenagers. So be careful. What I came to talk to you about is different. I don't want to leave town without you having some means of transportation and money. Please let me set up a checking account for you and give you a car," he said.

She shook her head. "No, thank you, Daddy."

"Okay, then, have it your way. But when we get home, we are going to discuss a job in the family business. You can start at the bottom and learn every facet of it from there on up to the CEO position, if that's what you really want," Dill said.

Her mother said that she loved her, and her dad was about to take her side and give her a job. Oh, yes, sir. This surely meant she was supposed to stay in Bloom.

"And what does Mama say about this?" she asked with caution.

"You let me worry about Charlotte," Dill answered. "I'll have a few days in Vegas to warm her up to the idea. And besides, she called me on her way home after you two had lunch and told me that she admired you for your determination. I think she's comin' around already. I'm glad that I didn't sell the company last year after all."

"You really thought about it? What did Mama say?" Jennie Sue asked.

"She threw a fit," he admitted. "I'm ready to retire. I realize I'm not that old, but I'm tired of the stress. I'd hand the whole company over to you today if I could."

For the first time, Jennie Sue could see that her father had aged more than normal in the last year. More lines etched his face, and his eyes looked tired.

"I don't want money or a car right now, Daddy. I'm doin' fine with my two jobs, and Miz Lettie lets me borrow her truck when I need it. I'll think about your offer until you get home. I could use the time. There's a fair amount of pride in working for what I need," she said.

Dill moved closer to her and draped an arm around her shoulders. "What turned you this way?"

"Percy. I was dependent on him for a living, and had to do what he said or else disgrace the Wilshire name with a divorce. After he left me and I lost the baby, I made up my mind that I'd finish my degree and no one would ever control me like that again," she answered.

He pulled her closer to his side. "I love you, Jennie Sue, and I'm so proud of you. If you don't want the company job, I'll support your decision in whatever you decide to do."

Tears flowed down her cheeks, and she sniffled. "I love you, too, Daddy. I promise I'll give it some serious consideration. If I do take a job, I want it to be on the lowest level possible. No nepotism."

"Can't promise no nepo-whaddyacallit." Dill whipped out a white handkerchief and handed it to her. "You are my daughter. Can't change that."

She wiped her tears away and handed the hankie back to him.

"Keep it. You might need it again." He grinned. "I've got a meeting, so I should be going. You can go on back to talking to yourself now."

She hugged him one more time. "Thanks for understanding."

"That's what daddies do. See you later." They exchanged waves as he left the store, and she tucked the hankie in her purse, hoping that she didn't need it again for a long, long time.

Chapter Sixteen

Snow cone and a drive? The text came from Rick as she was finishing up at Nadine's house.

Was this a date? Should she tell him that she didn't have time? She worried with it a full minute before she typed slowly, Ten minutes?

The answer came immediately: I'm outside. No rush.

She finished putting away her cleaning supplies and left a note on the cabinet for Nadine.

> Locking the door behind me. See you later.

Rick was leaning against the truck when she reached the driveway. He flashed a brilliant smile, but he had sunglasses on, so she couldn't see his eyes. Opening the door for her, he said, "That was the shortest ten minutes I've ever had to wait on anyone."

"You had me at snow cone, but Rick, are you sure about this?" she said.

"Hey, it's not dinner and a movie. It's just a snow cone after a long, hot day of work. What's your favorite flavor?" He slammed the door shut.

She laid her arm on the open window. "Rainbow. Cherry, banana, and grape. I like that you don't have AC in the truck. It reminds me of Frank's old vehicle when I was a kid. I liked to hang my arm out the window and catch the wind."

"I've saved enough money to buy a newer truck, but just can't make myself let go of it when this one is runnin' good except for the air. The heat works fine in the winter, so we don't freeze. But—" There was that sexy grin again. "I remember when the heater went out in Dad's old truck. Cricket and I were little kids, and Mama would bundle us up in quilts when we went anywhere. When he finally bought a newer model, we both cried and wanted our quilts back."

"It would be like going for an open carriage ride in New York City in the winter, all bundled up in blankets. Daddy and Mama came to visit me the first New Year's that I lived in New York, and we went on a carriage ride. It's one of my favorite memories," she said.

"Didn't you do things like that with Percy?"

She shook her head. "No, he liked limos more than carriage rides, and parties with lots of people more than anything else. When it came right down to it, he wasn't very romantic, at least not with me. Maybe he's better with whoever he's with now."

"He's an idiot," Rick growled as he got in line

behind half a dozen cars at the snow-cone stand. "Did you see lots of snow-cone stands in the big city?"

"Not in my part of the place. I haven't had one since I left Bloom to go to college," she answered. "So I want a large one, and add a stripe of lime to it with the other flavors. What are you havin'?"

"The same thing you are. It sounds great," he answered. "I feel like a little kid every time I get a snow cone." He moved up in the line, but there were still two cars ahead of him.

"Me, too," she said, but her mind settled on the little unmarked grave. That baby would never grow up to be a little kid or eat a snow cone or go to proms or pick peas in the garden. She would never cry or laugh or pull her first tooth.

"I had a baby daughter," she blurted out.

Rick reached across the console and tucked her hand into his. "Did your husband get custody?"

She shook her head. "He left when he found out I was pregnant and didn't want anything to do with her."

"Where is she?" Rick asked.

Jennie Sue felt as if there was a brick on her chest. Maybe it wasn't the right time to tell Rick. Maybe *never* would have been a better time, but the old proverbial cat was out of the bag now.

"She was stillborn. Mama and Daddy brought her to Bloom to bury her," she whispered.

“How? What?” he sputtered.

“I guess if you’ve got enough money, secrets can be kept, even in Bloom,” she said.

“Have you been to the cemetery?” he asked.

She held up two fingers. “Twice. The first time, I couldn’t even get out of the truck. The second was the day we almost collided. I feel so guilty that there’s not even a stone to mark her grave. It’s like I’m ashamed of her. Once we get a snow cone, maybe you better just take me home.”

“I’ve got a better idea.” He finally pulled up to the window and ordered.

“And that is?”

“Let’s go to the cemetery together. We’ll sit right there beside her, and you can tell me all about what she looked like,” he said.

For the second time that week, she was stunned speechless. That was the absolute last thing she’d expected him to say.

“Are you sure?” she asked.

He handed her the first snow cone that came through the window. “Of course. You need to talk about her, and I’m here to listen.”

“I’m not sure what I’d say to her,” she said.

“Not *to* her.” He took his snow cone and let go of her hand. “*About* her. I never felt right talking to my mama’s or my dad’s tombstone, but talking about them is a different matter.”

A wrought iron fence surrounded the Bloom cemetery, and huge oak trees located among the graves shaded much of the place. Rick drove through the gates and down to the first narrow road that divided sections.

"Where to now?"

"Left." She pointed. "To the Baker graves right down there."

"What's her name?" he asked as he parked the truck.

"Emily Grace." She carried her snow cone with her to the end of the plot and sat down on the grass.

Rick sat down beside her and draped an arm around her shoulders. "How much did she weigh?"

"Eight pounds even."

"Is she named after someone?" he asked.

"No, I just thought the name sounded southern and pretty. I could picture her in a pink lace dress on her first Easter with a little bonnet," she answered. "She had a lot of jet-black hair and a little round face with cheeks made for kissing. I got to hold her for an hour before they took her away. I sent the dress I'd planned to take her home in with Mama, but I don't even know if she buried her in it. I got a horrible infection and had to stay in the hospital a whole week. By the time I went home alone, she was already put away." Jennie Sue swallowed hard, but the lump in her throat wouldn't go down.

Rick moved closer to her and drew her to his

side. She leaned her head on his shoulder and let the tears flow freely.

"I just let Daddy and Mama take over the arrangements, and I buried myself in college classes. Mama said that she didn't want anyone to know because it could ruin my chances of finding another husband."

He patted her on the back. "I'm not sure I understand that reasoning, but your mother thinks different than I do."

"Seems like years ago," she said.

"It's a wonder you kept any sanity at all. We'll come every week from now on and bring flowers for her grave. She'll never be forgotten," he promised.

She nodded in agreement. "There's going to be a stone with her name on it, too."

His phone rang, and without letting go of her, he worked it out of his hip pocket. "Sorry about this," he said to Jennie Sue before answering the call. "Hello? I'm pretty busy right now, Cricket."

Several long seconds passed before he said, "Are you absolutely sure?"

When he finally shoved the phone back into his pocket, he grabbed Jennie Sue and held her so tightly that she thought she'd smother.

"Is everything all right?" she asked.

"No, it's not, and I don't know how to tell you," he whispered into her hair. "Oh, Jennie Sue, I'm so sorry."

"Is it Cricket? Did she fall on that bum ankle?" she pushed back and asked.

He shook his head.

"Spit it out," she said.

"Your dad's plane crashed about a mile from the runway."

"Was anyone hurt?" Her heart moved up into her chest, and she remembered that it was Thursday. Her parents had left for Vegas that morning.

"Your parents were in the plane. I'm so sorry." His voice cracked.

"Where are they? Where did they take them? Will you drive me to the hospital?" The words tumbled out of her mouth.

He shook his head, and a moan came from deep inside her chest—a sound that she didn't even recognize. He wiped the fresh tears from her face with a handkerchief that appeared from nowhere, and she remembered her father doing the same thing.

"No!" she muttered. "Please tell me they're not—" She couldn't make herself utter the word.

"I'm so sorry, but they were both killed when the plane crashed," he said.

"Take me to Mabel," she whispered. "And stay with me, please."

He stood up, bent forward, and picked her up, cradling her in his arms. She felt like a rag doll as he put her into the passenger seat. The trip from the cemetery to the house only took five minutes, but it seemed like they'd driven for hours, and she was totally numb when they reached the house.

Rick didn't even ask if she could walk but carried her across the cobblestone walkway to the porch. When they reached the door, it swung open and Mabel ushered them inside, wiping her tears on the tail of her apron the whole way into the living room.

"Lay her on the sofa. I'll get her a shot of whiskey," Mabel said.

Jennie Sue was in denial when he laid her down. This had to be a nightmare. It couldn't be real. Her mama said she loved her. She couldn't be dead. They had to build on that love and start a new relationship.

Rick bent and kissed her on the forehead. "I should go. You've got things to do."

She sat up, took his hand, and pulled him down beside her. "Tell me that you'll come back tomorrow and help me."

"Anything. Just tell me what to do," he said.

The doorbell rang and Mabel disappeared, coming back with Lettie, Nadine, and Cricket behind her. Nadine rushed across the room and knelt in front of Jennie Sue. "We had to come. We just couldn't stay away, but it doesn't feel right for us to be here, so we'll just give you a hug and leave."

"I'm so glad you are here. Sit, please." Jennie Sue motioned toward another sofa and love seat across from where she and Rick were sitting. She felt like she was floating above her actual body. The only other time she'd experienced that strange feeling was when she came home to an empty apartment and walked into the nursery. She'd picked up a children's book and sat on the floor beside the crib, reading it and pretending that Emily Grace was in her lap.

"Thank you." She laced her fingers in Rick's hand.

"What can we do? What do you need?" Lettie moved across the floor to take a place on the sofa beside Nadine.

"Would you ladies stay with me tonight? I don't want to be alone in this house," Jennie Sue said. "And, Mabel, I don't want to see anyone else."

"The Belles," Mabel started.

"Tell them to come tomorrow. I can't handle them today," Jennie Sue said. "Call Belinda. She'll get the word out to all of them."

Cricket crutched across the room and sat down in one of the wingback chairs. "I don't know what to say," she muttered.

"Me neither, Cricket. You just being here with me is a comfort."

"How can you say that after the way I've acted?" Cricket asked.

"Because it's the truth. You've lost parents," Jennie Sue said.

Lettie pulled a tissue from her purse and wiped her eyes. "I'm so sorry that I let things be the way they were between us and your mother. I should have taken care of that instead of bein' so stubborn."

Frank came in from the kitchen with his hat in his hands. "Darlin' girl, what do you need me to do?" His bent shoulders and the expression on his face said that he'd aged ten years in the past hour.

"Nothing right now. I want things to go on here in the house like normal until I can figure things out. Rick, you've got things to do."

"It can all wait," Rick said.

"There'll be talk if we stay here," Nadine said.

"I don't really give a damn." Her parents were gone forever. She could never talk to them or see them again. What people said didn't make a bit of difference to her. "Please stay with me."

"Of course we will," Lettie said.

"There's goin' to be so much to do these next few days. Lawyers and insurance and coroners and accident reports. Are you sure you don't want me to call the Belles to help you get through it all?" Mabel asked.

"Not tonight. I'll face it tomorrow. Tonight, I just need Nadine and Lettie and you, Mabel."

"Okay, then, I'm going to the kitchen and make food for y'all. When my mama died, I cooked and cooked and then cooked some more. Folks thought I'd lost my mind, but it was the only thing that brought me any kind of peace. And right now I need to find that peace," Mabel said.

"When Flora died, I made jam," Nadine said. "I was so angry with her for letting the cancer get so far gone before she went to the doctor that I made jars and jars of plum jam."

"She hated plum jam," Lettie said.

"That's why I made it, to punish her for dying."

"I made bread-and-butter pickles." Lettie nodded. "For the same reason. She loved them and could eat a pint a week, so I made them because she could never eat them again."

Jennie Sue squeezed Rick's hand. "You and Cricket can go, but please come back tomorrow morning."

"We'll be here," Cricket said. "And if you change your mind and want us to spend the night, just call and we'll be here in fifteen minutes."

"Thank you," she said.

The phone rang as they were leaving. Mabel answered it in the kitchen, took it to Jennie Sue, and whispered, "It's the lawyer, Justin Rhodes. He just heard and would like to come by for a few minutes."

"Tell him to come right now." She was totally

overwhelmed. There would have to be funeral arrangements tomorrow morning, and God only knew what else would require her attention as the only surviving child.

"We need to make a trip back into town for our overnight things," Nadine said. "But we'll be back within the hour."

Jennie Sue nodded. She had to stiffen her spine. "Mabel will be here, and I'll deal with the lawyer while you are gone."

The two ladies were only gone a few minutes before the doorbell rang and Mabel ushered the lawyer into the room. He greeted her as he opened his briefcase and brought out a thick file.

"Jennifer, this is such a terrible shock to all of us. I can't imagine how you must feel," he said gently.

"Numb," she said.

"You poor thing." Justin patted her arm. "I could come back tomorrow, but these are important things that you should know before you see the coroner. However, if you aren't able right now . . ." He paused.

"Let's just get it over with," she whispered.

"If you are sure," he said.

She nodded.

"Okay, then. Your parents have an ironclad will. You inherit everything as the last surviving member of both the Baker and Wilshire families.

It's written in the will that they both want to be cremated and their ashes scattered wherever you think best. Your mother had something against her friends staring down at her in a casket."

Jennie Sue didn't doubt that for a single second. Charlotte wouldn't have trusted anyone to do her makeup or pick out the appropriate outfit—not even Jennie Sue.

"Did they have funeral wishes?" she asked.

"Your dad said whether or not you had a memorial was up to you. As soon as the coroner finishes with their bodies . . ." He paused again.

She grabbed a tissue and wiped her eyes.

He took a deep breath and went on. "They are to be sent to Sweetwater to the crematorium. You should be able to pick up their ashes next week. And those will be in urns that they picked out when they updated their will," he said.

"My beautiful mother." She wept into Rick's handkerchief.

Justin nodded slowly. "Will always be beautiful in your eyes. Remember her the way she was when you saw her last. The rest of this can wait a few days. Just call me when you're ready to talk about the business, and I'll deal with the insurance people and all the accident reports. That's part of my job as the company lawyer."

His suggestion made sense, but she wished

that she'd insisted they spend the whole day together, not just an hour for lunch. And her dad, trying to help her with money and a car—she would have taken both just to make him feel better.

Chapter Seventeen

Rick and Cricket showed up right after breakfast the next morning. Jennie Sue answered the door and pulled him down beside her on the sofa.

"What day are you thinking about for the funeral?" Cricket asked as she sat down across from them.

"No funeral and no memorial. They left instructions to be cremated and for me to choose the spot where I want to scatter the ashes," she said in a hollow-sounding voice.

Lettie and Nadine came in from the kitchen, where they'd been helping Mabel clean up after breakfast. They sat in the two chairs that completed the seating arrangement.

"I heard that you got the news when you and Rick were at the cemetery," Lettie said. "That seems kind of strange."

"It was surreal and still is even this morning. I was visiting my daughter's grave," Jennie Sue answered.

"Jennie Sue, are you okay?" Cricket asked.

"Why?"

"You don't have a daughter, honey," Lettie said gently.

"Yes, I do," Jennie Sue said. "Emily Grace was

stillborn a few months after Percy left me in New York. Mama wanted to keep it all a secret so if I got married again, it wouldn't be an issue. My daughter is in the Bloom cemetery in the Baker plot. I guess there was one secret that no one in town knew about."

"Sweet Lord!" Lettie laid a hand over her heart.

"He left you when you were pregnant? What a bastard!" Cricket snapped. "Did he come back and support you when the baby was born?"

"I didn't even know where he was at that time. He left when he found out I was pregnant, and I haven't heard from him since," Jennie Sue answered.

"I'm so sorry. I didn't know," Cricket whispered. "I won't tell anyone about the baby."

"You can tell whoever you want. I will be putting up a tombstone as soon as I can arrange for one. I'm just glad that Percy let me take my maiden name back so I can have her stone engraved with Emily Grace Baker and she won't have to have anything of him on her grave," Jennie Sue said.

Jennie Sue went through the clothes that she'd left behind in her closet and found the simple blue dress her mother had reminded her she'd worn to her senior tea. She chose that one to wear to the coroner's office that morning. He'd called and said that the bodies were ready to deliver to the crematorium, but she wanted to see them. Maybe it would bring some kind of closure. She slipped her feet into a pair of white sandals. Her mother would've preferred that she'd chosen a pair of white leather pumps with maybe a three-inch heel with the dress, but after Percy left, she'd sworn that she'd never wear heels again.

Nadine, Lettie, Rick, and Cricket were waiting in the living room by the time she made it downstairs. Rick wore a pair of jeans and his customary long-sleeve shirt with pearl snaps. Cricket was in the same outfit she'd been wearing when she twisted her ankle.

"You look lovely," Rick said.

"You always look so put-together and classy," Cricket said.

"Thank you both, but jeans and flip-flops are more my style. I guess I didn't wallow around in the Wilshire gene pool nearly long enough," she said. "Are we ready to do this?"

"If you are," Rick said. "Mabel says that your mama's friends insisted on coming tonight, so we'll clear out before they get here."

"No, Belinda called to change it. They're coming tomorrow evening at eight and bringing refreshments with them, since Baker Oil employees will be dropping by, too. It's only for an hour, so please don't leave me alone with them." Jennie Sue handed him the keys to her mama's car. "If you'll drive, please, I'd appreciate it. And this car will be easier for Cricket to get in and out of."

"Rick and Cricket can be here tomorrow night, honey, but not us. Those women would barricade the doors and shoot us on sight," Lettie said as she got into the back seat of the Caddy, with Nadine and Cricket right behind her.

"I'm not sure . . . ," Cricket started.

"Please," Jennie Sue begged.

"Okay, if you are sure about it," Cricket agreed.

Rick touched her on the arm. "Yes, we will stay."

"Thank you both. I just need to get through this thing with the Belles tomorrow night, and then I can go back to my apartment," she answered.

"You're kiddin'," Cricket said. "Why would you do that?"

"Because I like my apartment better than I like that big house," Jennie Sue answered. "And I'm rattling on about plans because I'm dreading this part so much. Until this minute, I could kind of pretend that it was just a bad dream. I'm glad y'all are goin' with me."

It was only a short drive to the coroner in Sweetwater. He met them in the outer office. "I'm Dr. Wesley Johnston. Which of you young ladies is Jennifer?"

She stepped forward and stuck out her hand. "I am Jennie Sue Baker."

He pumped her hand once and dropped it. "Are you absolutely sure you want to see your parents? It's not a pretty sight. You might want to remember them the way they were the last time you talked with them."

"Yes, sir," she said. "I need to see them."

"Okay, then, follow me."

She grabbed Rick's hand and held on tightly as they entered a long hallway. The doctor turned a corner and then opened the first door on the left, with Jennie Sue right behind him. Rick let go of her hand and stood back to let her go inside alone with the doctor. Her chest tightened when the doctor shut the door, leaving her friends on the other side.

I can do this alone. I need to do this alone. It's the only way I'll ever have closure, she told herself.

"Are you ready?" he asked.

She nodded, and he carefully pulled back the first sheet. "Your mother sustained a head wound and was killed instantly. She did not suffer."

She stood there for a long time, tears running in rivers down her cheeks and dripping onto her dress. Finally, she reached out and touched Charlotte's hair. "My beautiful mama. You won't ever be old or have to worry about wrinkles again. You'll always be young and gorgeous. I love you, Mama."

"Ready to move on?" the doctor asked.

She nodded. “Goodbye, Mama,” she said softly as she took two steps to the other table.

When she saw her daddy, so still and lifeless with a huge cut on his chin, she groaned and let the next batch of tears loose.

“His neck snapped when the plane crashed. Death was instantaneous for him, too.”

“See you later, Daddy,” she whispered as she bent and kissed his cold cheek.

Chapter Eighteen

Cricket was dressed and trying to do something with her unruly, almost curly, not quite straight, hair when Jennie Sue rapped on the bedroom door. Wearing a cute little sleeveless black dress that stopped at her knee and a pair of plain leather flats, Jennie Sue looked like she'd just stepped off a fashion runway.

"Need some help with your hair? We've got thirty minutes before the Belles arrive, and I'm antsy," Jennie Sue asked.

"I'd love help, but you're always so cool and collected. I can't even begin to imagine you nervous," Cricket said.

"Those women are going to try to make me join their club. It's written in the charter that when a mother passes, her daughter steps up to take her place. I'll get the curling iron from my room and be right back."

For years Cricket had wondered what it would be like to be in the circle that Jennie Sue ran in. To be invited to slumber parties where they'd all fix one another's hair and do makeup. Now it was happening, and she wasn't so sure how she felt about any of it. Maybe it was because she and Jennie Sue were both twenty-eight. All that high school popularity didn't matter anymore.

"Got it." Jennie Sue plugged the iron into the wall and laid it on the vanity. "Have a seat in front of the mirror."

Cricket sat down and sighed at her reflection. She should just pull her hair up into a ponytail. It didn't matter if she was a wallflower that evening—this wasn't about her. It was about helping Jennie Sue get through the whole night with a bunch of people that she wasn't comfortable around. "Why don't you want to join the Belles? Your mama would want you to carry on her legacy."

While the curling iron heated up, Jennie Sue ran a brush through Cricket's hair. "Yes, she would. Just like my grandmother expected Mama to fill her shoes. But I'm just not Belle material. I might have been ten years ago or even six years ago, but not now. I've got an idea—you can join the Belles in my place."

"Not me. Those women intimidate me," Cricket laughed. "Look at us bein' good enough friends that you are offerin' me your place on the Sweetwater Belles."

"Honey, that probably means that we are what they call frenemies these days. I was teasin'. I would only wish that on my worst enemy." Jennie Sue laid the brush aside and picked up the curling iron.

"That bad, huh?"

"Worse." Jennie Sue shivered. "Big bouncy curls or straight?"

"What?"

"Your hair? How do you want it?"

"Curls." Cricket felt more than a little guilty about Jennie Sue styling her hair. "I should be fixin' your hair. How do you do it?"

"What? Fix hair or not fall to pieces right now?"

Cricket pointed at her hair.

"I had to learn. Percy didn't like the way the beauty shop did it, and it had to be perfect—always—not only when we went out or had an event. He had his good points, but somehow they got lost in his controlling nature." Jennie Sue tamed Cricket's hair with a few twists of the curling iron and then twirled the stool around to look at her work. "You have the most unusual shade of green eyes. With just a touch of dark-green eye shadow, they'd pop right out."

"I've always worn blue," Cricket said. "But I was talkin' about you takin' care of everyone else when we should be takin' care of you."

"You are takin' care of me," Jennie Sue said. "I'd be all alone if you and Rick weren't stayin' with me, and if you didn't let me go to the farm, I'd probably be crazy." She picked up a palette of eye shadow from the vanity. "Mind if I try green?"

"Not at all." Cricket couldn't very well tell her that the reason she'd worn blue since they were in school was because that's what Jennie Sue wore all the time.

When Jennie Sue finished, she swung her around to face the mirror. "I applied a little blush to your cheeks."

"Oh. My. Goodness!" Cricket gasped. "I'm almost pretty."

"You are beautiful with or without makeup." Jennie Sue flipped one curl forward over Cricket's shoulder.

Cricket felt the heat rising to her face but could do nothing about it. "I'm just a plain Jane, but you've done wonders."

"You are whatever and whoever your self-confidence allows you to be, Cricket. When you walk into a room, act as if you own the whole house, not just that room. Paste on a smile, even if it's fake, and never tug at your skirt or mess with your necklace. That shows insecurity," Jennie Sue said. "That comes straight from my mother on my way to my first Belle meeting when I was sixteen."

"So the daughters get to go to the meetings?"

Jennie Sue sat down on the end of the bed. "Once a year at Christmas, so that we'd learn the ropes."

"Did the husbands get to go to the meetings?"

"Nope." Jennie Sue shook her head, and not a single curl fell out of place. "They were allowed to attend the July Fourth barbecue here at our place, but that was the extent of their participation in the Belles. You got to remember, though, they started the club when women didn't work and needed women friends so they could bitch and moan about their husbands and relatives."

"And now?"

"Some of them have jobs, but the bitchin' and moanin' stayed the same."

"Then, no, thank you. I'll just be a member of the book club at Amos's store and call that enough. My nerves couldn't handle all the stuff that goes on to be a Belle," Cricket said.

"Tell me something. What changed your mind about me?" Jennie Sue asked.

"Lettie and Nadine did. It just took a little while for what they said to soak in. Again, I'm sorry for being rude."

"So you don't hate me anymore?"

Cricket shook her head and answered honestly, "Not as much as before."

Jennie Sue stood up and straightened a simple gold chain around her neck. "Fair enough."

Cricket rose up off the vanity stool. "Don't mess with your necklace. It shows that you don't have self-esteem."

"Noted." Jennie Sue nodded and smiled at Cricket echoing her words.

Sugar and Mary Lou arrived first again, each carrying a fancy platter with food. Sugar had cute little chicken-salad sandwiches cut in perfect triangles with the crust removed. Mary Lou brought in iced sugar cookies with a fancy *C* monogram on each one. They went straight to the dining room, put their offerings on the table, and then turned to have a group hug with Jennie Sue.

"Oh, darlin', this just breaks our hearts. We've done nothing but weep for two whole days. Charlotte was the very center of the Belles, and we don't know how we'll be able to go on without her." Sugar sniffled.

Mary Lou took a step back and kissed her on the cheek. "You will simply have to fill her shoes. I'm sure you know exactly where her scrapbook is, and you'll keep it up to date. We'll have an induction ceremony at next month's meeting. And who is this?" She turned her attention to Cricket.

"My friend Cricket Lawson. She and her brother are staying with me until tomorrow." Jennie Sue made introductions.

"Are you from New York?" Sugar eyed Cricket from her toes to her hair.

"No, she's from right here in Bloom. I graduated from high school with her. Y'all might remember her father, Richard Lawson. I believe he went to school with my dad and some of you, and he played basketball," Jennie Sue answered.

"Nope, the name doesn't ring a bell," Mary Lou said. "What's the matter with your foot?"

"I fell," Cricket answered. "I'm not sure who's takin' care of who, but we're managing, aren't we, Jennie Sue?"

"You bet we are. Oh, there's the doorbell. Excuse me." Jennie Sue turned to Cricket and said under her breath, "If it gets to be too much, slip out to the porch. There's a bar out there, too."

Escaped that, she thought as she took a deep breath and opened the door to find Belinda with her plate of vegetables and dip.

"Oh, Jennie Sue, how are we going to get through this? Charlotte's such a good friend and a wonderful person and I can't imagine life without her." She leaned in to kiss Jennie Sue on the cheek. "Charlotte does—I mean, did—help with so much." She handed the plate to Jennie Sue and dabbed her eyes with a linen handkerchief. "I just can't think of her in the past tense."

"I may never be able to think that way," Jennie Sue admitted.

Mabel laid a hand on Jennie Sue's shoulder and whispered, "I'll take over the job of manning the door now. I'm finished in the kitchen."

"I'd rather man the door or hide in the corner," Jennie Sue said.

"But that's not what you should do. You go on and visit with everyone. This is a good thing you are doing. It will bring a little closure to a lot of people." Mabel put her hands on Jennie Sue's shoulders and turned her toward the living room. "It's only for an hour or so."

She did what she was told. She mingled among the people, hugging some and shaking hands with others. She caught bits of conversation as she moved around the room shaking hands, giving hugs, and being nice. Folks wondering if she'd be able to hold the oil business together, if Percy would come back and try to win her heart again, what she'd do with the big house, and if she'd still continue with her silly house cleaning jobs.

Finally, after a while, she escaped to the porch. She'd bypassed the bar and headed straight to an empty lounge chair when Cricket reached up and touched her hand. "Hey, aren't you supposed to be playin' nice with all the people?"

"I can't stand any more. Move over and share the lounge with me."

Cricket scooted to one side, and Jennie Sue stretched out beside her, finding comfort in being close to a new friend—one free of the history foaming in the other room.

"Want a beer?" Cricket asked. "I helped myself to a bottle."

"I don't want to get it. Someone might see me, and the party will flow out here," Jennie Sue whispered. "I'd just rather sit here beside you for a while."

Cricket handed her bottle over to Jennie Sue. "We can share."

She took it from her and downed several long gulps. "You're not afraid of my uppity germs?"

"Not if you aren't afraid you'll get cooties from me," Cricket said. "I'm not sure what I expected tonight, but it wasn't this."

She handed the bottle back to Cricket. "Me neither. Most of them aren't even talkin' about Mama or Daddy."

"Someone asked me if you were going to run the company yourself or if you would only be a figurehead," Cricket whispered.

"I haven't let myself think about that. I'm just trying to get through the funeral. What would you do?" Jennie Sue asked.

Cricket took a drink and passed the bottle back to her. "Don't ask me about a decision that big. I might give you the wrong advice. Just this house intimidates the devil out of me. I can't imagine owning it and the cars and a multimillion-dollar oil company."

"Me neither," Jennie Sue sighed.

"I heard one of those Belle ladies fussin' about there not bein' a memorial. She thought it was disgraceful and totally inappropriate," Cricket said. "I thought about tripping her with my crutch."

"Tough. I bet they won't like it when I pass on joining the Belles, either." Jennie Sue finished off the beer and set the bottle on the floor. "Money is not the most important thing in the world. I've proven that these past few weeks."

"But it's nice to have enough that you don't have to worry whether to buy fries with your burger at the café," Cricket told her.

Jennie Sue let that soak in for a few minutes before she slung her legs to the side of the lounge and said, "Let's don't think about pennies and dimes tonight. Let's get through this next half hour. They'll all leave by then, and Rick will be back from the farm pretty soon. I vote that we have a late-night swim in the pool."

She knew he had to harvest. After all, he'd let it go the night before, but she missed him. He steadied her nerves just by standing beside her. This was the last night she planned to stay in the house.

"Can't go swimming. No bathing suit," Cricket said.

"There's plenty in the bathhouse. All sizes and shapes." The thought of skinny-dipping and a picture of the swimming hole flashed through her mind. Then she felt guilty all over again for thinking of that at such a time.

"Then you've got a deal as long as I can stay out here and not have to go back in there with the mob." Cricket grinned.

Jennie Sue sighed. "Mob is right, in more ways than one."

Just as she'd predicted, the house was empty in another half hour. She sent Mabel home with the promise that she'd put away the perishable snacks before she went to bed. "And you stay home tomorrow. If we want something to eat, we'll either eat what's here, cook for ourselves, or go to the café. Besides, I'm going back to my apartment tomorrow, so you don't have to cook for anyone or do much around here."

"No arguments here," Mabel agreed. "I'm so tired, my butt is draggin'. I may not even make it to church tomorrow. I overheard lots of talk about what you intend to do with the company tonight. My advice would be to listen to your heart."

"I intend to do just that, now shoo! Go home and get some rest." Jennie Sue hugged her.

"And don't get in a hurry about anything, darlin'. You need to think about things before you act," Mabel said as she headed out the back door.

"Yes, ma'am," Jennie Sue called out.

Rick came inside seconds after Mabel left. "I stopped to talk to Frank in the garage just as the last of the cars left."

"Hungry?" Jennie Sue asked. "There's lots of food left."

"Yep." He nodded.

"Me, too," Jennie Sue said. "All those people made me nervous, and I couldn't eat. Let's go sit down at the table and have some food. I'll get Cricket in from the porch, and after we eat we're going swimming."

“No bathing suit,” he said.

“No worries. We keep a closet full of them in the bathhouse.”

Rick’s hands began to sweat, and suddenly he didn’t think he could swallow a single bite of food. He’d always worn long-sleeve shirts to cover his scars, only rolling them up halfway to his elbows when it got really hot. Jennie Sue knew he had scars, but she’d only seen the one on his jawline. What was between him and her would be over before it had hardly even gotten started if she saw his body. He needed more time with her before he took this step. He couldn’t go out there in swim trunks—he just couldn’t.

It’s time to come out of your shell. It sounded an awful lot like his father’s voice in his head. *It’s part of you.*

“I can’t,” he whispered.

“Can’t what? Are you hungry? I couldn’t eat with all those people here, so we can have something together.” Jennie Sue took him by the hand and led him to the dining room table.

“I should wash up.” He avoided answering her questions. “I’ll be right back.” He escaped to the restroom, where he spent several minutes staring at his reflection in the mirror and trying to think up a plausible excuse for not swimming.

You are acting like a sophomore with a pimple at prom time. This time it was his mother’s voice in his head. *Jennie Sue has proven to be an amazing, compassionate friend. Get over yourself.*

"Okay," he said. "I guess it's time to swim or drown."

Cricket and Jennie Sue were already eating when he arrived at the table, so he took a seat across from them and picked up a plate. "It all looks good. Where do I begin?"

"With those little chicken sandwiches," Cricket said. "I wonder who made them. They are scrumptious. I've had half a dozen, but they're only bite-size, so it's really not even a whole sandwich."

Jennie Sue reached for another tiny sandwich. "Come on, Cricket. You know who makes these. You work for Elaine. Surely, you've eaten them before. Sugar has been buying them for years, even back when Elaine did some catering for a few choice folks. She also made those cookies and those pinwheel-rollup things with the cream cheese and ham and the little thumbprint cookies. And the vegetable tray and the fruit tray."

"Nope, I had no idea Elaine did anything like this on the side. She should put these on the menu," Cricket said.

"How do you know all this?" Rick asked.

"There's a secret to this kind of thing," Jennie Sue said. "You pay someone else to do the work. Then you put it on a fancy platter and make it look all pretty, and the last thing is to slap a fancy little sticker on the bottom with your name on it so the person can return the plate. Mama's famous for her fried chicken, but she's never stood over a skillet of grease in her life. It comes from Kentucky Fried Chicken in Sweetwater."

"Well, thank you, Elaine, for being such a good cook." Rick loaded up his plate a second time. "Maybe we'd better put off swimming since we're supposed to wait half an hour after eating."

"Drink a beer," Jennie Sue said.

"What?" Cricket raised an eyebrow.

"Proven fact. Eat. Drink at least part of a beer and you won't drown. The bubbles in your stomach will keep you afloat," Jennie Sue answered. "It also works when you're hiding from people, right? And I've been wonderin', is Cricket your real name?"

"It's your name, so you can tell her the story," Rick said.

Cricket rolled her eyes toward the ceiling. "The name on my birth certificate is Edwina Lucinda Velma Lawson. Don't even crack a smile, because it could've been worse. I was named for two grandmothers and Daddy's favorite aunt. But I could've been Beulah Oma Lucille Lawson."

"How did you get Cricket out of that?" Jennie Sue asked.

"When Mama brought me home from the hospital, she told Rick to be gentle with me because I wasn't any bigger than a cricket, and it stuck. Rick gave me the nickname, and thank goodness, no one even remembers all those other names," she answered.

"And I thought Jennifer Susanne was a mouthful." Jennie Sue finished off the last cookie on her plate. "Let's pop the tops of three beers and go swimming. I need something to settle my mind. It's buzzin' around in circles. I never knew that people could ask so many questions. Thank goodness Justin is takin' the business burden off me or I'd be completely overwhelmed."

Rick pushed his chair back. "Think we should clean up this table first?"

"We can do that afterward. All we have to do is put away what's left of the perishable stuff for tomorrow's lunch, then throw a tablecloth over the rest," Jennie Sue said. "Come on. I'll show y'all the way to the bathhouse where we can all change."

"Are we doing something wrong? This feels kind of hypocritical. We were talkin' about the people that came tonight acting like this was a party," Cricket pointed out.

"No, we are not," Jennie Sue declared. "I'm sure the enormity of what lies before me is going to overwhelm me in a couple of days, but I have to focus on one thing at a time to get through this. I want a swim and a beer to unwind. To work the tangles out of my brain and my body. But I have been thinking about doing something for underprivileged folks with part of the inheritance I'll have."

"That doesn't surprise me a bit," Cricket said.

Rick couldn't have denied Jennie Sue anything, up to and including starting a walk across the Sahara with only half a canteen of water. "Then let's go swimming. We'll get through these next two days, and then maybe things will get back to normal."

"I hope so." Jennie Sue slid the doors open out onto the big porch/patio and laced her fingers in Rick's. "Please don't think I'm callous or uncaring for doing something frivolous like going swimming. I just have to deal with this my way."

"Everyone deals with grief in their own way." He squeezed her hand.

He let go of Jennie Sue's hand and darted into the men's side of the bathhouse. He found the closet with a variety of bathing suits and chose a dark-green one. Stripping out of his clothing, he folded each piece neatly and laid it all on a shelf. At least the dark-green suit covered up part of the scar on his leg.

He couldn't make out the words, but he could hear the conversation on the other side of the wall. Cricket would be uncomfortable in a bikini, so he hoped there was something a little more modest over there for his sister. But at the same time, he sure wouldn't mind if Jennie Sue came out wearing a two-piece—the skimpier the better.

He inhaled deeply and let it out slowly, avoided the long mirror on the back of the door, and went outside. Jennie Sue and Cricket appeared in the moonlight almost as quickly, wearing identical black one-piece bathing suits. His pulse raced—his heart threw in an extra beat. No bikini in the world could make Jennie Sue look a bit sexier than that simple suit did.

"Oh, my goodness!" Jennie Sue stopped in her tracks when she saw him.

There it was. The repulsion that he'd been expecting, but he didn't think she'd be so blatant about it. He cringed inside, but he squared his shoulders like a good Army Ranger and got ready for what was coming.

She rushed to his side and touched the biggest scar on his side and then ran her hand down his rib cage to each and every one of them. "Oh, Rick, 'thank you for your service' doesn't begin to cover this. Or this one on your leg, either." His whole body vibrated when she bent forward and touched his leg. "You should wear these proudly, not cover them up. They say that you are a hero."

"That's what I've told him ever since he came home." Cricket dived off the side of the pool into the water. "Let's swim now and not think about scars or sad things."

Rick scooped Jennie Sue up in his arms and

whispered, "Thank you," just before he fell backward into the deep end of the pool with her in his arms.

When they surfaced, she pushed her hair out of her eyes and splashed water in his face. "That was mean. I didn't even have time to get my hair up in a ponytail."

"I'd apologize, but I'm not sorry. You're beautiful with your hair in your eyes."

He swam to the other end, where he propped his elbows on the side and waited for her. Cricket did laps in beautiful form while Jennie Sue made her way to him, swimming underwater the whole way and stopping to kiss the scar on his leg before she surfaced.

"I wasn't shootin' you a line of shit about your scars," she said.

"I wasn't shootin' you a line when I said you were beautiful with messy hair and smeary eye makeup, either," he told her.

"That's hard to believe," she whispered.

"Welcome to the real world, darlin', where we speak the truth and don't put much stock in what other people think." He brushed a strand of hair back behind her ear. "At least, some of us are of that mind. There are those that still thrive on small-town rumors."

"You got that right." Even though her heart was still numb from the shock and the pain, everything made sense.

Chapter Nineteen

Rick took a long, hot shower and crawled into bed that night, but he couldn't sleep. He laced his hands behind his head and, like other folks in town, wondered exactly what Jennie Sue would do about the oil company and all the property. She'd shown that she was strong by taking her own way and making her own decisions, but this had to be overwhelming.

Tomorrow she'd be back in her apartment and he'd be in his house. In his world, things would be back to normal—hers would never be the same. He shut his eyes and replayed every moment he'd had with her.

When a soft knock landed on his door, he sat straight up and was slinging his legs over the side of the bed when Jennie Sue eased it open and peeked inside. "Rick, are you awake?"

"I'm right here," he whispered. "What can I do?"

"Hold me?" she said.

He stood up and met her halfway across the room with open arms. She walked into them and laid her head on his bare chest. He cupped the back of her head with one hand and slipped the other around her waist. "The nights are always tougher than the days."

"I did it pretty much alone when I lost the baby, but this is different," she whispered. "That time I buried myself in schoolwork. Now, there's so many decisions . . ." Her voice trailed off.

He took a step back, tucked both her hands in his, and led her to the bed. She sat down on the edge and then eased back on the pillow where his head had been. The thought of getting into bed with her was more than a little intimidating.

"Maybe we should go down to the living room," he suggested.

She scooted over and rolled to her left side. "This is fine. I just want to go back to that safe place that I remember so I can sleep."

He settled in behind her and gathered her tightly to his chest.

"Like this?" he asked.

It's natural to be aroused with a woman snuggled up against me, he thought. *But this isn't the time or the place. She's too vulnerable.*

"Just like this." She wiggled in closer to him.

Good Lord, let her go to sleep and not realize the effect she's having on me, he prayed for the first time in ages.

Evidently, God heard him, because a soft purrlike snore said that she was out. It took a long time for him to reach the same state.

Jennie Sue reached across the bed to touch Rick when she awoke the next morning, but all she got was a handful of air. She sat up with a start and saw him sitting over beside the window with a book in his hands. He was reading by the light coming in through the window on that rainy morning.

"Good mornin'," she yawned.

He laid the book aside. "Did you sleep well?"

"I did, and thank you again. I thought I was okay after we got out of the pool, but when I got into bed, I remembered the hankie that Daddy gave me just before he left. I lost it, and it brought on more tears."

He moved to sit beside her on the bed. "That's the way grief works. One minute you think you've got it all under control, and then the simplest thing will set you off, and you're a mess again. A month after he passed away, I found Daddy's little notebook where he kept all the phone numbers of places he liked to buy his seed, and just looking at his handwriting tore me up. I bawled like a baby."

"Then I'm not completely insane?"

"No, darlin', you are not." His deep drawl soothed her.

She turned so that she could wrap her arms around Rick's neck. "You are the best thing that ever happened to me."

He tipped up her chin, and before their lips ever even touched, she felt as if she was drowning in his dark-green eyes. The kiss started out as a sweet brushing of lips, then it deepened into a fiery-hot passion.

Jennie Sue pulled away when she heard the bathroom door at the end of the hallway close. She stood up and tugged at the bottom of her nightshirt. "I'd better go on back to my bedroom."

"Jennie Sue, it may be the wrong time to ask, but what are we going to do about this thing between us?"

She bent down and kissed him. "I'm going to hope that it's more than a passing fancy for you."

Cricket was waiting in the dining room when Jennie Sue arrived with Rick right behind her. She barely glanced up as she kept putting cookies in plastic bags. "I can't stand the idea of wasting a single bit of this food."

"Have you had breakfast? I'll be glad to make us bacon and eggs or whatever y'all want," Jennie Sue asked.

"I would love pancakes," Rick said.

"Something neither of us can make unless we use that mix that you just put water in." Cricket kept right on working.

"Pancakes it is. Bacon, sausage, or both?"

"Bacon," they said at the same time.

"What can I do to help?" Rick asked.

"Can you fry bacon?" She nudged him with her shoulder.

"Yes, ma'am."

"Then you can do that while I make the pancakes." She sniffed the air. "Do I smell coffee?"

"I made a pot. Hope that's okay," Cricket answered.

"It's better than okay. It's great. We'll have a cup while we are getting breakfast ready. And while we eat, I want you both to be my sounding board. While I was getting dressed this morning and packing a suitcase of things I want to take to my apartment, I came up with some things I need to bounce off you," she said.

"Ideas about what? You really need to take time to think about everything and not rush, Jennie Sue," Rick said.

"Mabel told me to listen to my heart, so that's what I'm doin'," she replied.

He followed her into the kitchen and asked, "What if this chemistry we have is just a passing fancy for you? You now own a huge company, not to mention this house and property. What if I'm only—"

She turned around and wrapped her arms around his neck. "Rick, what we have has nothing to do with money. It's something deeper than that, something in our hearts. To me, it's not a passing fancy. It's like the seed that you plant in the spring. With some tender care, it could grow into something fruitful."

"I think we can work with that." He kissed her on the forehead. "Now, where's a good cast-iron skillet so I can do my part about gettin' breakfast ready?"

"Under that cabinet." She pointed and then set the electric griddle in the middle of the table.

When he'd fried a pound of bacon and they were all seated, she poured the batter out in six perfect circles. A picture of Percy throwing away the first pancakes she'd made after they were married because they weren't perfectly round flashed through her mind. She quickly hit the mental "Delete" button, determined that she was never going to think about him again.

"Okay, I can already see that those are the lightest pancakes I've ever seen. What's the secret?" Cricket asked.

"I only give out my recipe to people who don't hate me," she answered.

"Okay, okay, I don't hate you anymore." Cricket grinned.

"So are you only my friend because I make good pancakes, because you feel sorry for me, or because I like your brother?" She flipped two pancakes onto Cricket's plate.

"All of the above. When did you start liking Rick?" Cricket asked. "I thought y'all were just friends."

"It's been a slow process. And the secret to good pancakes is beating the egg whites until they are almost like meringue and then folding them in gently. Gives them little air pockets that make the pancakes very light. I'll text you the link to the recipe. I found it on Pinterest." Jennie Sue put two on Rick's plate.

"Oh, my!" Cricket moaned when she took the first bite. "These are fabulous."

Jennie Sue slathered her pancakes with butter and poured syrup over them. Then she flipped the ones on the griddle before she took the first bite.

"I know it's quick, but I want some things settled and off my mind. So I'm askin' Justin to call a meeting for the board of directors and the vice president of the oil company on Monday morning. I know there's a lot of worry about jobs and what's going to happen, and the sooner I can put employees' minds at rest, the better. I am going to sell the company to the highest bidder. Daddy told me a while back that two major oil companies had approached him to buy it, so that shouldn't be a problem. He was ready to retire, himself."

"You sure you're ready to do that? You have a business degree. You could learn to run it yourself," Cricket said.

"I thought about it last night before I went to sleep. I don't want a job that requires that much commitment, so I'm selling it. I feel right about my decision."

"You'll be a multimillionaire," Rick muttered.

"Yes, I will, and the money can sit in the bank until I decide what I want to do with it. And this house is going on the market next week. I do not want to live here," she said.

"Why? It's a beautiful home, and you have a staff here to do all the work," Cricket said. "Granted, it's too big and intimidating for me, but you grew up here. It's your childhood home. Don't do something you will regret."

"It's time for Mabel and Frank to retire. They should've done it years ago. I'm going to ask Justin to set up a severance package that will keep them comfortable and doing anything they want the rest of their lives," she said. "And I'll give the other people who work here a nice bonus with their last paycheck."

"You've got until tomorrow to think about this before you go to that meeting." Rick held out his plate for more pancakes. "You could change your mind."

"Maybe, but I don't think so." Jennie Sue slid the other pancakes off the griddle onto a plate. "When we get finished here, can we go out to the farm? We could take a picnic from the leftovers from last night to the creek."

"If that's what you want," Rick said.

"Not me," Cricket said. "I'm not crutchin' it out that far. Drop me at Lettie's house. Do you mind if I fix up a basket of leftovers to take to her place?"

"Take whatever you like. Why didn't they come around last night?" Jennie Sue asked.

"They were afraid that the Belles might drown them in the pool. It wasn't just your mama that couldn't get along with those two. It was the whole Belle group. When your great-granny started the club, she wouldn't let their mama join it. That could be why Flora did what she did," Cricket explained.

"What a tangled mess." Jennie Sue picked up a piece of bacon and bit off the end. "Perfect. I love it like this. Floppy bacon never did appeal to me, but Daddy loved it."

"So did my dad, but Mama liked crispy," Rick said as he put another two pancakes on his plate. "We could wrap up any leftovers of these with bacon in the middle and take it to the creek for our picnic. I bet they're just as good cold as they are hot."

"Anything would taste good if we eat it by the creek." Just making that much of a decision took a burden off her chest. And the fact that Cricket hadn't gone up in flames when she said that she liked Rick was an added bonus.

Cricket rapped on Lettie's kitchen door and then opened it a crack. "Hello. Anyone home?"

"In the living room. Come on in here and tell us about the party last night. We were hoping you might sneak away and come by or at least call,"

Lettie said. "Get yourself a glass of sweet tea on the way, and bring the pitcher to refill ours."

Cricket set the brown paper bag holding several baggies full of goodies on the cabinet and yelled, "Can't carry this much. Y'all come and help me."

"We forgot that your foot is messed up." Nadine's voice preceded her into the kitchen. "And what is this?"

"I brought the party to you since you couldn't come to it," Cricket said.

Lettie came in right behind her. "I'll take that to the living room. We was sittin' in there, tryin' to decide whether we wanted to make us a fresh tomato sandwich or go to the café for some lunch. It was so crowded after church that I just brought us on home. Now we can put all this out on the coffee table and have us a picnic."

"So start tellin' us about the party while we get things done." Nadine got out the pitcher of tea from the refrigerator and carried it, plus an empty glass, with her. "Come on, girl. I'll give you the recliner, and me and Lettie can take the sofa and spread out all these goodies."

"Well, I think Jennie Sue and I have gotten past the hate stage. She fixed my hair last night and even helped with my makeup. I had no idea that green eye shadow would look so much better on me." Cricket set her crutches to the side and hopped over to the recliner. "And we went swimming after everyone left, and Rick even wore a swimsuit."

"What did Jennie Sue do?" Lettie popped open the bag of leftover chicken salad and the one of pimento-cheese sandwiches and helped herself to a couple of each.

"She didn't freak out. And this morning at breakfast, she admitted that she liked him. I hope he's not in for a broken heart. When you think about the difference in what she's inherited—well, it could change things." Cricket took a sip of her tea while they opened all the lids on the leftover containers.

"Go on." Nadine crossed forks with Lettie's when she tried to get a bite of the shrimp cocktail. "You can have that chicken stuff. I like this better."

"Too bad. I'm having at least one bite of the shrimp," Lettie said. "Now tell us, who all was there, and what did they talk about?"

"I didn't know a lot of them, but . . ." Cricket went on to talk about the party atmosphere, and what all she'd heard while everyone there ignored her.

"Where's Rick and Jennie Sue now?" Nadine asked.

"At the farm. They took a picnic to the creek. Jennie Sue said bein' there calms her down."

"Her granny Baker was a farm girl," Lettie said with a bob of her head. "So what's going to happen to the oil company? Is she going to run it?"

"Not a word can be said outside this room." Cricket went on to tell them what Jennie Sue planned to do.

"Bless her darlin' heart." Nadine wiped a tear from her cheek. "That she's thinkin' of doin' something like that for Mabel shows that her heart is in the right place."

"And what's she going to do with all that money if she does sell it all?" Lettie asked.

"She says that she has a plan. I don't think she'd go back to New York, but she might go to one of those third-world countries and help the women and children by building clinics and schools," Cricket answered.

Lettie set her mouth in a firm line. "What are you going to do if she asks you and Rick to go with her?"

Both of Cricket's palms shot up. "No, no, no! I'm not cut out for a clinic in a third-world country. I can't even look when the doctor has to give me a shot, and I'm sure not smart enough to teach if she decided to build a school or something like that."

"What if Rick goes with her?" Lettie asked. "He seems to be pretty struck with her."

"Then I guess I'll hire a good-lookin' feller to help me run the farm." Cricket winked. "And maybe he'll like women who are curvy instead of skinny as a rail, and we'll get married and have lots of babies."

"Sounds like a book I just finished. Someone left it in my lending library out in front of the house. You should read it, Cricket. You might get some bedroom pointers. It gets pretty damn hot in places. I got hot flashes so bad I almost called Lettie to bring me one of her pills."

"I ain't had a hot flash in years"—Lettie popped her on the knee—"but I would like to read that book to see what one feels like."

"You'll have to get in line," Cricket said.

Chapter Twenty

It's not a memorial. It's just a gathering of friends. These are the people who didn't get to come to the one with the Belles and the other folks. We want to be there for you," Lettie said.

"Promise you won't go to a lot of trouble," Jennie Sue said.

"We promise," Nadine told her. "You get a good night's rest up and sleep in as long as you like. It's just Amos, the Lawsons, us, and maybe the preacher if he hasn't made other plans. That's all."

"Okay." Jennie Sue nodded even though she really would rather have spent the afternoon at the farm with Rick.

"So how did the picnic at the creek go?" Lettie asked.

"It was amazing. So peaceful."

"We'd like a few more details than that," Nadine pressed her.

"A lady doesn't kiss and tell." Jennie Sue grinned.

"So there was kissin'?" Lettie popped the footrest down on her recliner and leaned forward.

"A couple of times, but that's all. He took a quilt from the house, and we had lunch, a long nap, a few kisses, and then we gathered in the garden stuff," she said.

Lettie put the footrest back up. "If I'd gotten a feller that handsome out by a creek on a summer mornin' at your age, I believe I could've done better than that."

"You always have to dredge up the memories," Nadine told her. "So you like him for more than a friend?"

"I do, but this whole relationship thing is pretty new, so I'm afraid if I talk about it, I'll jinx it for sure. Right now, I'm going to take what I brought from the house up to the apartment and unpack it. I may need y'all to help me when it's time to go back out there and go through personal things," she said.

"Anytime," Nadine said. "We're here for you, and I'm sure Mabel is, too."

Jennie Sue stood up from the sofa and glanced around the small living room. She liked a small house so much better than that huge thing out there in the country. When she built her own place, it was going to be just a house, maybe with a creek running close by. "Good night, ladies. I'll see you tomorrow afternoon, and thank you for everything you've done for me."

"It's been our pleasure, darlin'," Nadine said.

Lettie nodded in agreement. "If you need anything or can't sleep tonight, you just call me, and we'll get out the cards or dominoes."

"If you do that, y'all better come and get me," Nadine fussed.

"Sure thing." Jennie Sue waved goodbye, knowing that if she couldn't sleep, she'd call Rick before she called anyone.

When the lawyer, Justin, had laid out the basics of the will, he'd eyed Jennie Sue like she was a piece of ripe fruit. Several times Rick had caught his eyes roaming from her toes and going all the way up to her eyebrows. It didn't take a rocket scientist to know that he liked what he saw. And it sure didn't take one to know that every man in West Texas was going to be on her doorstep when they found out just how rich she was.

That was what was on his mind as he parked the truck beside the Cadillac at Lettie's place. Just seeing the car sitting there reminded him she was out of his league, no matter what she'd said about them being in the first stages of a relationship. That could simply be grief talking—the need to have someone to hang on to until she could get past it.

An ironclad guarantee for happily ever after did not come with life. Life simply happened. A person accepted his fate and moved on. Those were his mother's words, and that day as Rick got out of his truck, he understood the meaning more perfectly than ever before.

"Isn't that Frank's truck?" Cricket asked. "I didn't know they were going to be here."

"Yep, guess the party grew a little bit," Rick said.

"Are you okay? You've been pretty quiet all mornin'." Cricket tucked the crutches under her arms, and he shut the door for her.

"I'm fine, just a little worried about Jennie Sue," he said.

"Hey, Rick, come sit on the porch and join me and Frank while the ladies put the finishing touches on the food," Amos called out.

He hung back and let Cricket crutch inside the house before he sat down on the top porch step. "Looks like it might rain."

"Be a good thing for the crops, wouldn't it?" Frank asked.

"Oh, yeah! We never complain about rain this time of year." Rick glanced up at the kitchen window to see Jennie Sue.

He waved, and she returned the gesture. They'd been up until almost dawn, talking on the phone because she couldn't sleep. He'd offered to come to her apartment and had asked her out to the farm, but she'd said just hearing his voice was enough.

"Are you lookin' at Jennie Sue?" Amos asked.

"Yes, sir, I was, but she's disappeared now," he answered.

"Did you hear that she might sell the company and the house and run off to some third-world country to set up clinics for the needy folks?"

Amos asked. "Someone told Lettie that she would be leaving by the end of the month. I'd sure hate to see that happen. She's such good help at the bookstore and, well . . . ," Amos sighed. "I'd kind of thought maybe I'd sell it to her, and carry the note myself. I think Iris would be proud for her to have it."

"You goin' with her on that crazy trip?" Frank asked. "Me and Mabel wouldn't worry about her so much if you was around to protect her. You never know what might happen off in them places. You hear about kidnappin' and such on the news all the time."

"Jennie Sue hasn't mentioned anything like that to me," Rick said. There was no way he could go with her, even if the rumors were really true. Before he died, Rick's father had made him promise that he would take care of Cricket. But then, he couldn't see his sister leaving Bloom to go halfway around the world, live in a hut, and work with underprivileged people.

"Lettie is going to try to talk her out of it. I figure she'd be more likely to go back to New York City if she goes anywhere," Amos said.

"I doubt that happens—not for a little while, anyway. She's got a lot of stuff to settle before she goes anywhere," Rick answered.

"Nadine says that she's goin' into that meeting tomorrow, and turnin' it all over to her lawyer and then she'll be gone by the end of the week," Frank said. "Me and Mabel are goin' to miss her so much."

"I wouldn't put too much stock in rumors. They're about as trustworthy as that weatherman who said today was going to be sunny and hot," Rick said.

"Well, he got half of it right. It is hot and humid. Hope them clouds comin' in from the southwest ain't just teasin' us," Amos laughed.

Rick felt like a stone was tied to the bottom of his heart. But if Jennie Sue had confided in someone that she had a desire to do something meaningful with her life, like help out overseas, it might make things easier for him. Seeing her about town and knowing that they were worlds apart would be tougher than remembering the amazing time he'd had with her.

Something wasn't right. Jennie Sue could feel it in her heart, but she couldn't put a finger on what it was. She paced the floor in her tiny apartment and finally went out onto the balcony and searched for constellations in the sky.

She went back over the day and finally pin-pointed the exact time that things began to go downhill. It had been when Rick came inside the house after sitting on the porch with Frank and Amos. From then on, he'd been standoffish and quiet.

Finally, she picked up her phone and sent a text: Are we all right?

A reply came back immediately. Are we?

She hit the icon to call him.

He picked up on the first ring. "What's goin' on?"

"Are you mad at me for something? You hardly spoke at the lunch, and then you and Cricket left, and you didn't even say goodbye, much less give me a hug or a kiss. And when I told you that I wanted to go to the garden with you, you said that you had it covered," she said.

"I couldn't kiss you in front of all those people," he stated, almost as if he were reading from a speech, it was so flat.

"Are you ashamed of me?" she asked.

"No, I am not, but think about it, Jennie Sue. We can't live in a pipe-dream bubble our whole lives. I am who I am and you are who you are. We can't change that."

"Why would either of us want to change?"

"Think about it for a few days, and then we'll talk again. Good night, Jennie Sue," he said, and the phone went dark.

She went inside, stripped out of her clothing, and took a long, cool shower before she crawled into the middle of the bed and sat cross-legged. "Think about what?" she said aloud.

Her decision to sell the company. Suddenly, she had misgivings about that. Should she try to keep it and learn the ropes? Percy had put a fear into her that she couldn't do anything right. What would happen if she made mistakes that cost the company millions, or worse yet, cost people their jobs? Could she live with that?

The rumors about her leaving Bloom—the only difference between one place and another was the population and terrain. Desert? Mountains? Prairie? Rolling hills? What made one area better than the other was family and friends. She liked her new friends, and she had no intention of leaving Bloom.

She was rich now and Rick was still a farmer: That was what she was supposed to think about, wasn't it? She should have seen this coming.

She fell back on her pillow and pulled the edge of the chenille bedspread around her body. When she opened her eyes the next morning, she picked up the pillow she'd been hugging and threw it across the room, knocking a can of hair spray and her makeup bag off the dresser.

"Dammit, Rick! I don't like waking up without you," she muttered as she got out of bed and retrieved the pillow. "If you're being stubborn because of money, I'll give away every damn dime to charity."

She talked to herself as she got dressed, went down the stairs, and all the way to Lettie's, where she rapped on the kitchen door.

"Come on in," Lettie called out. "I was hoping you might come by this mornin'."

Jennie Sue got a whiff of fresh cinnamon and coffee blended together when she entered the house. Lettie motioned toward the table. "Pour a cup and have a seat. I just took three nice slices of french toast from the skillet, and the warm maple syrup is on the table."

"You're goin' to put a hundred pounds on me." Jennie Sue refilled Lettie's cup and then poured hers.

"You need a good breakfast before you go to the bookstore." She pulled out a chair and sat down across from Jennie Sue. "I've got news. Amos told Frank out on the back porch yesterday that he'd love to sell the bookstore to you. He thinks Iris would be happy if you owned it but that he wouldn't sell it to anyone else. But me and Nadine told Mabel that was silly, because your days of cleaning houses and working at a bookstore were probably at an end. If you work at the oil business, you'll set your own salary, and if you cash in, why would you ever sell used books?"

"Happiness isn't measured in dollar bills," Jennie Sue said between bites.

"Nope, it sure ain't. If it was, there'd be a helluva lot of unhappy people in the world." Lettie took a sip of her coffee. "So the rumors are all untrue, then? You've made up your mind to stay here, and you aren't moving away to set up clinics for folks?"

"What are you talking about?" Jennie Sue asked.

"You mentioned doing something for underprivileged folks, and well . . ." Lettie shrugged. "You know how gossip is around here."

"I have made up my mind to stay right here," Jennie Sue answered. Rick Lawson had better get used to the idea, because she wasn't going anywhere.

"And you don't have a meeting with the directors this morning?"

Jennie Sue took a sip of coffee. The taste of good strong coffee mixed with cinnamon and warm syrup was too good for words. "That part is true."

"You decided what you're going to say to all of them?"

"Pretty much," Jennie Sue answered. "I'm going to think it all over one more time before I walk into that meeting."

"Honey, you do know you will have to clean out that house if you decide to sell it, right?"

"I know, and it won't be easy going through Mama and Daddy's personal stuff, but I can work on it a little at a time. It's past time for Mabel and Frank to retire, and they'll both think they have to keep workin' if I live out there. The first order of business when I go into that meeting is that I'm going to make sure they have a severance package that will take care of them the rest of their lives. They've given their lives to my family for years. It's time for them to enjoy life without having to work every day."

Lettie laid a hand on her shoulder. "You are a good person."

"Thank you. Please keep that between us until I get the details lined out with the lawyer. Now on to a different subject. Did you notice how quiet Rick was yesterday?"

" 'Course I did. I figured you two were arguing about something. But Frank told Mabel that he didn't say much out on the porch. Maybe he's worried that you'll really take off halfway around the world, and he won't ever see you again." She lowered her voice to a whisper. "He's got a thing for you, you know."

"We're the only two people here. Why are you whispering?" Jennie Sue glanced around the room.

"You never know who's listenin' in on that phone you carry around with you. Could be that's where all these rumors got started. There might be one of them roaches inside it," Lettie said.

"Roaches?" Jennie Sue frowned.

"Bugs," Lettie said.

"I see." Jennie Sue bit back a grin. "I should be going. The meeting starts in half an hour. Thanks for breakfast and for listening. I'll call as soon as I'm back in the bookstore, and you and Nadine can come down for a visit."

"I'll already know what happened. I heard they've hired Elaine's cousin to serve finger foods, and she'll keep her mama informed. Her mama will call Elaine, and I've made a deal with her to call me. So don't say nothing you don't want repeated."

"Small towns. Sometimes they're great, but other times not so much," Jennie Sue sighed.

"Got to love 'em no matter what, though, don't you?" Lettie called after her as she left by the back door.

Chapter Twenty-One

As she was walking out the door, Rick's truck came to a screeching stop not a foot behind her mother's car, where she'd parallel-parked it against the curb. She was so happy that he'd come to give her a little bit of last-minute moral support that she didn't care if he buckled the rear end of the Caddy. But it wasn't Rick who crawled out of the driver's seat—it was Cricket.

Disappointment filled her heart but was soon replaced by worry. "Is something wrong? Why are you driving? Is Rick hurt?" The questions tumbled out of her mouth faster than her pulse.

"I didn't figure on it hurting to pump the brakes and almost smashed into your car. Nothing is wrong. I'm driving because Rick is a stubborn-headed jackass today. He stormed off to the creek when I told him that we should at least check on you this morning. So I got in the truck myself, and here I am. Are you on the way to the big meeting?" Cricket asked.

Relief, pure and simple, even if Rick was a jackass, swept over her. He could get over his pissy mood, but being hurt or even dead was a different thing altogether. "Yep. You want to go with me?"

"I'm not dressed for that. Besides, I'd be in

the way, and you don't really want me there, do you?" She paused at the last part.

"Yes, you are. No, you won't be, and yes, I do." Jennie Sue opened the passenger door to the Cadillac for her. "When the gossip starts the minute I walk out of the company, I'll need a witness to repeat exactly what I decided. Weren't you the one who snapped a dozen pictures of me getting off the bus on the day I came back to Bloom?"

"Twenty-two, but I deleted the ones that were blurry," Cricket answered as she handed her crutches to Jennie Sue and got into the car. "You are welcome."

"See, you were my friend before you even knew you were." Jennie Sue slammed the door shut. Cricket gave her confidence and strength to stand up to the board of directors and do things her way.

"I wasn't really your friend when I deleted the pictures," Cricket said as soon as Jennie Sue was in the driver's seat and had turned on the AC. "I just didn't want anyone to think I was a bad photographer."

"You are full of crap, Cricket Lawson."

"No, I'm not, but my brother sure is this mornin'. You might change your mind about likin' him when he gets in moods like this," she said.

"Is that very often?" Jennie Sue asked. Not

even Rick being in a bad mood could make her not like him, but it might make her argue with him.

"Not so much lately, but when he first got home, they came on a daily basis. I thought he was making big progress until this morning," she answered.

The car didn't even have time to cool down when Jennie Sue pulled over to the "Reserved for D. Baker" spot in the parking lot. She retrieved Cricket's crutches from the back seat and handed them to her when she hopped out of the car on one foot.

"You're getting pretty good at that," Jennie Sue said.

"Can't wait to get my boot on and throw these things away. They're death on the underarms." Cricket got them into position. "I hope they've got an elevator."

"I thought I'd get behind you and push you up the stairs." Jennie Sue's voice went high and squeaky with nerves.

"Don't know about you, but I've got the jitters about going with you into the Baker castle, so don't joke around about it."

Jennie Sue swung the door open for her. "Elevator is straight ahead, and it opens right into the conference room. And between us sisters, I'm terrified, but I don't intend to let anyone know it."

"I'm not your sister," Cricket protested.

"But I'm the one who took you to the hospital, remember?" Jennie Sue pushed the button for the elevator and tapped her fingers on the wall while they waited.

"You really are nervous, aren't you?" Cricket asked as they waited for the elevator door to open.

"I vowed when Percy left that I'd never let anyone make me tense like that again. This isn't the same, but . . ." She stepped into the elevator and pushed the second-floor button when Cricket was inside.

"He must've been a devil to live with," Cricket said.

"He was fine when everything was perfect, but when it wasn't, he was a basket case. His therapist said he had the worst case of control issues she'd ever seen. I don't ever have to be perfect again."

Cricket's eyes started at her sandals and traveled up to her hair. "I can see that."

"Disappointed in the way I'm dressed?" Jennie Sue asked.

"Nope. I'm glad you are being yourself," Cricket answered.

The doors opened before Cricket could answer, and at least twenty sets of eyes tracked them. The room went so quiet and still that Jennie Sue wondered if they'd all been struck dead and simply hadn't fallen down yet.

"Hello, everyone. This is my friend Cricket Lawson. I asked her to accompany me today," Jennie Sue said.

"Honey, we don't allow extra people in these meetings," Lawrence O'Reilly, the vice president, said. "Your friend can wait in my office just down the hall."

"Why?" Jennie Sue asked.

"Because we will be discussing things of a sensitive nature." He looked over the top of his glasses at her as if she were a child.

"Then why are the caterers allowed to stay in here?" Jennie Sue asked. "I do believe this is my company now. Here, Cricket, you sit right here." She pulled out the seat at the head of the table and motioned for Cricket to sit down. "Where is Justin?"

The lawyer came in from a side door. "I'm right here. Needed to print a new copy of one of the papers. Shall we all sit down and begin?"

"You are sitting in my chair." Lawrence glared at Cricket.

"You won't be stayin', so it doesn't matter," Jennie Sue said and waited until Justin was seated just to Cricket's left before she took a place across the table from him. He was the one she wanted to talk to, not the other people.

"Okay, Jennie Sue, you need to start signing papers at the orange tabs. These are simply saying that you are receiving the company, your parents' checking account, the stock portfolio, and their savings. All in all, it's merely transference of everything they owned into your name, as stated in the will."

She spent the next fifteen minutes signing her name and then stood up. "I want to thank all of you for your loyal service to this company. Now you can all leave, because I'm calling an executive meeting with Justin. You can wait in your offices until he calls you to return. At that time he will tell you my decisions."

"But—" Lawrence started.

"No buts," Jennie Sue said before he could go on. "I've made up my mind, and I won't be long. The caterers can stay in the office with you until I finish, and then they can come back and y'all can have finger foods while Justin explains my plan."

Lawrence's lips set in a tight line in his big, round face as he stormed out of the conference room. "I told all of you that she was crazy."

"That might not have been a wise move," Justin said. "He's already putting out feelers for another position, because he says your lack of big business sense is going to be the downfall of this company."

"I'm sure it would be. So get your notebook out and start writing. Number one. I expect that most of the business will be concluded in six weeks, tops, other than the sale of the company. There will be audits and all kinds of things I don't even know about that will take a while."

"Whoa!" He threw up both hands defensively. "Selling the company? This quick? That's a really rash decision, Jennifer."

"Didn't I just sign papers saying all of this belongs to me?" she asked.

"Yes, but you need some time to grieve and to think about what you are about to do," he answered.

She folded her arms over her chest. "I can always get another lawyer if you don't want to take care of my business."

He took out a yellow legal pad and poised a pen above it. "Go on."

"My house is for sale. I'm asking Mabel and Frank to stay on for one month. That's how long I'm giving myself to clear out what I want. Then your job is to hire an auction company to take out the rest of the stuff or to offer the property as is. I really don't care how that part is taken care of."

"I've heard that millennials are sizing down from what their parents and grandparents thought were heirlooms." He talked as he wrote notes.

"I'm of the same opinion. It's all just stuff. I will be living a simpler life. The next item is that I want to give Frank and Mabel a really good severance package that includes insurance and a paycheck to equal four times what they make in a month, plus Frank can have Daddy's new truck," she said. "Set up a fund for that, however you do it."

Justin nodded. "Next?"

"Daddy told me two years ago that Texas Red had approached him more than once with an offer to buy the company. Mama wouldn't have any part of it, and since she basically held the purse strings, he couldn't do it. But he was ready to retire. So contact them and sell them the company at a fair price. If they make noises like they want it for a fraction of what it's worth, then put it on the market."

"Okay, but please, please, wait at least six months before you do this." The color faded from Justin's face, and he looked like he might faint right there in the conference room.

"I have thought about it, and this is what I want. You can advise me through the process, and when it's done, I will want your input along with my CPA's to help me decide where and how to invest the money. Next, I want whoever buys the company to either retain the employees that are here or else give them at least six months' salary and benefits to last until they can find something else—that includes Lawrence, even though he's a son of a bitch."

Justin laughed loudly. "That he is, but he's a smart businessman. What next?"

"Are the savings accounts and checking accounts available to me at this time?" she asked.

"Yes, they are," Justin said.

"Okay, that's enough for me to buy the bookstore."

"Why would you do that?" he gasped.

"I like to work there," she answered. "Oh, and I want you to hire a carpenter to go over to Lettie's place and measure that little lending-library box beside her mailbox. Then I want an ad put in the *Bloom Weekly News* saying that all a person has to do to get one like that in the color of their choice is to come into my bookstore and fill out a form. As I get the completed papers, the carpenter can build and install them."

"Again, why?"

"Because that's a dream of Rick's, and he is my friend," Jennie Sue answered.

"What else?" Justin asked.

"That's enough for today. If I think of anything else—I need your card. I don't have you on speed dial like Daddy did. His office isn't to be touched by anyone. I'll be cleaning that out before I do anything else." Her confidence was building with every single argument. "I don't want anyone to go through his computer or his other things, understood?"

"Yes, ma'am," Justin said. "Is that all?"

"For today. I'm sure I'll think of smaller things along the way. When I do, I'll call, or when you have news about the sales, then let me know. No doubt about it, we'll be in close touch. You can call them in here and relay what I'm doing now. Cricket and I won't be stayin'. We're having milkshakes at the Main Street Café. You will let me know about Texas Red as soon as you get in touch with them, right?"

"I'll talk to them tomorrow morning. Until the papers are all signed, it will be business as usual, right?" Justin said.

"That's right, with Lawrence running things. He's a good vice president, and I'm sure he'll manage things fine," she said.

Cricket got to her feet and picked up her crutches. Jennie Sue followed her to the elevator and pushed the "Down" button. The doors opened immediately, and Jennie Sue let Cricket go inside before her.

"I can't believe you just did that," Cricket said.

Jennie Sue leaned against the elevator wall and sucked in big lungfuls of breath. "I couldn't have gotten through it without you, Cricket. Every time Justin argued, I just thought, *What would Cricket do?*"

"Hey, don't fool yourself. I would've folded if he'd glared at me like he did you." Cricket shivered.

The doors opened, and they stepped out of the elevator and headed toward the door. "I'm glad it's done," Jennie Sue said.

"Do you realize what you are giving up? You could be the head of this company. You could live in that house and never have to worry about pickin' beans again. And what if the new company brings in a whole new crew? Bloom depends on the jobs that this place offers."

Jennie Sue helped Cricket into the car and then got into the driver's seat. "Pickin' beans is exactly why I made those decisions. I want a simple life. And I hope that the new company will recognize good help when they see it and keep most of them on. Now, do you want to go back to the café when the doctor releases you, or will you come to work for me at the bookstore?"

"You are offering me a job?" Cricket's voice shot up several octaves.

"I was going to ask Amos about a story hour two days a week through the summer for the little kids. But now that I will own the store, I realize I'll need help." Jennie Sue made plans as she drove toward the café.

"I can't believe you'd be willin' to work with me every day."

"Why?" Jennie Sue snagged a parking place in front of the café. "We're both up-front and honest, and that makes for good business partners."

"You'll own it. I'll be an employee, not a partner," Cricket said.

"I'll make you a full partner if you agree to help me."

"I'll think on it until I get a doctor's release and you actually buy the store," Cricket said.

Jennie Sue got out and held Cricket's crutches until she hopped up on the curb and got them situated. When they entered the café, the silence that greeted them was almost as deafening as the company conference room's had been an hour before.

Then Amos waved from the back of the place and headed their way. Cricket chose the booth closest to the door as chatter started up again and set her crutches against the wall. Jennie Sue took the other side from her, and Amos pulled up a chair to the end.

"So how did it go?"

"My lawyer will be calling you in the next day or so to ask about buying the bookstore," she said. "I hope you were serious."

"Well, hot damn!" Amos yelled. "Iris is smilin' down from heaven. I know she is. I'll make you a real good deal." His face went from smiling to serious. "You're not doin' this and then hirin' someone to run it, are you?"

"No, sir. I intend to be there most of the time, but I have asked Cricket to work with me and buy into the store as my partner. One or both of us will be there all the time. I might leave a little early every now and then during the summer to pick a few beans." She winked.

"Then tell that lawyer I'm ready to deal." He pushed up out of the chair and headed back to the table of elderly men.

Jennie Sue leaned over and whispered, “That’s one bit of news that Amos gets to spread before the caterers do.”

“Pinch me. I think I’m in a dream right now,” Cricket said.

Jennie Sue reached across the table and pinched her on the arm.

“Ouch. That was mean,” Cricket yelped.

“Proves you aren’t dreamin’.” Jennie Sue’s heart felt lighter than it had in months.

Elaine came over, took their order, and was on her way to the kitchen when Rick stormed inside. It didn’t take a genius to know that his tomato-red face wasn’t due to sunburn. There went the happy mood that Jennie Sue had been enjoying.

“What in the hell do you mean, takin’ the truck? You aren’t supposed to be driving,” he hissed when he stopped by their booth.

“I told you I was coming to town, and you were too stubborn to bring me, so I drove. I did fine until I braked and nearly rear-ended Jennie Sue’s Caddy,” she said. “Sit down and cool off. How’d you get to town, anyway?”

Lettie arrived right behind him, looked around, and slid into the booth beside Cricket. “I drove out there and gave him a ride. I needed some strawberries. What are y’all havin’? I could use an order of sweet-potato fries. What do you want, Rick?”

"Nothing. I'm going home. I've got work to do," he growled.

Jennie Sue caught his eye, but he looked away. If he wanted to play that way, then she'd let him—but not for long. If he didn't come around by the next day, it would be time to pay the fiddler, as Mabel used to say.

"I've been to the meeting. Aren't you even going to ask me about it?" she said.

"I don't give a damn about the meeting. Come on, Cricket." He turned around and headed outside.

"I've ordered a milkshake, and I'm not leaving until I finish it," she said.

"Then you can walk." He left without another word to any of them.

"I'll bring her home," Jennie Sue yelled. "Want us to bring you a burger for lunch?"

He didn't even glance their way as he passed the diner window, but a few minutes later, his truck rumbled down Main Street.

"Jackass. I thought he was makin' progress, but he's acting just like he did when he first came home," Cricket said.

"He is, honey. He just don't know how to handle it." Lettie patted her on the hand. "Give him some space."

I'll give him space, Jennie Sue thought. *But not for long.*

Chapter Twenty-Two

After another sleepless night of wondering if she'd done the right thing and if she'd regret the decisions she'd made and whether Rick was still angry, Jennie Sue made it to the bookstore at exactly nine o'clock to find Amos already there.

"Good mornin'," he said entirely too cheerfully for that time of day. "Coffee is made and there's doughnuts in the office. Ledgers are all out and on the desk. Never could figure out that damn computer even after I bought one, so that part is on you. Combination to the safe is written on the first page of the ledger. All the keys to the place are over there by the cash register."

"What are you doing, Amos?" She frowned.

"Selling you the store." He grinned. "When Justin gets all the paperwork in order, call me. I talked to him last night, and we settled on a fair price."

"And that is?" She was suddenly fully awake, her mind running in circles.

"He'll call you later, but don't fuss—Iris told me to do it this way."

"And how's that?"

"When I thought about the price, I didn't feel peace until I got to the right number. Sometimes it takes a while for her to get through my thick skull. I'm happy you have the store, and so is she. I'll pop in every few days, and if you have any questions, you can always call me," he said. "Now hug me and don't argue with the way I'm doing this."

She wrapped her arms around him. "Thank you, Amos. There's two places that I've been truly happy. One is out on the Lawson farm. The other is in this store."

"You are so welcome." He took a step back, looked around the store, and said, "I can't help but wonder what all those lending libraries will do to the business. And to the library as well. Folks might stop coming to buy or check out books if they can just grab one on the street corner."

"They'll make both businesses even better," she said. "Because they will teach people to love to read, and that will bring them into the store and to the library for the authors that they like. I'm thinking of putting up a little section of brand-new books, too."

"Iris really is smiling." He waved as he left the store.

A moment of instant panic set in. She went straight to the office, poured a cup of coffee, and called Lettie. "Guess what just happened?" Her voice sounded shaky in her own ears.

"Amos turned the store over to you, and you can't clean for me and Nadine anymore. Don't worry, honey, we saw this coming. One of Elaine's cousins has agreed to come work for us. I'm sure she won't do things like you, but that's all right. We can live with a little less than perfect."

Jennie Sue took a sip of coffee. "The other shoe is going to drop. This is all too good."

"Nadine and I'll be down there in thirty minutes, and we'll talk. I've heard at least twenty stories this morning about what went on in that meeting yesterday," Lettie said. "And we've got some confessions to make of our own."

Had she really made the decisions that she had? That was what was on Jennie Sue's mind as she waited on Lettie and Nadine. If she decided to back out of selling the company and the house, she could always sell the store to Cricket.

But if the books on a small business like this scare you, what's a multimillion-dollar company going to do? Mabel's voice was in her head as she picked up a chocolate doughnut.

"I went too fast, didn't I?" she said aloud.

No, you didn't. You listened to your heart, and I'm proud of you. This time it was Dill's voice. *Do what makes you happy, and tell the rest of the world to go to hell. Life is short. Live it the way you want to, baby girl.*

She sat down at the desk and opened the ledger. Other than the fact that it was on paper and not a computer screen, it wasn't so different from the mock-ups that she'd worked on in her online classes. Covered with dust, the laptop sat over on the end of the oversize desk. She flipped it open and turned it on to see what programs had been installed. Nothing but the basic things that came on the computer—no wonder Amos couldn't figure out what to do with his bookkeeping.

She went back to the ledger, and right there on a sticky note in spidery handwriting was the number for a CPA. Jennie Sue poked the numbers into her cell phone, and a lady answered on the second ring.

"Good morning, this is Drummond CPA service, Annie speaking. What can I do for you today?"

"I'm Jennie Sue Baker and—"

The lady butted in before she could finish. "Amos has already called me. I will be glad to continue to do your books. But I hear that you are really smart, so you might just want to invest in a program and take care of them yourself."

"If you do them, I'll have more time to do what I want," Jennie Sue said.

"Okay, then, I like to have them quarterly, by the first of the month, so I can get your taxes ready every three months. I'm in Sweetwater," Annie said.

"I see your card stuck under the sticky note. So you'll want them on the first of September. Do you want the journey tapes for the month, also?"

"You *are* smart," she said. "Yes, the tapes from the cash register and the ledger and for goodness' sakes, let's get this stuff on the computer as soon as possible—then you can simply email me the whole thing."

"I agree," Jennie Sue said. "By the time everything is due again in January, I'll have it transferred."

After goodbyes, she'd just gotten off the phone with Annie when the bell rang in the front of the store. She picked up her lukewarm coffee and hurried that way. Lettie and Nadine had both already reached the sofa, and one look at their faces said something was terribly wrong.

"I don't think I can take any bad news." She slumped down in a chair.

"Did your first thoughts go to Rick?" Nadine asked.

Jennie Sue nodded. "He hasn't called, and I've been worried about him."

Lettie wrung her hands. "Well, it's not him, but Cricket says he's still an old bear, so she's stayin' out of his way. It's us, and we don't even know where to begin."

"At the beginning." Jennie Sue figured that they were going to offer to keep the bookstore for her on Thursdays and Fridays if she would clean for them.

"It all started a long time ago," Nadine said.

Looked like it wasn't going to be a problem

with the house cleaning business after all, and it wasn't Rick or Cricket. Jennie Sue's heart and pulse slowed down to normal.

"Oh, we don't have to go back to the first chapter of Genesis, when God created dirt," Lettie fussed. "Everyone in town knows that we have an interest in Texas Red."

"That's where all that money comes from, but they don't know how deeply we are into it. We own a major percentage of the stock there, and we've tried to buy Baker Oil for years, mostly because we were enemies of the Wilshires. Your lawyer called our CEO this morning. We don't feel right buying it without tellin' you because of all the past problems with the families."

"And you are our friend, so you should know," Nadine said.

"I knew you weren't poor, but I'd forgotten about your family and Texas Red. I remember Daddy talking about it when the company was mentioned in oil-magazine articles." Jennie Sue stumbled over the words.

"We inherited the shares when our parents died. Baker Oil and Texas Red were started the same year. Our parents bought into one, and the Wilshires into the other," Lettie said. "Our parents didn't believe in spoiling kids with material things, so all three of us girls worked."

"And, just like you, we like a simple life, but we do a lot of good with what we have. Scholarships at the Bloom school for girls who can't go to college without help—Texas Red money built the library in town. I'm not braggin', but just wantin' you to know some of what we do, so you won't . . ." Lettie had wrung the handkerchief in her hands so much that it was nothing but a knot.

"Your friendship means more to us than buyin' Baker Oil. We'll back off if you have a single problem with it." Nadine finished the sentence for her sister.

"Would you buy a watermelon from me if I had a vegetable stand on the side of the road? Would you buy a book in my store?" Jennie Sue asked.

"That's kind of an irrelevant question," Lettie said. "But of course we would. We already buy watermelons from Rick that you probably helped harvest, and we'll always buy used books in here because they are cheaper than buying new."

"Exactly. Watermelons, books, companies. They are all just things and should never come between friends. Buy Baker Oil if you want to expand. Tell the whole world that you did. Let's put an end to this crazy feud," Jennie Sue said.

Lettie glanced around the store, evidently making sure there were no cameras or listening devices. "We could tell everyone that you gave all the money away to charity."

Jennie Sue went to give them both a hug. "Except for what I kept back to build a house of my own. Do you know about any property in the country? Maybe five or ten acres so I could have a garden?"

Nadine nodded. "Well, I heard tell that there's five acres north of town that Amos's cousin by marriage would sell for a song."

"Why is he selling it?" Jennie Sue asked.

"He split up his property and sold it off in ten-acre sections. Trouble was, he wasn't thinkin' real straight, and that last five acres don't have access to a road. It would be a headache to get easements across other folks' property. But since it abuts the Lawson farm, you could get permission from them to cross their land in your vehicle and be just fine," Lettie explained.

"It's grown up in mesquite and cactus. You'd have to get enough cleared for a house and sink a well," Nadine told her. " 'Course I'm not sure right now is the time to approach Rick about it."

"Is that fence not far from the creek the one that separates that piece of property from Rick's?" Jennie Sue was already visualizing where she'd put the house and what way it would face.

"That's right," Lettie answered.

"I want it. I'm going to call Justin right now."

"And if Rick won't let you drive through his place to get to it?" Lettie asked.

"I'll buy a helicopter," Jennie Sue answered.

"That's the spirit." Nadine nodded in agreement.

"Hey, I need to go pick out a headstone after

work. I'll treat us all to supper at the café if y'all will go with me," Jennie Sue said as she dialed Justin's number.

"Love to. We'll be at Lettie's and ready when you get there," Nadine agreed without hesitation.

Jennie Sue used her lunch hour to go to the Baker grave sites. The big, gray granite stone in the middle was simply engraved with "Baker," but each person buried in the enclosed area had an individual headstone—great-grandparents and grandparents and the fresh grave on the other side of the grassy area where her baby was buried. That was it. There was room for her parents but none for Jennie Sue. Should she buy a headstone for each of them? Should she bury the ashes in the urns right there?

She sat down on the grassy lawn and flattened both hands out over her baby's grave. "My precious little darlin'. I will never understand why you didn't live. I'm so sorry if all the stress I was under caused you to have issues. I wanted you so badly, please know that." Tears rolled down her cheeks and dripped on the grass. "I love you so much, Emily Grace." She needed her baby to know that she was loved and wanted—to hear her say the words. Finally, she rose to her feet and promised that she'd be back soon.

She'd intended to get a sandwich at the café and eat it as she pored over the ledger that afternoon, but she couldn't have swallowed anything past the huge lump in her throat. She just made a fresh pot of coffee and sipped on it as she opened the ledger back up. When Iris had been there, the store had shown a nice little profit every year, but it had slowly been declining since Iris had passed away.

Jennie Sue dug around in her purse until she found her phone and called Justin. "I'm sorry to bother you again, but how much am I paying Amos for this store?"

"Fifty thousand. That's the building's appraisal for insurance. He's throwing in the inventory for free," Justin said. "It's a steal. With a little work, you could flip it for twice that in six months."

"I'm not interested in ever flipping it. Have we heard from Texas Red?"

"I was about to call you. They want to buy the company and the house for the CEO that they plan to send up here to take over Lawrence's position. He's asked to step down to a less stressful place, so Texas Red said they'd let him choose a new position before they make decisions about the rest of the staff. Looks like everyone will still have a job. It'll take a while for the official signing, so you've got some time to take care of the personal property," he said. "You still have time to change your mind. We can back right out of the deal if you want."

"No, thank you. My mind is made up," she

said. Now if only she could figure out exactly what she wanted to do with her folks' ashes, she'd have most of the big decisions made.

"Anything else?" Justin asked.

"Just that property I'm interested in," she said.

"I've made a phone call. That's in the works. Want to quibble with him over price? It's a little high, considering the fact that you'll have to have an easement to even get back to it," he said.

"Just give him the asking price and get the deed to it, but I do want all of it, mineral rights included," she said.

"Going to start your own oil business?" Justin asked.

"Nope. I don't care what's under the dirt and roots to the mesquite trees. But I don't want anyone else to ever come in there and tell me they're putting an oil well in my backyard, either."

"Smart woman. I'll get on that right now. Call me if you think of anything else," he said.

"Thank you." Jennie Sue touched the screen and slid the phone back into her purse. It hadn't even reached the bottom when it rang.

"You can't do this." Frank's voice cracked. "Your lawyer sent over papers for us to sign, and oh my Lord, Jennie Sue. This is too much. We can't take your money like this."

"You can and you will. You've given your whole lives to the family, and now it's your turn to do whatever you want with the rest of yours. I love both of you so much, and this makes me happy." Jennie Sue's eyes welled up with tears. "Please, Frank, don't make me all sad again. I've had enough of that."

" 'Thank you' isn't enough," Frank said.

"That goes both ways. I can't ever thank y'all enough for all you've done for me since the day I was born. Now start plannin' your bucket list, and then do whatever is on it," she told him.

"I couldn't ever tell you no."

"Then don't start now. Let me talk to Mabel."

"She says that she's crying too hard to talk to you now, but she'll call later."

"Tell her that I love her," Jennie Sue said. "See you later." Saying that brought her dad to mind and put still another lump in her throat.

"Yes, you will."

"So have you talked to Rick?" Lettie asked when she got into the front seat of Jennie Sue's car that evening to go to the Sweetwater Monument location.

"Not yet, but I'm going to tonight after we get this job done. We need to get things settled," she answered.

"You are right. Rick has wallowed around in this mood long enough. My opinion is that you should get up every morning and decide if you are going to be happy or miserable. Me, I choose to be happy most of the time. Evidently someone is going to have to kick Rick in the seat of the pants to get him over this attitude," Lettie said.

"When Lettie chooses to be miserable, I stay the hell out of her way," Nadine said from the back seat.

"Sometimes everything is like either a dream or a nightmare." Jennie Sue turned south toward Sweetwater. "I still have to tell the Belles that I'm not joining their club. I imagine Daddy smiling and Mama throwing things when I think about it."

"Sounds to me like you are keeping one foot in reality," Nadine said.

There was little traffic on the road from Bloom to Sweetwater that evening, so it didn't take long for them to arrive at the monument place. Jennie Sue got out and went straight toward a small heart-shaped white stone sitting on the lawn for display. "I want this for my baby."

"Then you should have it," a lady said as she came out of the small building. "I'm Rachel Carter. You must be Jennie Sue Baker. You mentioned the possibility of three when we talked. Do you have an idea about the other two?"

Jennie Sue took her phone from her purse and showed the lady the pictures that she'd taken. "As near like these as possible."

"I've got a whole book full of adornments. You

can have a rose or a book or even a deer or a bull on them if you want," she suggested.

"Just plain. Names, dates, and that's all. But I want my daughter's name on the front of the heart one, and on the back it should be engraved with 'Daughter of Jennie Sue Baker.' Can you do that?"

"I sure can. Let's go inside and we'll fill out the forms. I'll have them all ready in two weeks," she said. "I'll call before we deliver so you can have someone come and show us exactly where to set them."

"That would be Randall from down at city hall. He takes care of the cemetery," Nadine said.

"We'll be in touch, then. Anything else you need today?" Rachel asked.

"No, that should do it." Jennie Sue pulled out a debit card that she'd never used before. When she'd signed the papers to be included on her folks' accounts in case of their deaths, the bank had given it to her. Seemed fitting that the first time it was used was to pay for their headstones.

She made it to the car before she broke down. She wrapped her arms over the top of the steering wheel, laid her face on them, and sobbed. "I'm going to miss them both so bad. They weren't perfect and they drove me crazy, but I loved them."

Nadine patted one shoulder from the back seat,

and Lettie clamped a hand on the other one. "It's all right," they said at the same time.

"Let it out," Nadine said. "It's natural for little things to set off the grief."

Jennie Sue straightened up and hiccuped. "It's not fair." She slapped the steering wheel. "Mama was coming around to understand that I was my own person. It's not fair that I didn't have more time with her and that neither of them will ever see my children."

"Now, honey, that's not true," Nadine said softly. "They are with your little Emily Grace right now, taking care of her for you."

"Do you really believe that?" Jennie Sue asked.

"Yes, I do," Nadine answered.

"I want children," Jennie Sue said softly. "I want a whole house full of them, not just one, and I don't want to wait forever to start a family."

Lettie raised an eyebrow. "Are you tellin' us something?"

"No, but I wish I was."

Chapter Twenty-Three

A big lovers' moon hung low in the sky with a gazillion stars twinkling around it when Jennie Sue brought the Cadillac to a stop in front of the Lawson house. She fortified herself with a deep breath and slung open the car door. She stomped across the lawn, trying to build up a bigger head of steam with each step. Rick was not going to treat her this way. She refused to feel like something that had been thrown into the trash when it was no longer usable.

She rapped on the door frame and waited a few seconds. Then she grabbed the handle, determined that she'd go in without an invitation if she had to.

"Come on in," Cricket yelled.

She poked her head in the door. Cricket was sitting on the sofa with her leg on the coffee table. "He's not here. He's down at the creek pouting. And the deed to this place is in the name of Richard *or* Edwina Lawson. That means I have a say-so without his signature, and I say you can have an easement across the property if you want to build a house back there by the creek."

"Faster than the speed of light," Jennie Sue said.

"Telephone, telegraph, tell-a-woman. The three

things that are faster than lightning and twice as deadly." Cricket nodded.

"Thank you." Jennie Sue started to shut the door.

"Want to take a club with you? He's pretty hardheaded," Cricket yelled.

"Maybe I can handle it without violence." Jennie Sue closed the door.

"If you can't, call me. I'll bring my crutches."

Jennie Sue cracked the door back open. "Is he really that upset? And why?"

"He's in the same place he was when he came home from the service. He won't talk, and all he does is brood. If you can get him out of that, then you should put in a therapy room in the bookstore and hang out a shingle to help people," Cricket said. "And then I might even like you as a friend and not hate you at all."

"You'd do that for him?" Jennie Sue asked.

"Of course. He's my brother," Cricket answered.

Jennie Sue headed around the house toward the creek. She found Rick, sitting against the old oak tree with a mound of small rocks beside him. One by one he was tossing them out into the water. When he ran out of rocks, he waded out into the creek, gathered them back up in his shirttail, and went back to the tree to repeat the process.

If throwing rocks was therapy, then Jennie Sue figured that she should try it. "But I sure haven't got the time to gather up a whole pile of them," she whispered.

She looked around and found one the size of a softball and hurled it through the air. It hit the moon's reflection right smack in the middle and splashed water all the way to Rick.

"Well, that didn't cure anything. We still have to talk," she muttered as she started toward him.

"What are you doing here?" he asked gruffly.

"I came to talk, so you need to clean off a spot because I intend to have a hissy fit, and once a Wilshire woman sets her mind to have one of those, it takes some territory."

"Oh, really?" His tone didn't change.

"I've given you plenty of time to get over your pissy attitude and grow up, so now you have aggravated me, and you'll have to suffer the wrath of your stupidity." She sat down beside him but kept a foot of distance between them.

"I'm not stupid. I'm dealing with this the best way I know how," he protested.

"Is this about money?"

"I am a disabled vet, Jennie Sue. I won't ever be anything else. I grow vegetables and peddle them for enough money to keep the place running. My pissy mood will pass. It did in the hospital when I was injured, and it will again."

She slapped him on the arm. "That's not what I asked you."

"Yes, dammit! It's about the money. I won't have people sayin' that I'm a kept man."

"Did I propose to you?" she asked.

"No, you did not," he grumbled.

"Didn't you hear the latest news? I'm selling everything and giving it to the poor and needy. I am keepin' Mama's car, because I need something to get around in since you are being so hateful and won't give me rides in your truck. And I'm buying the five acres right behind that fence back there so I can build a small frame house just like I want."

"You did what?" He raised his voice. "And you call me stupid? That land has no road access."

"I'm going to come across your land," she told him bluntly.

"The hell you are. I'm not signing an easement."

"Your sister already said that she would, and it's a done deal. And for your information, I'm mad at you," she said. "Hell's bells, Rick Lawson, you let me think we had the start of a good relationship, and then you dump me. I must be worth less than nothing. One man gets paid to marry me and still leaves me high and dry when the money runs out; the next one that comes into my life leads me on and then throws me out like yesterday's newspaper because I have a little bit of money." She stopped to take a breath and then went on. "Looks like I can't win for losing. I'm leaving now. You can sit here in your self-pity and pout the rest of your life."

She'd taken about a dozen steps when suddenly she was lifted off the ground in a swoop. The hot night air blew her hair back away from her face as she struggled to free herself.

"Put me down right now," she screamed.

Her arms flailed against him, and when she could see his face, it was etched in stone. Finally, he dropped her right into the cold creek water. "That ought to cool you down."

She reached out with one hand and grabbed his good leg and gave it a hard tug. He landed right beside her. "You're the one who's all hot under the collar. And you are a self-righteous hypocrite."

"Oh, yeah, what makes me that horrible?" He pulled himself up on his elbow.

She splashed water in his face. "You've said at least twenty times since we've been friends that you don't like gossip, and now here you are fighting against what we have because people might have something to say about it."

He returned the favor, soaking what little dry threads were left on her shirt. She cupped his face in both hands and kissed him long and hard. And when that kiss ended, she shifted her weight until she was sitting in his lap.

"Did you really give all your money to a charity?"

She shook her head. “I didn’t. That’s just what we’re going to tell people.”

“Are you really going to buy that land and build a house?”

She nodded. “I can imagine my house sitting right back there, and it makes me happy. When I think of living anywhere else, I’m sad. Besides, from here, I can walk to the garden and not have to drive.”

He buried his face in her wet hair. “What if someday you have regrets?”

“I don’t think that day will ever come.” She snuggled down closer to his chest so she could listen to his steady heartbeat.

Cricket hit the “Snooze” button when the alarm went off. It was the day that she had to go to the doctor, and hopefully he’d give her a walking boot, and say that she could throw the crutches away. But the appointment wasn’t until ten o’clock, and she sure wasn’t looking forward to riding to Sweetwater and back with her moody brother.

When the alarm buzzed the second time, she put a pillow over her head and slapped it again. The third time, she threw the pillow across the room and turned it off. Jennie Sue had spent a long time with Rick at the creek the night before, so hopefully she’d gotten through to him on some level. If she hadn’t, Cricket hoped that she hadn’t mentioned the easement idea. That would be a huge sore spot.

"And I sure don't want to be stuck in a truck with him all morning in that case," Cricket mumbled as she headed toward the bathroom.

She was reaching for the knob when the door swung open, and there was Jennie Sue, wearing nothing but a towel around her body and a big smile on her face.

"Good mornin', Cricket. When you get back from the doctor's office, would you like for Rick to drop you at the bookstore? I could use the company," she said.

Cricket was speechless until she heard her brother whistling in the bedroom down the hallway. In that moment, she didn't care where Jennie Sue had slept the night before or what people would say about it. Rick only whistled or hummed when he was happy, and that was worth everything to her.

"I'd love to. Want me to bring some takeout Chinese from Sweetwater? I could pick it up after my appointment," Cricket said.

"Sounds amazing." Jennie Sue padded down the short hallway and closed Rick's bedroom door behind her.

Brushing her teeth and putting her unruly hair into a ponytail wasn't an easy feat while standing on one foot, but Cricket managed. When she finished, the aroma of coffee filled the whole house. She spent a little extra time getting dressed, halfway dreading the awkward moment when she made it to the kitchen. Would they be all lovey-dovey with each other, or would it be just winks and nudges? She finally headed that way, only to be surprised to find Rick alone when she arrived.

She looked around the kitchen. "Where's Jennie Sue?"

"She stuffed a biscuit with bacon and said she'd eat it on the way to work," he answered. "I hear you gave her verbal rights to cross our place to get to her land when she buys it."

"Yep, I did." She pulled out a chair and sat down. She absolutely loved this little house where they'd lived their whole lives. A cozy living room, small dining area, and kitchen built for two people at the most. Nothing like the huge place where Jennie Sue had grown up. Three bedrooms, one of which was still the same as the day her dad died, because she couldn't bear to change what had been his and her mother's. One bathroom that she and Rick had fought over in their teenage years. She'd sat in his bedroom for hours after he'd left for the military and wished that he'd stayed closer to home.

"So what are you thinkin' about right now?" He set a plate of food in front of her. "You look like you're seeing ghosts."

"I think I just might be. We didn't often have

friends that slept over, Rick. I don't know how to put it in words, but it doesn't feel weird that Jennie Sue spent the night, that we are sharing our home with her," Cricket said.

Rick turned around so quick that he almost dropped his plate of food. "Would you repeat that? I've been preparing myself for a lecture lasting from now until we get back from your appointment."

Cricket frowned at him. "Brother, after the way you've acted the past few days, I wouldn't fuss if you slept with the devil's sister."

He wiggled his dark brows. "Sleep?"

"I do not want or need to know details." She covered her ears with her hands. "La-la-la. Changing the subject—I'm sure hoping that the doctor lets me throw away these crutches today. And when we're finished, I'm buying Chinese takeout to bring to the bookstore to have lunch with Jennie Sue. Want to join us?"

"Love to, and since I don't have a bookmobile trip today, I might just hang around for a while. Are you really going to take that job and be her partner in the store?" he asked as he sat down across the table from her.

"Yes, I am. I made up my mind last night. And Jennie Sue says we might start some programs, like a reading hour, a couple of times a week for children. I'd love that," she answered.

"Think maybe I could read to them once in

a while? It'd be a way to get them to visit the bookmobile, too."

Cricket finished off the last of her biscuit. "I'm sure you could. If someone had told you a month ago that we'd be talkin' about these things, would you have believed them?"

"Nope." He set about eating his breakfast.

Lettie and Nadine were waiting by the bookstore door when Jennie Sue arrived that morning. Lettie had a covered pan of something that smelled like one of her famous breakfast casseroles, and Nadine carried a covered bowl of biscuits.

"You didn't come home last night. You are wearing the same clothes you had on yesterday morning, although they do smell like they've been washed and dried, and you've got a smile on your face that suckin' on a lemon couldn't erase. Open the door and let's hear all about it," Nadine said.

Jennie Sue found the right key on her mother's key chain to the door and stood to one side to let them enter first. "What happens on the farm stays on the farm, and I might not come home lots of times."

"Did you sleep on the sofa because your good friend Cricket said you could have the easement? Or did you get lucky and sleep somewhere else?" Lettie wiggled her finger at Jennie Sue after she set the casserole on the table. "I'll make some coffee and get plates."

"Like I said, what happens on the farm . . ." Jennie Sue followed her.

"It was somewhere other than the sofa or she wouldn't be grinnin'." Nadine was right behind them.

"How many times have either of you stayed out all night?" Jennie Sue turned the conversation around.

"We'd have to take off our shoes to count, but it's been years. We love living vicariously through you. So give us some details about something!" Lettie said.

"Well, Rick was whistling when I left, and when I was coming out of the bathroom with nothing but a towel around me, I ran into Cricket. And that's all the details I'm tellin'." Jennie Sue set three mugs by the coffeepot.

"Oh! My! God!" Nadine squealed. "I bet Cricket is givin' him hell."

"I don't think so. She didn't seem mad and even offered to bring takeout for us to share after her doctor's appointment this morning. Coffee is done. Let's go have breakfast." Jennie Sue picked up three disposable plates and some plastic cutlery.

Lettie swept a hand through the air. "The *Bloom News* headline of the day will read, 'Oil Heiress Loses Her Mind.' "

"And the picture would be one of you lookin' like a drowned rat when you got back to the farmhouse from the creek." Nadine filled three mugs.

Jennie Sue almost dropped the plates and forks. "How did you know that I got wet at the creek?"

"Didn't until now." Nadine picked up a couple of the mugs. "Never underestimate the powers of an old woman diggin' around for details."

All three of them went back to the front part of the store and took their seats again. Lettie took her place on the sofa and removed the cover from the food. Nadine pushed the mugs around to the right places. Jennie Sue set the plates on the small table.

"Do you love that boy?" Lettie asked.

Nadine dug into the food first. "She slept with him, didn't she?"

Lettie tucked her chin against her chest and looked over the top of her glasses at her sister. "Did you ever spend the night with a guy you didn't love?"

"More than once," Nadine said. "Sometimes it involved liquor, and sometimes it was just plain old lust. You want to talk about Everett Johnson?"

Lettie adjusted her glasses. "Maybe not Everett, but we could discuss his johnson."

"Lettie Clifford!" Nadine gasped.

"Well, you brought it up," Lettie argued, and then started laughing. Jennie Sue joined her.

Nadine slapped her on the arm. "Did you really have sex with Everett? Why? You never did like him."

"Liking him didn't have anything to do with it. I had a one-night stand with Everett to make Flora mad. She'd been trying to get him to ask her out for years, and he wouldn't. I didn't feel like I was as pretty as her, but then one thing led to another." Lettie shrugged.

"Why would you want to make your sister mad?" Jennie Sue asked, glad that the subject had shifted away from where she'd slept the night before.

"She borrowed my earrings without asking, and that night, she said that I was too ugly to ever get a guy," Lettie answered. "Here comes Amos. I swear, that man can smell food a mile away."

"Especially homemade. You could flirt with him. He likes to eat and you like to cook. Y'all would make a good couple," Nadine whispered.

"Sorry, but his last name isn't Johnson," Lettie told her as the bell above the door sounded. "Hello, Amos. Had breakfast yet? We've got plenty. Go get a plate from the office."

"Nope, I haven't, and yes, I would love to join y'all." He removed his hat and shifted his weight from one leg to the other. "I was down at the café this mornin', and I heard that you had a baby last year. I came to say that I'm sorry. If

I'd known, we would have come to the funeral," Amos said.

Jennie Sue stood up and hugged him. "Thank you, Amos."

"Bless your heart. Losin' your sweet little baby and then your parents all within a year. It's got to be tough, but we're here for you." He motioned to include Lettie and Nadine. "You just call us if you need anything."

"You got that right." Lettie nodded.

"I love every one of you," Jennie Sue said.

"And we love you, girl." Amos hurried off to the office and returned with a plate and coffee. "I heard that you're buyin' the property behind the Lawson farm. I'm glad you are stayin' close to home."

Home.

Mabel often said that home was where the heart was. If that was the case, Jennie Sue really was staying close to home, because her heart was right there in Bloom.

"And guess what else?" Amos went on as he piled his plate full. "I heard that Texas Red is buying Baker Oil and your house, too, for the new CEO they're bringin' in. Is that rumor or truth?"

"Truth." Jennie Sue winked at Lettie.

"Man, that is some fast business," Amos said.

Jennie Sue finished her food and put the trash in the can. She imagined her mother shaking her finger at her all the way from heaven, scolding her for all the calories and fat grams.

"It's not really so fast," Nadine said. "I'm sure it will take a few months to get all the paperwork in order. This isn't like selling a few bushels of beans at the farmers' market."

"Or a failing bookstore?" Amos glanced up at Jennie Sue.

"It'll be a thriving one before long. Please tell me that you didn't come in here to say you'd changed your mind." Jennie Sue sure didn't want to tell Cricket that she had to take back the offer of partnership.

"No way." He picked up another biscuit. "I drove past and saw that you'd put some nice stuff in the windows. Iris used to do that. And then I saw Nadine and Lettie out there on the sidewalk with what looked like food. I never miss an opportunity to partake of their cookin'. Reminds me of Iris's."

Jennie Sue wondered if Rick would ever say that about her. Would the time come when they were both old and gray and he'd still get a look of love in his eyes? Or was this just a passing fancy for both of them?

A sudden pang of jealousy shot through her at the idea of him having a wife and children that she'd have to see every day when she drove home from work. Maybe this big notion of buying land joining his property wasn't such a good idea after all.

• • •

Rick was glad that Cricket had finally gotten a walking boot, but he was even happier to hear that she could go back to work part-time if her job did not require her to stand. Unlike him, she'd never liked staying at home all day. She needed to be around people and was cranky when she was cooped up even over a weekend.

"I like this new Rick," Cricket said while they waited for their food order. "He reminds me a lot of the Rick I knew before the military got ahold of him."

"Oh, yeah?" He picked up the sack of food and carried it out to the truck. "Well, this new Rick feels more like he did then."

"Think we could shoot the other one if he shows his sorry face again?"

"Probably not. You could wind up killin' the wrong one. You've never been very good with guns. Seriously, sis, I'm happy right now. It proves that I don't have to fear happiness and that even with my scars, I'm not repulsive. For that I will always appreciate Jennie Sue."

Cricket reached over and patted him on the arm. "You are not repulsive, but I had no idea that you'd had that on your mind. Can you live with her having more money than God?"

"God doesn't have money. Why would He need dollars and dimes when He has streets of gold?" Rick asked. "I might always struggle with that.

I can't think of a better world than a wife who owns a bookstore, and the rest I just won't think about."

"Wife? So things have gotten that serious?" Cricket asked with wide eyes.

"It could be going in that direction," he answered.

"Promise me one thing," she said.

"What's that?"

"You won't name your first child after me."

"If that ever did happen, it's a long way down the road. I wouldn't worry about it." He drove into Bloom and parked in front of the bookstore.

"Come and see what I got," Cricket called out when the little bell at the top of the door announced their arrival.

Jennie Sue appeared from the end of the children's books. "Well, would you look at that? A walkin' boot that you can kick your brother with if he gets in another pissy mood."

"Come on now. Don't give the man grief that brought the food."

She looked over Cricket's shoulder into Rick's eyes. The world shifted in that moment back into the rightness it had contained before he got hurt.

Chapter Twenty-Four

Jennie Sue and her parents had seldom gone to church when she was growing up. Dill called them CEO Christians—Christmas and Easter Only. That was when her mother dressed her up in fancy clothes and took her to Sweetwater, where the Belles all met at the same big church for the holidays. Afterward, someone would host a fancy dinner—which meant sitting up straight and not spilling anything on her dress.

She had a whole different spirit that Sunday morning, sitting on the pew with Lettie, Nadine, Amos, and Rick lined up on her right and Cricket on her left. She wore a sundress that she'd found at the house when she and Cricket had cleaned out her closet.

"Good morning," the preacher said. "Welcome to everyone. Let's all open our hymnals to page 204 and sing, 'I Know Who Holds Tomorrow.' " The lyrics spoke to Jennie Sue's heart so much that tears formed in her eyes. She fished in her purse for a tissue and dabbed her eyes. It had been a tough two weeks since the plane crash. The tombstones would be delivered the next day.

Rick's arm circled around her shoulders and pulled her close as he sang in a rich baritone voice that every step was getting brighter and every cloud was silver lined. It had been a bittersweet time for Jennie Sue—losing her parents had been devastating, but gaining all the new relationships had been sweet. She truly knew what it was to see the silver lining in a dark cloud. She slipped her hand in his and whispered, "I'm glad that you are holding my hand."

She didn't care that the whole congregation and even God saw him kiss her on the cheek. If they knew what went on out at the farm every night, they'd be grateful that he didn't kiss her on the lips.

When the song ended, the preacher took the lectern. "Be glad that you can sing that song with conviction and that you know who holds your hand in times of trouble."

Jennie Sue squeezed Rick's hand. "Yes, sir," she whispered.

"Shh," Cricket scolded, and then winked at Jennie Sue.

The preacher went on to read scripture and then deliver a sermon. Jennie Sue caught an occasional word, but nothing that she'd be able to discuss later, because she was too busy counting her blessings. Rick Lawson was at the top of the list.

Amos was called on to deliver the benediction, and everyone said a hearty amen when he finished praying.

"Dinner is at my place today, and we've invited

the preacher." Nadine stood up and wiggled her head to get the kinks out. "I'm sure it was a good sermon, but I kept dozing off. Didn't sleep worth a dang last night."

Jennie Sue raised an eyebrow. "Dang?"

"Can't say *damn* in the church, especially on Sunday. God is pretty serious about his day," Nadine whispered.

"Rick and I won't be at the dinner today. We're going out to my five acres to see the land the tree cutters have cleared out. It'll be a while before the construction crew can start the new house, but they assure me I'll be in it by Christmas," Jennie Sue told her.

"Won't that be wonderful? You can have your first Christmas in your own house," Nadine sighed. "But we get you for Thanksgiving. No excuses."

"Yes, ma'am," Rick said. "We'll be there, and I'll even bring the pumpkin pies."

"Nadine is meddling," Lettie whispered in Jennie Sue's ear. "She thinks Cricket and the new preacher, Tom Davis, would make a good couple."

"Oh. My. Goodness," Jennie Sue gasped. "I can't see Cricket as a preacher's wife."

"Did I hear my name?" Cricket whipped around from the aisle line.

"Yes, you did. I said that Nadine should call me when you are ready to come home this evening and I'll drive in and get you," Rick jumped in.

"I could take you home," the new preacher said when Cricket put her hand in his. "And if you need a ride to Nadine's, I could give you a lift there, too."

"Well, thank you. That will save my sister a trip," Cricket said.

"Sister?" Jennie Sue asked when they'd gotten outside the church.

"Hey, you said it first, not me, so now you have to live with it," Cricket laughed. "Isn't this new preacher just the dreamiest man ever?"

"Nope, your brother is," Jennie Sue said.

"You're wearin' rose-colored glasses, and so is he. I'm going back inside to wait for the preacher," Cricket said.

"When you get home, I'll expect details," Jennie Sue said.

"I'll give you as many as you give me." Cricket waved over her shoulder.

"What happened back there?" Rick asked as he opened the truck door for Jennie Sue.

"Nothing except that Cricket thinks the new preacher is sexy. I was thinking that the talk of the town tomorrow won't be about us, but how unsuited Cricket and Tom are," she answered. "Can you see your sister as a preacher's girlfriend or wife eventually?"

He shook his head from side to side. "What'd be even worse is that he'd be my brother-in-law and I'd have to learn how to talk without cussin'. But let's talk about us instead of them."

"I like that subject much better. I'm so glad we're taking a picnic to the creek. It's the perfect way to spend a Sunday afternoon," she said.

"I couldn't agree more." He nodded.

Rick held Jennie Sue's hand all the way to the creek. She carried an old quilt, and with his free hand, he toted a basket of food that also had a pencil and several sheets of paper in it. Today she wanted to get Rick's opinion of the first draft for the house design. The contractor had said that, barring any really bad weather, it could be finished by Christmas. The one thing she was adamant about was that it have a big porch that wrapped around three sides.

Rick set the basket off to one side, and together they spread the quilt out under the oak tree. Sun rays found their way through the leaves, and the creek bubbled along like it had nowhere to go and all day to get there.

"Peace." Jennie Sue eased down in the middle of the quilt.

"Beauty." Rick did the same and kissed her. "I didn't hear a word the preacher said, because all I could think about was how lucky I was to have you beside me."

"It goes beyond lucky. We are so blessed to have found each other. I wish I'd have known you better earlier in our lives," she said. "I feel like we've wasted a lot of good years."

He tucked a strand of blonde hair behind her ear. "No, darlin', we haven't. Everything happens for a reason. We weren't ready to be together when we were young. We had to grow up and learn who we were and what we want out of life."

"How'd you get to be so wise?" Jennie Sue asked.

"It's only on Sundays. On Mondays I lose most of the wisdom," he answered.

"Okay, wise man, do you think Tom and Cricket are going to hit it off?" She opened the basket and set out the food.

"Nope. I didn't say anything because I didn't want to spoil Lettie and Nadine's fun, but the preacher has a girlfriend in Roby. I'm sure he was just being nice when he offered to drive Cricket to Nadine's, or maybe he's going to ask her to head the committee for the Christmas dinner again this year. I'm sure they'll find out pretty quick, though it gets Cricket out of the house today."

Jennie Sue squeezed his hand. "You're a sly one. How'd you know about his girlfriend?"

"I drive the bookmobile, remember? And there's some old guys up there that gossip as much as the old gals do here in Bloom," Rick answered.

"I want her to be as happy as I am," Jennie Sue said.

"When the time is right, she will find someone," Rick said. "But enough about them. Today is all about us."

He pulled a bottle of champagne from the basket and popped the cork.

"That's some expensive stuff," she said.

"There's two wineglasses in there, too. I'm courting you in style." He grinned.

"I love you, Rick, but I like beer better than this."

"Well, today we're doin' it up right, darlin'. You deserve the very best." His smile got wider.

"Why?"

"Because of this." He got up onto one knee and took her hand in his. "Jennifer Susanne Baker, will you marry me?" He pulled a velvet box out of his pocket. "You have put sunshine back into my life and melted the chains from around my heart."

"No, Jennifer Susanne will not marry you. But Jennie Sue will." She threw herself into his arms so hard that they both fell backward and the box flew toward the creek.

He quickly retrieved it and snapped it open to reveal a beautiful pale-blue stone surrounded by fifty tiny diamonds. He slipped it on her finger and said, "The blue is the color of your eyes. The little diamonds around it represent the fifty years I want to spend with you."

"And what if we're together longer than that?" she asked.

"I'll buy you another ring with more diamonds." The kiss was long, lingering and sweet. When it ended, he looked deep into her eyes and knew that he was a blessed man.

Epilogue

Jennie Sue picked up the *Bloom Weekly News* on her way to the bookstore on the day before Thanksgiving. Cricket entered the store behind her with a shiver. The north wind blew dried leaves down Main Street, swirled them around, and sent them into the store before Cricket could slam the door.

Jennie Sue went to the thermostat and turned on the heat. "We probably should have closed today, since everyone will be home getting ready for the holiday."

"I couldn't stand to spend the whole day cooped up in the house with you," Cricket said.

"Right back at you." Jennie Sue reached into her tote bag and brought out the paper.

Cricket curled up on the end of the sofa. "Does it have your wedding picture in it this week? I sent it to them in plenty of time."

"Guess it's my turn to get caught by the town." Jennie Sue sat down beside her and laid out the paper on the coffee table. They bent forward, taking turns reading the highlights and the first paragraph or two of each article.

SWEETWATER HOSPITAL
GETS NEW NICU WING

An anonymous donor has given the money for the hospital to build a new wing that will care for critically ill babies, to be called the Grace NICU Wing. It will have all the newest equipment and rooms set up for the parents of children to stay at the hospital. Construction could begin as early as next spring, with hopes of a finish date before the end of the year.

"I wonder who that anonymous donor is and if her name is Grace. You know it's going to drive the folks crazy trying to figure it out, don't you?" Cricket said.

"While they're talkin' about that, they'll be letting us rest. You still happy with the way we did things?" Jennie Sue asked.

"Wouldn't have it any other way," she answered.

LIBRARY GETS FUNDING

The Bloom Library will have a brand-new children's corner from a hundred-thousand-dollar donation. Along with a multitude of new books, it will have a cozy new seating area sized for small ones.

"Amos and Rick are both so happy about this, Jennie Sue. He's a firm believer in reading to children and teaching them to love books," Cricket said.

"Me, too. I intend to read to my children before they are even born," Jennie Sue said.

LENDING LIBRARIES GROWING

In the past four months, more than two hundred lending libraries have popped up beside people's mailboxes in Bloom. The town is setting a precedent for surrounding areas, and several inquiries have been made as to how other small towns can begin a similar program.

"And Rick is happy about this and the fact that a different donation has helped him take the bookmobile to three other towns," Jennie Sue commented as she turned the page.

"You're sure doin' a lot of good with your inheritance." Cricket leaned over and bumped shoulders with her.

"Well, thank you. I do it in hopes that you won't hate me," Jennie Sue said.

"Not damn likely that could ever happen

again," Cricket laughed, and pointed. "Look, you and Rick made the news, and with a picture."

"We really did. And look at that picture. It's really good," Jennie Sue said.

LAWSON AND BAKER WED

> Richard Lawson and Jennifer Baker eloped to Las Vegas last weekend and were married in the Double Heart Chapel. They are making their home in Bloom.

"Good picture of y'all, right?" Cricket said. "I did a better job than I did with the one when you got off the bus that first day back in Bloom."

"Yes, it is. Whatever happened to the ones you took of me back then?" Jennie Sue reached out and touched the newspaper picture, running her finger down the scar on Rick's face.

"Oh, I still have them. I might need them for blackmail someday. I'm glad you took Lettie, Nadine, and me to Vegas with y'all so we could be there at the wedding. But . . ." She looked around the shop and lowered her voice. "I think maybe you turned a monster loose. They're planning to go back next weekend and want me to go with them."

"Go on and have a good time. I can hold down the store while you are gone," Jennie Sue said.

Cricket turned the page and pointed at the next headline. "Would you look at that?"

SWEETWATER BELLES INDUCT NEW MEMBER

The Sweetwater Belles had a formal ceremony to welcome Danielle Crossett into the club last Friday night, filling the opening left by the death of Charlotte Baker.

"Does that make you sad?" Cricket asked.

"Not one bit. I'm just glad they weren't able to put me on a guilt trip like they tried to do when I refused to join in Mama's place. And, speaking of the Belles, look at this one." Jennie Sue pointed to the next headline.

BABY SHOWER GIVEN

The Sweetwater Belles hosted a baby shower for Belinda Anderson on Sunday afternoon. All twelve members were in attendance.

"I'll give you a baby shower when the time comes," Cricket said. "Think that might be any-time soon?"

"How about in seven and a half months?"

Jennie Sue laid a hand on her flat stomach.

Cricket turned the page and then gasped. "What did you just say?"

"That I'm six weeks pregnant. Rick wanted to tell you the day I took the test, but I was afraid I'd jinx it until I saw the doctor and he confirmed it. We'll be out of your house by the time the baby is born, so don't worry about diapers and sleepless nights," Jennie Sue told her.

Cricket grabbed her in a fierce hug. "Oh! My! Goodness. I'm so excited I can't breathe." She fanned herself with both hands. "This is the best Thanksgiving ever."

"We've got so much to be thankful for, don't we, sister?" Jennie Sue said.

"What was that about being thankful?" Rick, Lettie, and Nadine all pushed their way into the store.

"I'm going to be an aunt," Cricket squealed.

Rick crossed the floor and kissed Jennie Sue. "And I'm going to be a dad, and this baby is going to have the best mama in the world."

"Well, how about that?" Nadine grinned. "We are going to be grandmothers, Lettie."

"I'll start knitting a blanket next week." Lettie fished two dollars from her purse and handed it to Nadine. "A week ago she said you were pregnant, and I told her she'd been listenin' to the aliens in her sleep."

Lettie clapped her hands like a little girl. "I'm

so happy I could dance a jig, but my old knees would give out."

"You ready now that we've dropped this bombshell on them?" Rick asked.

She put her hand in his. "It's time, isn't it?"

"If you are ready, but there's no rush," he said.

"Sure you don't want us to go with you?" Lettie asked.

"No, I need to do this by myself," she said. "Thanks for helping Cricket with the store today so Rick and I can have the day to ourselves once we get finished."

"Honey, we're glad to help," Nadine said.

"Caddy or truck?" Jennie Sue asked when they were on the sidewalk in front of the store.

"Caddy—you're carrying precious cargo, and it's an easier ride," he said.

She handed him the keys, and he opened the door for her. She fastened the seat belt and looked over her shoulder. Rick had carefully pulled the seat belts around the two silver urns so that they wouldn't tip over. The tombstones had been in place for months, but Jennie Sue had procrastinated. She'd gone back and forth between burying them or combining the ashes and scattering them somewhere that had been special to them both. In the end she'd decided that burial was the best decision, and what better time to do that than right before Thanksgiving.

"It's your last ride, Mama, and it seems fitting

that it's in your Caddy," Jennie Sue whispered as Rick rounded the back of the car and got into the driver's seat.

They were at the cemetery in only a few minutes. Rick helped her out and then handed her the urn with her mother's ashes. He picked up Dill's urn, and together they carried them to the two holes dug to the right depth for that kind of burial.

"One more time," he said. "You're sure this is what you want?"

"Yes." She nodded. "I want them to be here with Emily Grace so I can put flowers on their graves and remember them. I want to bring our children here and tell them about their sister and grandparents," she said as she knelt down and put the urn inside the hole. "Rest in peace, Mama. You will always be beautiful in everyone's memories."

Rick handed her Dill's urn next, and she did the same.

"See you later, Daddy."

When she straightened up, Rick drew her close to his side, and then he worked his phone from the hip pocket of his jeans and laid it on Emily Grace's tombstone. Vince Gill's "Go Rest High on That Mountain" seemed to fit her feelings about Emily Grace and her parents better than any church song that she'd thought about playing that day.

Tears flowed when the lyrics said that their lives on Earth had been troubled, but she kept her eyes locked with his and found strength and happiness there. When the song ended, Rick put the phone back in his pocket. He turned to face her and took both her hands in his. They bowed their heads at the same time and said a silent prayer.

"Amen," they whispered at exactly the same time and looked up at each other.

He pulled her toward him and whispered, "I'm the luckiest man in the whole world."

"And I'm the luckiest woman. Let's go home now and take a quilt to the creek," she said without a single doubt about any of her decisions and so much peace in her heart that she knew she'd never have a single regret.

"That sounds like the perfect finish to this day." He tipped her chin up and kissed away the tears.

Acknowledgments

Dear Reader,

I've lived most of my life in small towns. They have a heartbeat and pulse of their own, and I love them. When you read in my biography about everyone knowing everyone else, knowing what they are doing, with whom and when they're doing it—and they read the local newspaper on Wednesday to see who got caught—that is the truth in a nutshell.

It's fall here in Oklahoma as I finish this book and have to say goodbye to Jennie Sue and all her new friends in Bloom, Texas. Putting the last words to a story is always tough for me, because by then I've made such good friends with the characters. But in order for them to move on with their lives, and for me to move on to writing the next story, it's necessary. You'll be reading the book in the summertime, so pour a glass of sweet tea or lemonade and find a cool spot—like maybe under a shade tree beside a babbling brook—and enjoy your visit to the small town of Bloom, located just north of Sweetwater.

I'm a very fortunate author to have such an amazing team at Montlake Romance. They take my ideas and help me turn them into a finished product for my readers. From edits to covers to publicity, they are all amazing, and I appreciate them more than words could ever express.

Special thanks to my editor Megan Mulder, who continues to believe in my stories; to my developmental editor, Krista Stroever, who always manages to help bring out every emotion and detail in my books; to my awesome agent, Erin Niumata; and to Folio Literary Management. And once again, my undying love to my husband, Mr. B, who never complains about takeout food so I can write "just one more chapter."

And thank you to all my readers who buy my books, read them, talk about them, share them, write reviews, and send notes to me. I'm grateful for each and every one of you.

Until next time,

Carolyn Brown

About the Author

Carolyn Brown is a *New York Times*, *USA Today*, *Publishers Weekly*, and *Wall Street Journal* bestselling author and a RITA finalist with more than ninety published books, which include women's fiction and historical, contemporary, and cowboys-and-country-music romance. She and her husband live in the small town of Davis, Oklahoma—where everyone knows everyone else and knows what they're doing and when—and they read the local newspaper on Wednesday to see who got caught. They have three grown children and enough grandchildren to keep them young.

Books are produced in the United States using U.S.-based materials

Books are printed using a revolutionary new process called THINKtech™ that lowers energy usage by 70% and increases overall quality

Books are durable and flexible because of Smyth-sewing

Paper is sourced using environmentally responsible foresting methods and the paper is acid-free

Center Point Large Print
600 Brooks Road / PO Box 1
Thorndike, ME 04986-0001 USA

(207) 568-3717

US & Canada:
1 800 929-9108
www.centerpointlargeprint.com